A HEART BESIEGED

A HEART BESIEGED

Veronica Heley

CHIVERS

British Library Cataloguing in Publication Data available

This Large Print edition published by AudioGO Ltd, Bath, 2013.
Published by arrangement with the Author

U.K. Hardcover ISBN 978 1 4713 5399 4
U.K. Softcover ISBN 978 1 4713 5400 7

Printed and bound in Great Britain by TJ International Limited

CHAPTER ONE

The Lady Ursula de Thrave was being prepared for her betrothal. Her honey-coloured hair had been freed from its silken sheath and combed out till it fell beyond her hips and tangled with the buttons at the wrists of her long, tight sleeves. Her aunt placed a garland of yellow roses on Ursula's head, and stood back to admire the effect.

'Now don't crush that silk, child. This is the most important day of your life and a creased gown will not help. And leave the talking to me. If only you could manage to weep, as other maidens do on these occasions . . . but you were always a stubborn fool, and will fail us, for sure.'

'I will not fail you.'

Lady Editha adjusted her rings. She had become so thin of late that her rings were loose, and she was constantly checking on their presence.

'You should never have been allowed to run wild. I told your grandfather it was not seemly, but no-one ever listens to me! Did your father listen to me, when I advised him not to wed a dowerless girl? Did he heed me when I told him not to go on the Crusade? And as for taking his bride along with him . . .' She tugged her wimple awry. 'I knew how it would be.

I told your grandfather we would never see either of them again, and neither did we.'

Ursula put her arm round her aunt. 'But you had me.'

'More of a boy than a girl, climbing cliffs and riding bareback . . .'

'Not for a long time now.' Ursula kissed her aunt's soft cheek. 'Come now. Smile for me?'

'How can I smile, when we are brought to such a pass? And how can you talk of smiling, when at this very minute your grandfather may be fighting his last battle?'

'Aylmer will help us. Has he not promised to drive the wolf from our door?'

'You make a jest of everything.'

'I am not as careless as you seem to think. I know very well that we are in trouble, and that it is up to me to rally support for our cause. Our treasury is empty, the enemy sits outside our gates, and therefore I am to sell myself in marriage to the highest bidder.'

Lady Editha shrieked. 'If my lord Aylmer should hear you!'

Ursula had the grace to blush. 'Well, is that not the truth? Is grandfather not besieged in Salwarpe, and all our lands overrun by Hugo de Frett? If you and I do not find allies here, will not Salwarpe be lost to us, and we be turned adrift on the world without a penny?'

'Salwarpe is strong and your grandfather has been a notable soldier in his day. Salwarpe will not fall, and you are yet its heiress.'

'And luckily for us both, my lord Aylmer desires to make me his second wife. Heigho! Am I not a lucky girl?'

'Ursula, you do not intend to slight him!'

'No, aunt. I agree with everything you say about him. He is a big man, and I like a man who stands taller than I do. He is a rich man, and I am not averse to eating off gold plate. More, he is a kind man, and his servants obey him with a smile.'

'You forget the most important thing in his favour; after his offer to help Salwarpe, that is. His first wife bore him no children, and therefore the children you bear him will inherit all this . . .' The Lady Editha indicated the richly furnished room in which they stood and, by implication, the wealth of castle and estates around it.

'It is your good fortune that he is wealthy,' said Ursula. 'I do not marry him for that. I marry him because he can save Salwarpe and also—yes, I will agree that there is something about him which pleases me . . . an air of authority . . . a fine figure . . .'

'It is a good thing you look older than you are. At eighteen you could pass for a woman in her early twenties. It will make the contrast between you less obvious.'

'Why, my lord is a handsome man, and I am half in love with him already. What is more, I have no idea when he was born, and I beg of you not to tell me. I shall say to myself that he is in the prime of life and if that satisfies me, then who shall dare to remind me that he is forty-one, or two or three?'

'Forty only, I believe. But no one thinks he looks his age.'

Someone was at the door. Aylmer had sent a distant kinswoman, who had been acting as châtelaine for him since his wife died, to escort his guests down the stairs and into the Great Hall. There in the late summer sunshine were signed such papers as confirmed the betrothal of the Lady Ursula de Thrave of Salwarpe, to Baron Aylmer de Rathe . . . the titles of whose estates took up no less than three lines of parchment on the deed. Aylmer took the quill from the hand of the clerk, and signed his name with deliberation. Then he handed the quill to Ursula, indicating where she should also sign . . . or . . .

'A cross will do,' he said, in a low voice. Few women knew how to read or write.

Ursula took the quill with a smile. She understood that he had meant to spare her embarrassment, and she appreciated his kindliness. She felt a wave of gratitude to Providence for giving her to this man. How very much worse things might have been . . .

She signed her name, and underlined it with a flourish. He should see that though she was bringing him a dowry encumbered by problems, yet she did have some gifts for him. His handclasp was warm as they stood together before the priest to exchange vows. This ceremony was almost as binding as marriage, even though she could not yet call herself his wife.

Aylmer stood with his feet apart and his head thrown back. He always stood like that. He was a big-boned man and well-made, with a fine head of corn-yellow hair and a well-trimmed beard to match. His hair was slightly darker in colour than Ursula's, but there were only a few white hairs over his ears and some fine lines about his eyes to show that he was old enough to be her father.

There was nothing of the paternal in his attitude to her, though. His eyes were warm as he bent to kiss first her hand, and then her lips, at the conclusion of the ceremony.

For the first time Ursula felt ashamed of the bargain she was making. She was honest enough to want to give good value for what she was about to receive. She had thought he was marrying her because he needed an heir, and also because she was young, comely and of good family.

His fingers twisted in hers, and she looked up to see him smiling down at her with an expression of amused understanding. Did he really understand? He was no fool. He must have realised that she was selling herself to save her family.

If there was much that was untamed in Ursula, there was also much generosity. She lifted his hands to her lips, and bowed her head.

'My lord, I am not worthy . . .'

A murmur of approval rose from the company around them. How touching! How charming! The suppliant girl, and the man who would no doubt grant his bride anything she asked . . .

She had not meant to shed tears. She brushed them away, to see her aunt smiling and nodding to her. Her aunt would think she had cried on purpose, for effect, and yet it had not been so.

Let them think what they might! She, Ursula de Thrave of Salwarpe, would repay her husband by being a loving and loyal wife.

She put her hand on his arm and leaned against him. His people were coming up to them, one by one, to be introduced to her.

Grave faces passed before her, bowing over her hand, unsmiling . . .

Four knights, tenants of Aylmer's, owing him fealty; they had been summoned to his betrothal to hear from Ursula's own lips of the danger in which her people lay. Without their support, Aylmer could not mount the sort of force needed to dislodge Hugo from the township under the walls of Salwarpe, and raise the siege.

They looked on Ursula and, while acknowledging her grace and beauty, they clearly reserved judgment as to the wisdom of fighting for her.

'These are not all my knights,' said Aylmer, drawing Ursula apart. 'Two more are expected to arrive later today. You know one of them already, I believe?' Aylmer looked self-conscious. 'Ah, but young Reynold will be angry that I have stolen a march on him, will he not? We shall have to find him some other beautiful young heiress to marry.'

'Reynold de Cressi?' She had indeed met him earlier that year, at the same tournament which had brought her to Aylmer's notice. Reynold was a young widower, tall and red-headed. He had made himself conspicuous in the lists by challenging one of the most experienced of the jousters, and been lucky enough to unseat his opponent at the third run with the lances. Subsequently Reynold had sent Ursula various tokens of his regard, to wit some verses and a garland of flowers, and she had smiled at him in return. But the affair had gone no further than that.

She slipped her hand within Aylmer's arm. 'A most reckless young man, is he not?' It was possible that Aylmer might be jealous of Reynold, and so she spoke of him as she would of a wayward child.

She had taken the right line. The stern look on his face vanished.

She said, 'I thought him most gallant. I have always admired tall men. One day he might even come to look like you.'

'Clever Ursula.' Had he really said that? She gave him a sharp look.

'I meant it,' she said. 'It is true that I said that partly to please you, but I did mean it. I always say what I mean.

'Yes, I really think you do.'

'There is something else I want to say. It is generally understood that I am marrying you to save Salwarpe. I want you to know that that is not true . . . or at least, only partly true. I do want to help my grandfather, of course. But I wish with all my heart that there had been no trouble at Salwarpe. I wish I could have come to you with a dowry which would cost you nothing. If you take me as I am, without dowry . . . if you take no action about Salwarpe, I want you to know that I will be just as true a wife to you.'

He put his hands on her shoulders, and said, 'I am a lucky man, indeed!'

A page came tumbling into the room.

'They come, my lord! They come!'

Aylmer laughed. He gathered Ursula within his arm and hustled her out of the room and along a covered passageway. Now they overlooked the courtyard. Below servants were preparing to receive the party which was even now clattering over the drawbridge.

First came a squire, bearing a pennant of green and silver stripes . . .

'Reynold de Cressi,' said Aylmer.

A red-headed man in a brilliant green and

silver striped surcoat over chain-mail came into sight. He was riding a mettlesome horse, but had it well under control. His chin was on his shoulder, looking back the way he had come.

Aylmer said, 'He is watching out for Benedict, no doubt.'

'Benedict?'

'Benedict de Huste. They are enemies, Reynold and Benedict. And there lies my dilemma, Ursula. Those two men are the key to the relief of Salwarpe; Benedict is your man for a siege, and Reynold for fighting on horseback. If you can win them both to your side, then you will save Salwarpe. If not . . .'

'I do not understand. Can you not command them to obey you?'

'At harvest-time? Can I force them to take their men away from the fields at harvest-time? No. Can I force them to go into battle again, when they have already completed their service for me this year? Assuredly not. I cannot compel them to anything.'

Ursula bit her lip.

Aylmer nodded to where another pennant was being dipped to clear the portcullis. 'Yet they come. They come to my command, and they will listen to what you have to say, and to what I have to say. Then they will decide what they will do. If words of mine can win them to your side, then those words will be spoken.'

'But you think it will be more difficult to

woo men from the harvest, than knights to battle?' She bit her lip. 'Well, I said it would make no difference to my vows, if Salwarpe were not to be regained. You have put me to the test sooner than I thought, but I will not fail you.'

'Do not be so hasty, child. All is not yet lost. Benedict is a man of subtle mind. Win him to your side, and he may yet find a way for us to raise the siege.'

Reynold had reached the mounting-block and was sliding out of his saddle. A body-servant was unbuckling saddle-bags from a packhorse, while Reynold's squire took charge of his master's helmet and shield.

But, 'Where is Benedict?' said Aylmer.

A riderless horse appeared in the courtyard, led by an elderly servant in a livery of azure on black. Aylmer strode to where steps led down into the courtyard, and Ursula followed him.

'My lord Aylmer . . .' Reynold was bowing before them. He spoke to Aylmer, but his eyes were on Ursula. 'Reynold, I thank thee for coming so soon. But where is Benedict?'

'Making a fool of himself, as usual.' Reynold's eyes had not moved from Ursula's face, and he smiled, showing pointed teeth. His eyes were a warm brown and expressed not only homage to her beauty, but also something which was not quite—but very nearly—impudence.

'A child tumbled down the bank on the road

outside. Some scullion's imp, sent out to look for herbs. And what a wailing there was! Right under my horse's hooves. And so, of course, Benedict had to interfere. He told me to go on, and make his apologies.'

'And here I am!'

No-one had noticed Benedict's entry into the courtyard. He had walked in bearing a small child in his arms. Two or three more children hung about him, at once helping and hindering him in his errand of mercy.

Unlike Reynold, Benedict was dark. He was not a tall man, but he had wide shoulders and gave the impression of being at once awkward and immensely strong. He had taken off his surcoat to wrap about the injured child, and there were streaks of blood and dust on his tousled hair and swarthy cheek. Like Reynold, he had worn chain-mail in which to travel, but, unlike Reynold, his armour looked as if it had seen much wear.

He seemed not to notice Ursula, but ducked his head at Aylmer.

'My lord, forgive me if I take the child away, and reassure his mother. He is more frightened than hurt, but there was a lot of blood . . .'

'Give him to one of the servants,' drawled Reynold. 'This is not the time to . . .'

Benedict turned his back on them and spoke over his shoulder. 'You will excuse me, then.'

Aylmer was at Benedict's side, turning him

so that he might see the child for himself. 'Why, it is the washerwoman's son . . . that's right, lad! You are in good hands. Benedict, I am glad to see you.'

'And I to see you,' said Benedict, his dark face transformed in a sudden smile. 'Aylmer, I cannot say how pleased I am to hear you intend to marry again . . .'

'And this is the lady,' said Aylmer, discovering Ursula close at his side.

'Will you not allow me to help?' said Ursula, smiling at Benedict.

'No, no.' Benedict's smile vanished, and he brought up his shoulder, as if to protect the child from her. 'We will do well enough.'

His manner was so abrupt as to be insulting. Ursula was hurt. She looked at Aylmer for support, but he was shaking his head at her, and pushing her towards the stairs.

'I will go with Benedict,' he said. 'Reynold will escort you back to the others, and I will join you there anon.'

'I am skilled in such matters,' said Ursula, protesting.

'So is Benedict,' replied Aylmer. He was rewarded with a quick smile from Benedict.

Ursula, withdrawing from the courtyard, caught both the smile and Benedict's subsequent flashing glance in her direction. His eyes were so light a grey that they appeared to blaze.

She could not remember when she had last

felt so rejected.

Now that she had retired from the scene, the children were all jumping up and laughing. Even the injured boy was raising his head and looking about him. Servants were coming up, all of them smiling, greeting Benedict. Aylmer had his arm round Benedict's shoulders.

She was forgotten.

But not by all. Reynold said, close in her ear. 'Did you not know he was afraid of women?'

'Who? Benedict?'

Reynold laughed. Benedict had turned and was walking away . . . no, not walking, but limping. His left leg was crooked, and shorter than the right.

Did you not know?' said Reynold. 'They call him The Lame Knight . . . among other things.'

CHAPTER TWO

'First we will feast, and then we will talk,' said Aylmer. He led Ursula to the place of honour on his right at the top table. 'I want everyone to see how highly I value my bride. They cannot praise you too much, for me. I am out of practice in such courtesies. Perhaps they can teach me the trick of it once more. I did know how to please a lady, once.' Here he sighed.

Ursula knew that he had loved and

mourned his wife Joan, who had died the previous year.

She said, 'It will not be easy for an untried girl to take the place of your lady wife. You will forgive me if I make mistakes, at first?'

His hand pressed hers. 'She begged me to remarry, when she knew she was dying. She said I must look for someone young, beautiful and kind. I did not think I would ever have such good fortune . . .'

Ursula frowned. 'I will admit to you, my lord—and only to you—that my so-called beauty lies chiefly in my hair. It is long and thick and of a good enough colour. Men look only at that, and think "There goes a great beauty!" And yet it is not so, for when my hair is close braided as it is at home, I excite no great admiration. Or perhaps—what a humiliating thought!—I have been raised to the position of "Beauty" because I am to marry you? Naturally your wife must be worthy of you, and possess all the accomplishments in the world. I daresay that is why they say I am beautiful.'

He lifted his cup in a toast to her. 'Not only beautiful, but also witty and modest! With every word you cause me to value you more.'

'Yet you would not allow me to help with the injured boy this afternoon. I assure you I am no idler. I have been used to dealing with all the hurts and fevers of the castle.'

'It was not that. I could see you spoke the

truth, but . . .' He looked down the table. Reynold was seated on the far side of Lady Editha, and beyond them were the four knights she had met earlier. At the end of the table was an empty chair, where Benedict should have sat.

The steward, hovering behind Aylmer's chair, bent forward to say that Sir Benedict had gone to see his old tutor, who was now bedridden. He had sent word he might be late.

'Ah, of course,' said Aylmer. 'I might have guessed.' He turned back to Ursula. 'No, I did not mean to slight you, but . . . how can I explain it to you? Benedict is not at ease with women.'

'Reynold said he was a ward of yours. Could you not arrange a suitable marriage for him, to correct that fault in his education?'

'I did. He married a young girl of good family—another ward of mine—when they were both eighteen. The marriage did not turn out well, and Benedict has been left with a dislike of women which I doubt even you could overcome.'

'Do you wish me to try?'

At that moment Benedict limped into the room, stuffing a small book into his wallet. He smiled as he bowed to Aylmer, did not smile as he ducked his head to Ursula, and went to take his seat.

Servants sprang to bring him dishes. He greeted each by name, and they smiled as they piled food on his platter. Then he addressed himself to his meal, talking now and then in a low voice to his neighbour, a grizzled knight of considerable girth.

The rest of the party had donned brilliant clothing in honour of the betrothal feast, but Benedict wore black, without so much as a jewel on his hands or a gold chain round his neck to relieve its severity. Although he had presumably washed his face and hands and combed his hair before he came to table, he still looked unkempt.

Yet Ursula's eyes strayed to where Benedict sat, even while she listened to the talk of those about her, and applauded the acrobats in the body of the hall below.

'My lord Aylmer,' said the Lady Editha. 'When shall we celebrate the marriage proper? As you know, we came away in haste.'

'Ursula shall have everything she wants,' said Aylmer. 'I have sent for the women who acted as attendants to my late wife, and they should be here tomorrow. Trinkets, gowns . . . order whatever you wish, my dear.'

'But when will the ceremony take place?' Editha was persistent. 'Two days? A week? You know that my father looks to you for help. He has but one carrier pigeon left, which will fly to our good neighbours at Spereshot. They are still true to our cause. They will send us any news from Salwarpe, and we can send news to Salwarpe through them. I will write tonight to tell him that we are safe, but when should I tell him that help will arrive?'

Uneasy looks passed around the table, and there were mutterings about 'the harvest' and 'impossible!'

Aylmer said, 'We will adjourn to the solar, if you please, where we can discuss the question of Salwarpe in private.'

Once more Aylmer seated Ursula on his right, and Editha on his left. Once more Benedict sat far back in the shadows, saying nothing.

Aylmer put the case for relieving Salwarpe well. His family and that of the Lords of Salwarpe had long been friends and allies. The lands around Salwarpe were rich, the township and harbour below the castle were prosperous and the family's present predicament due to the greed of a villain called Hugo de Frett.

Hugo was a man of whom men spoke ill. He was faithless, unscrupulous and rich. Some years ago the Lord of Salwarpe had thwarted a scheme of Hugo's whereby the latter had claimed the goods and chattels of a prosperous merchant by falsely claiming that he was a villein, and no free man. When Hugo had lost his case, he had sworn vengeance on Salwarpe in general, and on Henry, Lord of Salwarpe, in particular.

Now Hugo's father had married a distant cousin of Sir Henry. Both parties to the match were long since dead, but Hugo now laid claim to the Salwarpe estates, claiming that Ursula had no right to them, and that he did.

Hugo's claim was preposterous, but since he was rich and powerful, he had made out a case of sorts to present to the King. Everyone knew that it might be months before the case was heard, and that Sir Henry—being temporarily short of funds—could not fight a lengthy duel in the courts. To defend his suit, Sir Henry would have to travel with the Court wherever it went, waiting and greasing palms, till such time as the King condescended to listen to his plea. Hugo knew that Sir Henry could not afford to do this.

It was at this juncture that Sir Henry played his last card. He sent his daughter Editha out into the world with Ursula, to see if the girl's beauty could attract a champion to Salwarpe. And at the tourney in York Aylmer had seen Ursula and spoken for her.

Sir Henry could not have dared hope for such luck. Although Aylmer and he were neighbours—not more than twenty miles separated their estates—yet Aylmer could have looked to ally himself with the highest in the land.

On learning of the proposed marriage, Hugo might have been expected to withdraw his claim, but he did not. The man had the instincts of a gambler. He staked everything on one last throw. There were mercenaries in plenty to be hired once the summer's campaigning on the Continent was at a close. Hugo knew that Aylmer could not put another force into the field at harvest-time, and he did not think he would employ mercenaries.

So one day Sir Henry found the town below the castle invaded by hostile forces, who swept on up the road to the very gates of the castle . . . and stayed there.

Lady Editha and Ursula had been out riding when Hugo arrived, and, warned of his coming, had fled through the forest to Aylmer for help. Now there was no way in or out of Salwarpe, except by carrier pigeon.

Aylmer's audience shook their heads. It was a dreadful affair, they agreed. No one had a good word to say for Hugo, save for the grizzled knight who remarked that he was an experienced soldier. Why, said one of the others, did not the ladies take their case to the King?

'The King is abroad for the winter,' said the Lady Editha, removing all her rings in her agitation and dropping them onto her lap. 'By the time we reach him, and gain a hearing, Salwarpe may have fallen, and our case be lost. If Hugo once gains entry . . .'

'What precisely does he mean by saying that he is the rightful heir to Salwarpe?' said Reynold. 'Surely the Lady Ursula is the rightful heir?'

'He pretends to believe that she is not legitimate,' said the Lady Editha. 'But there is nothing in it.'

Ursula blushed. She could feel them all looking at her, and wondering if she really were legitimate or not. It would be so much easier for them, if they could convince themselves there was something in what Hugo said. For if her cause was bad, then there would be no need for them to trouble themselves in the matter.

Aylmer put his hand over hers. 'No knight worthy of the name believes that story. In fact, it merely makes me the more anxious to champion Sir Henry's cause. Well what of it, friends? I speak to you as comrades, and not as your liege lord, for I know full well that you have already paid what duty you owe me this year. I also know that I have torn you from your manors at a time of the year when you most wish to be at home, supervising the harvest. I considered both those facts when I summoned you, and I felt that out of the love I bear you, and out of the love and loyalty which you owe me, you would come and advise me truthfully and bravely.'

One or two heads nodded, but the oldest of the knights cleared his throat and said, 'My cousin and I have already taken counsel on this, my lord. We are very willing to follow your lead in raising the siege of Salwarpe, but we cannot put any company of men into the field until the harvest is in.'

'That is so,' said another knight. 'Fifty

men will I bring here on Michaelmas Day, or seventy by mid-October, on St. Luke's Day.'

'And I will bring one hundred on Michaelmas Day, or one hundred and thirty on St. Luke's Day,' said another. But earlier . . .' he shrugged.

'Then my father is a dead man, and Salwarpe is lost to us!' cried Lady Editha. In her distress she stood, scattering her rings over the tiled floor.

In silence the knights retrieved the rings, and handed them back to the Lady Editha. They avoided her eyes as they resumed their seats.

'Very well,' said Aylmer. 'I accept that, and I thank you for what you offer, which is more than I could have compelled you to do. Let us now consider another way of raising men. Hugo has employed a force of mercenaries to lay siege to Salwarpe. Can we raise enough money to do the same? I will waive some portion of the fees owing to me next year, in order to hire mercenaries for our side.'

'My rings!' cried the Lady Editha, holding them out to him. 'You shall sell my jewels as well!'

The knights still looked grave. 'My lord,' said the oldest, who seemed to have been deputed as spokesman. 'We also considered this course of action; but bearing in mind that the news from France is not good, and that we will undoubtedly be forced to mount another expedition next year, we do not think we can afford to do as you ask. We cannot afford double taxes; and as for raising a small levy now, we would be hard put to it to do so, with the harvest not yet gathered in.'

'Besides which,' said another, 'mercenaries are unreliable. They work for the highest bidder, and are not particular how they complete their contracts. Suppose Hugo offers them a better deal, once they are in the field against him? And who would lead them, anyway?'

'I would,' said Reynold de Cressi. 'What! Ye dolts! Here is a chance to see some stout work, and ye hang back, talking of stooks and sheaves, and let the chance of glory slip through your fingers!'

'Glory is all very well,' said the greybeard. 'But glory will not fill the stomachs of our men when they come to exchange blows with Hugo de Frett!'

'If my manor were but larger,' said Reynold, striding up and down, 'If I only had more men to put into the field . . . !'

'But you have not.'

A large knight stirred uneasily. 'I would we could do it. It would be a man's work, to relieve Salwarpe and cross swords with Hugo de Frett! But we must see the harvest through first.'

Aylmer went to lean on the stone hood over the fireplace. During the previous conversation he had several times glanced in Benedict's direction, though the latter had not spoken. Now Aylmer turned to Benedict for help.

'Well, Benedict? You have not spoken, yet of all my counsellors you are the one upon whose judgment I would choose to rely. What do you say in this affair?'

Ursula looked at Benedict, as did everyone else. He was turning his book over and over in his hands, and frowning at it. He did not look at them, even now, but spoke to his hands.

He said, 'I have only seen Salwarpe in the distance. I have never met Hugo de Frett, though I have heard of him—as who has not? You say his reputation is bad, but among soldiers his name is respected. He has done much campaigning in France. To besiege a castle is nothing new to him. Once he is in Salwarpe, Sir Henry's cause is lost . . .'

'Faintheart!' said Reynold.

'On the other hand,' said Benedict, in the same even tone, 'I have also heard that Salwarpe is a strong castle, and well-manned. Is this true? What are its defences? When was it built? How is it garrisoned, and what store is there in its granaries?'

'It is well built,' said Aylmer. 'On a natural hill overlooking a tidal marsh on one side, and the township and harbour on the other. There is a curtain wall around the top of the hill, and within is the old keep, built some century or so ago. There are also other, lesser buildings . . . granaries, stabling and so forth. There is a well within the castle . . .'

'It never fails,' said the Lady Editha, leaning forward. 'Even in the hottest weather! And our granaries are well stocked.'

'The condition of the walls?' said Benedict. 'The number of trained soldiers in the garrison? What officers have you?'

'The walls are in good repair,' said Lady Editha, 'Although there has not seemed to be any need of recent years to effect improvements. There is a double gatehouse, with portcullis and drawbridge.'

'Access?' said Benedict, becoming ever more abrupt.

'A steep road up from the township, passing under the two sets of gate towers. The outer and inner sets of towers are joined by walls, topped with ramparts, so that if invaders force the portcullis in the outer gatehouse they are hemmed into a square pit, and archers can shoot at them from the walls above.'

'That is the only way into the castle?'

'Yes. The sides of the hill are steep, and the walls high.'

Ursula stirred. Benedict pointed a finger at her. 'Yes?'

'There is a postern gate in a tower, overlooking the marsh.'

'Don't be ridiculous, child!' said the Lady Editha. 'Of what good is that to a force of mounted men?'

'Show me on a map,' said Benedict.

Aylmer stooped, took a charred brand from the fire and drew with its charcoaled tip on the stone hood of the fireplace. First he drew the circle of the hill, crowned with walls, and enclosing a smaller circle for the ancient keep. Then he drew a winding road which bent this way and that across the steep face of the hill, until it led into the town below. The road went into the town and stopped.

'That is the harbour,' said Aylmer. 'The river is very wide at this point, and at every tide the marshes which surround the castle on three sides are flooded with water. As I remember it, the depth of water which floods the marshes is not sufficient to allow boats to approach the castle, save by the harbour. And Hugo now sits in the town and, presumably, also in the harbour.'

Ursula went to look at Aylmer's map. It was reasonably accurate, for a man who had not been to Salwarpe for years. She thought she remembered him coming to visit her grandfather, years ago, when she was a child . . . he had given her a cup and ball to play with . . . or perhaps it was not he, but another . . .

She said, 'There is a channel from the river across the marshes to the foot of the hill, here.' And she pointed to a spot on the opposite side of the castle to the town and harbour. 'It is a narrow channel, but it will admit small boats, if you know the way.'

'A channel for wildfowlers and unruly children,' said Lady Editha.

'She means me,' said Ursula, trying not to blush. 'I used to steal out of the castle by the postern gate. There is a gully below the postern, and we kept ropes there, to let ourselves down onto the marsh. And a flat-bottomed punt, for fishing. But small boats can come up to the foot of the hill at high tide if they know the way.'

'Hugo has a guard on the channel?'

'I doubt he knows of it. It is known to very few people. Local fishermen, and the like. There is nowhere on the marshes where he could station soldiers, and it is often covered with mists . . .'

'The ropes are still there?'

'I am not sure. I used to climb down that way with one of the pages when I was a child—a long time ago. Then he slipped one day and broke his leg . . . I went that way a few more times by myself . . . and then I suppose I grew out of it.'

Reynold cut short their exchange. 'Of what use is it to talk of secret posterns and punts? We are soldiers, not fishermen. Can we relieve the siege by taking a large force over the marshes? Sooner give them webbed feet, and teach them to swim!'

One or two men smiled, but Aylmer still looked at Benedict, who continued to study the map. He limped over, considering it first from this side and then from that.

'How did you say the place was garrisoned? What officers have you, accustomed to siege work?'

'The garrison is made up of stout-hearted men,' said Lady Editha, 'And my father was a notable warrior in his day.'

'I have heard tales of him. How old is he?'

Lady Editha flushed. 'He is not in his first youth, of course.'

'Age?' Benedict looked at Aylmer.

Aylmer shrugged. 'His spirit is stouter than his frame. I doubt he fills out his armour very well nowadays, but equally I doubt not that he still wears it on occasion.'

'Experience of siege work?'

'None.'

'What officers has he, accustomed to siege tactics?'

'None that I know of.'

'That is not true!' cried the Lady Editha. 'There is our sergeant of arms, a most worthy man, who was twice in Gascony in the war, and many others . . .'

'Sir Henry has not been on any campaigns, nor sent any men to war since his son died in the last Crusade,' said Aylmer. 'He had not the heart for it, since so many of his best men, and so much of his wealth, was lost on the path to the Holy Land. He has commuted his knight service for money since then. If he has any men in the garrison now who have seen service, they must be men past their first youth.'

'What matters that?' said Reynold.

'It is the crux of the matter,' said Benedict. 'Sir Henry has no officers accustomed to siege work, and no experience of it himself. If we can solve that problem, we can save Salwarpe.'

He looked at the blank faces around him. 'Surely it is quite plain what we must do? Salwarpe is well provisioned, and has a stout-hearted commander. Hugo cannot storm the walls, if the garrison be but half as true as their lord. Therefore at first he will be content to wait, denying access, hoping to starve the garrison out, or frighten them into submission.

'Soon, though, he will learn that the Ladies of Salwarpe have gone for help, and that Aylmer will give that help. He will hear of our gathering today. He will learn that we cannot mount an expedition to relieve Salwarpe until after the harvest, and so he will do one of two things. Either he will retire, and pretend he never wanted Salwarpe in the first place . . .'

'I doubt if he will do that,' said Aylmer 'So near to success . . . and he a headstrong and determined man.'

'Then he will attack the castle first by land, and then by the river route. Let us not underestimate him. He will have learned all about that "secret" channel by now. He is no fool. More, he is experienced in siege warfare, which the lord of Salwarpe is not. Therefore I say to you that unless Sir Henry is able to recruit officers who are also experienced in siegework, then Salwarpe will fall.'

'Shame!' cried Lady Editha.

'I agree, Benedict,' said Aylmer. 'But how do you propose to get your relief force into Salwarpe, and where will you recruit them?'

Benedict smiled. 'Be sure we will not approach through the town. We must go secretly by night over the marshes, using the hidden channel from the river. And we must climb the hill by the ropes to the postern gate.'

'Have you gone mad?' cried Reynold. 'How could we transport even twenty men by such a route without rousing the enemy? And where, pray, would we obtain boats for so many . . .'

'One experienced officer,' said Benedict. 'That is all that is needed. A skiff, a guide for the hidden channel; these things can be hired at Spereshot, which lies between us and Salwarpe. Spereshot is on a tributary of the same river that circles Salwarpe, is it not? So I shall go to Spereshot, hire a boat and a guide, and take to the river by night. I shall not need my squire. He is getting on in years, and I doubt he could manage the climb up the cliff.'

'One man!' Lady Editha was outraged. 'I ask for help, my lord, and you give me one man!'

'This is not a situation in which numbers count,' said Benedict. 'Siege warfare demands a certain endurance, a certain knowledge of tactics, and patience. That is all. You see, I only have to show your father what to do, and then sit it out till Michaelmas, when my lord brings up his force.'

'You make it sound easy,' said Aylmer. 'Yet I am reluctant to give my consent to your plan. I, too, have sat out a siege in my time. I know what it is like to sit there and be attacked, day after day, night after night, without sufficient sleep . . . counting off the hours till dawn, and then counting off more hours of daylight . . . knowing that help cannot reach you for so many days, and that your stock of weapons is running out . . . not easy, Benedict! I agree that your solution is a good one, and possibly the only one. That you should offer to go to Salwarpe yourself is no more than I would have expected of you, and yet . . .'

'You know that I prefer to keep myself occupied,' said Benedict.

Aylmer put his hands on Benedict's shoulders. Being a tall man, he looked down into Benedict's face.

'I owe you so much already,' said Aylmer. 'I am not sure that I ought to permit this.'

'You cannot prevent me,' said Benedict. His eyes seemed to flash silver, and then he turned away, ashamed, perhaps, at having displayed his affection for Aylmer so openly.

'No, I cannot prevent your going,' said Aylmer. 'But I can ensure that you get a good night's sleep now and then while you are in Salwarpe. You must take a second officer with you, to share the command.'

The grizzled knight nodded. 'I will go, my lord.'

'I have more experience of such work than you,' said another.

'We will throw dice for the place,' said Aylmer. 'He who throws the highest number will go with Benedict, and share the command with him.'

Reynold laughed 'Then I shall go, for I always win. Always.'

His eyes were warm as they rested on Ursula.

Reynold won.

CHAPTER THREE

Ursula woke early, braided her hair in a single plait and slipped it into the silken tube which kept it neat during the day. She was lacing up her old woollen gown before her aunt was properly awake.

'Ursula, you are never going out like that!'

'Why not, aunt? I cannot be comfortable in that borrowed silk . . .'

'Child, remember your new position . . .'

'Oh, but I do. I suppose when I am married I shall have to wear stiff silks every day . . .

heigho! . . but although I have been duly betrothed with bell, book and candle, I am still a maid and for today I shall wear what I like.'

'You should be considering what my lord likes.'

Ursula held out the skirts of her gown. It was not torn, nor even dirty. The colour became her, being neither peach nor pink nor honey, but something between the three. The cloth had been bought of a passing merchant last Michaelmas, and because it almost matched her hair, and because the wool was so fine, she wore it nearly all the time.

'My lord did not seem to dislike me in this gown, when we rode in from Salwarpe, even though we had but two of our men at our back. I do not think he cares so much for appearances as you seem to think.'

'Not all of his men are as happy about this match as is my lord Aylmer.'

'Now what are you hinting at? Are we not to be wed within the week, and is my lord not sending help to Salwarpe?'

'I would be happier if it were any other man he were sending.'

'Which man? Reynold?'

'No, no. Not he. Sir Reynold is a proper man, and courteous to the ladies. No, I was referring to the favourite, Benedict. Did you not know that Aylmer planned to make Benedict his heir, till he saw you at the tourney? It would not be wonderful if the cripple disliked you, and had some dark plan to thwart your marriage, would it?'

'Did Reynold tell you that? I do not believe it. Benedict does not resent me because I am to marry Aylmer, but because I am a woman. Aylmer said so and, after all, he ought to know. Benedict was warm in his congratulations to Aylmer on his forthcoming marriage. No, no! You are mistaken, I am sure.'

'I think not. Sir Reynold told me the man was very deep. He rid himself of his wife, you know . . .'

'I do not understand you and, what is more, I do not want to hear any more!' She tugged at her plait and frowned. 'I do not like the man—his manners are appalling—but he seems to have the knack of inspiring loyalty in the servants here, which is a good sign, surely!'

'In servants who expected him to succeed Aylmer? Why, of course they jump to obey him. His own servants were too loyal for their own good, too. I warn you, Ursula, they will take orders from him rather than from you, if you are not careful. His wife, the Lady Idonia—may God have mercy on her soul—offended him, and was found lying in a ditch at dawn, with a fever . . . whereof she shortly died. And she not nineteen years of age!' The Lady Editha gave a nod, as if to say that that clinched the matter.

'And did he put her in the ditch? And if so, why did she not climb out? And did he give her a fever? And how, pray, can you give anyone a fever?'

'By ill-treatment, they say. She was a great beauty, rich and of noble family. She had many suitors, of course, but she was one of my lord Aylmer's wards, and he decided to marry her off to his favourite, Benedict. At one point the Lady Idonia said she wished to marry someone else, but since she was already betrothed to the cripple she was persuaded to go through with the match.'

'I don't understand how a woman can change her mind about marrying a man so quickly. Is a contract of betrothal not as binding, almost, as marriage?'

'Ah, but they say Benedict treated his wife badly from the very beginning. Who can wonder at her disliking to be tied to such an ugly, awkward creature? I am sure I do not wonder at it. He may be all very well on the battlefield, but in bed . . .' She shrugged. 'Unable to perform, I believe.'

'If that were true, she could have obtained an annulment.'

'I believe she wanted one, but he would not agree. He went away to the wars, and left her all alone in a poor sort of manor-house, with servants to watch her every movement. If he was so fond of her, why didn't he leave her here with Aylmer's wife? Would that not have been more suitable? Eh? Answer me that! But, no! He has to pack her off to an isolated estate of his, far from her friends. I am sure it would have been nothing to wonder at if the poor girl had committed suicide . . .'

'Make up your mind, aunt. Suicide or murder?'

'I am not saying it was either. All I say is that the girl was found one morning at the edge of the moat, in mysterious circumstances; and that she had a fever, and died.'

'What are these mysterious circumstances?'

'It was said that she was trying to run away at the time, and fell into the moat, and got wet. Hence the fever. They do say she had been writing in secret to someone, had been intending to meet him . . . had talked much of him. You may be quite sure those servants knew more about her death than they let on.'

'Well, you may be quite sure I will not be found floating in the moat one morning. It sounds to me that your Lady Idonia was no better than she ought to have been. You would say that she had a lover, within a year of her marriage? How could she break her marriage vows so quickly, even if the man did repel her? Ugly though he is, cripple though he may be, yet surely she need not have created a scandal.'

'Oh, that sort of man has no scruples, you know. They say he was very pleased to hear of his wife's death, which to my mind proves the case against him. She was rich, and he inherited everything, you see. I can't help remembering the Lady Idonia, when I think how you now stand between him and Aylmer's inheritance.'

'Well, he will be gone by nightfall, and we will see no more of him.'

* * *

The previous evening they had sent off a carrier pigeon, carrying a message of hope to Salwarpe. Ursula followed the pigeon's swoop in her mind as it winged its way first across the forest, and then over the low-lying hills around Spereshot, before it descended at last onto the roof of its cote. From Spereshot another pigeon would relay the message to Salwarpe. Even now her grandfather might be taking the message from the cylinder attached to the pigeon's leg, and unrolling the fine paper within.

Benedict had wanted to work out a cipher for the message, but Aylmer and Lady Editha had been so anxious to reassure Sir Henry without delay, that the message had been sent in clear. Now Ursula was full of doubts. Suppose Hugo's men had been on the look-out for a pigeon, and shot it down, before it got to Salwarpe? Hugo would be able to read the message, then. He would learn that Aylmer would not be able to bring any force of men to Salwarpe until Michaelmas. He would also learn that Benedict was going to try to get into Salwarpe by the river route.

Ursula tossed her head. It was not like her to be so pessimistic. She would go to look for the chapel, and kneel before the Rood, and say a prayer.

'Please, God! Don't let Salwarpe be taken, and make me a good wife to my lord, and don't let Benedict hate me . . .'

Or something like that. She wasn't accustomed to making up prayers, and wasn't sure she had much faith in them when she did. But she did intend to be a good wife to Aylmer.

This train of thought reminded her that Aylmer had promised to show her the garden of the castle that morning, so she sped down the stairs in search of him.

* * *

He was there, waiting for her, by the gate into the garden. High brick walls surrounded a quiet green place. There were espaliered fruit-trees round the walls, heavy with fruit and the hum of bees. Down the centre of the garden ran a shallow canal, and over the water were low arched bridges. It was a pleasant place, drowsy with the heavy scent of late roses, honeysuckle and lilies.

Aylmer had had a gardener pick a posy of mixed flowers for Ursula. He kissed her hand as he closed her fingers around the flowers, and she was amused to see that her skin was as brown as his.

'Now you see me in all my morning glory,' she said, 'with my hair in a plait and wearing an old gown. Do you still think me beautiful?'

'Beauty you have in plenty; but you have something more than beauty, and it is that which first attracted me to you. You have the air of one who enjoys life.'

She sobered. 'And yet now and then it stabs at me, thinking of Salwarpe. How can I be happy . . .?' She brushed her sleeve across her cheek. 'But I will not cry this morning. Are you not doing everything possible?'

'I wondered if you thought I ought to go to Salwarpe, instead of Benedict.'

'Oh, no. How could you? That would not be right, indeed it would not. I would have no rest, if you were to go. Besides, who else could muster men to relieve Salwarpe at Michaelmas? Did I sound ungrateful? I did not mean it. Tell me; I was trying to remember . . . was it you gave me a cup and ball years ago, when I was a child?'

'Why, yes! Your grandfather and my father were good friends, and before your father died we were often guests at each other's expense. I thought you would have forgotten that little toy, it was so long ago . . . soon after I wed Joan . . .'

He looked pensive and she sought to distract him. She put the posy to her lips and kissed the flowers, smiling at him over their petals.

'Then you will remember that we do not have as big a garden as this at Salwarpe. In fact, we do not have a proper garden at all—only a sheltered corner in which grandfather likes to sit and hear me tell my lessons. Sometimes he tells me stories there, too. We do not have any lilies there, but strangely enough there is a rose like this one here, and also a bower of honeysuckle. When you gave me these flowers, it was as if you were making me a gift of Salwarpe.'

'And so it shall be. Your grandfather taught you how to say pretty things. Now will you tell me why you frown?'

She put her hand within his arm, and sighed. 'Is it so obvious? I try not to worry. I tell myself that you know best, that it is none of my business . . .'

'. . . but . . .?'

'. . . is there not a saying "divide and rule"? I wonder how your lieutenants will fare—how Salwarpe will fare—under a divided command. You told me yourself that Sir Reynold and Sir Benedict were enemies.'

'Do you think that had not occurred to me? Aye, and kept me awake a large part of the night, too. I would it had been any other man but Reynold to win the place! It was in my mind at first to declare the dice faulty, and select some other man to go with Benedict. Then it came to me that perhaps here was a chance to heal the breach between them, which time alone has failed to do.'

'Perhaps we might leave it to chance, if this were an unimportant matter, but it is an affair of life and death.'

'I realise that. There was an easy way out of the difficulty, of course. Knowing Benedict, I guessed he would seek me out early this morning . . .'

'To request that Reynold be placed under his command, or removed?'

'Why, no. You misread his character. No, Benedict offered to resign the mission altogether. He said almost any other of my knights who had had siege experience would do as well as he, and would—being senior to Reynold—automatically take the command.'

'You accepted?'

'I refused. There is no other man I would trust in this as I trust Benedict.'

'I heard a rumour . . .' She stopped, biting her lip.

'Ah. I saw Reynold whispering in your aunt's ear, and guessed how it would be. You heard that Benedict was jealous of Reynold, on account of Idonia? Well, there is some truth in the story, though not as much as people make out. Benedict took his wife away before there was any actual damage done—except in my eyes and the eyes of my wife, of course.'

'Do you always take Benedict's side?' Her

tone was neutral, but she removed her hand from his arm.

He swung her to face him. 'Ursula, I do not know what tale you have heard, but it is best we have this matter out between us. Benedict's father was my dearest friend, and when he died I willingly took the boy into my household. His estate was not of any great size but sufficiently well-ordered to make the boy of interest on the marriage market. Idonia was the only surviving daughter of a distant cousin, whose wardship passed to me when the girl was twelve. She had been brought up in a convent. I knew little of her, save that she was beautiful and considered sharp-witted.

'When Idonia came to join my household from the convent, there were many young men anxious for her favours, and of these she liked Benedict and Reynold best. Now Reynold's marriage was already in the process of being arranged by his family—he was a squire in my household at the time. If Idonia had shown a clear preference for Reynold at the time, we might perhaps have rearranged matters . . . but she decided to take Benedict. And knowing both young men well, I thought she would be best off with Benedict. So the betrothal took place. They both seemed well pleased; Benedict could not take his eyes off her, in fact.

'Then everything went wrong. There was a bad storm one night. It rained so hard that day and the next that we could barely crawl about. On the third day we went to inspect what damage had been done . . . floods everywhere . . . crops beaten down . . . cattle drowned. There is a wall below the castle, holding back the road. A spring had broken out behind the wall, and it was bulging outwards. As we returned, the wall came down on us . . . stonework, earth, water . . . flinging clear across the road. Benedict caught me up and threw me forward, but was trapped by one leg himself. Where I had been standing . . .' He swallowed. 'I would have been killed, for sure.

'It was thought at first that Benedict's leg must be amputated, but with careful nursing it was saved. Only it did not set straight. And while he was in pain, unable to rise from his bed, Reynold flirted with Idonia.

'Some women are not good at nursing the sick. She would not sit with Benedict or try to help him. She began to speak carelessly to him, and then hurtfully. She would whisper with Reynold, glance at Benedict, toss her head and say something designed to make him feel badly. If he had not loved her so much, he would not have cared. But he did love her, and he did care.'

'Why did you let them go through with the marriage?'

'You cannot break the bonds of betrothal for a whim. Reynold was formally betrothed to someone else by that time. Idonia was young, and once removed from Reynold's side, safe in Benedict's hands . . . for I knew him to be trustworthy and kind . . . I thought—we all thought—that the marriage would turn out well enough. She agreed she might as well marry Benedict, since she could not have Reynold.'

'But he failed her in bed?'

'I am not sure. She said so. He became a grim and silent man, overnight. She . . . she was found in Reynold's arms within a week of the marriage. My wife told Benedict to give Idonia a good whipping. My wife was the mildest of women, who could hardly bear to chastise a puppy, but she refused to have Idonia about the castle any longer. She was very fond of Benedict, you see. She blamed Idonia for everything. I warned Reynold to be more careful. I told him it would be as well if he accompanied me to France that year, to give Benedict and Idonia a chance.'

'Then Idonia was not running away to be with Reynold?'

'Most unlikely. Although . . . well, it was not Reynold who accompanied me to France, but Benedict. Reynold went off to a tournament here, a tournament there, winning laurels everywhere. It was Benedict who came with me to France. And I was with him when the news came that Idonia had caught a chill and died.'

'I must ask this. Was he surprised?'

'Surprised? He was stunned. He could neither speak nor hear. He just sat there. I could not get him to speak of her then, or since. It is my belief that he loves her as deeply now as he did then.'

'And you would send this man into Salwarpe with Reynold on equal terms?'

'No.' He led Ursula to where a marble bench had been strewn with bright cushions, and seated her. 'I asked them both to join me here in the garden at noon to discuss the matter. And here they come.'

Reynold was striding towards them, plucking at his belt, his lower lip jutting. His eyes were everywhere, but each time they passed over Ursula his lips formed a smile which seemed to say, 'I would say such things, if I were alone with you . . .'

Benedict arrived at their bench, without their having seen him approach. One moment he was not there, and the next he was standing with folded arms, and his crooked leg thrust forward, his eyes on the gravel at his feet.

'Reynold and Benedict. Well met.'

'It is not to be borne!' cried Reynold, frowning and smiling at one and the same time. 'I have slept on it, as you bade me do, and I say it is not to be borne that I should serve under Benedict! Of what use is a cripple in an assault? What experience has he of the tournament? Would he be able to withstand more than one pass with the lance? It is absurd even to think of it!'

Aylmer held up his hand and Reynold came to a halt. 'Benedict has already offered to resign, and I have refused to let him do so. It is true he has little experience of tournaments, but his experience of siege warfare and of life in the field is extensive. Moreover he is not a man to be baited easily, as you may have observed. If you find it impossible to serve with him, may I suggest that you consider following his lead and . . .'

'Allow the Ladies of Salwarpe to point the finger at me as a coward? Never! I will fight for them to the last!'

'Then will you not look on this as a holy cause? Will you not take Benedict by the hand, and let bygones be bygones, that you may both serve me in this matter?'

'If he will acknowledge me as commander of the garrison,' said Reynold, 'Then I am willing to take him with me.'

Benedict lifted his head from contemplation of the ground long enough to say, 'Surely the Lord of Salwarpe is commander of the garrison, and we but his lieutenants?'

'Oh, in theory; yes,' said Reynold. 'But in practice . . .'

'He is advanced in years, of course,' said Benedict. 'But in his prime he saw much service in France. I heard legends of his prowess when I was a boy. Legends such as that are worth a hundred mercenaries. I say that not only is he commander of the garrison now, but that he must remain so.'

'We will see to that when we get there,' said Reynold.

'Enough!' cried Aylmer 'Either you compose your differences, or neither of you shall go!'

There was silence, full of unspoken objections. Aylmer took a hasty turn around the bench. 'It was in my mind,' he said, 'That we could ride to my hunting-lodge in the forest this afternoon. Any news from Salwarpe or Spereshot must pass through the forest along the road which skirts the lodge, so that you would be half a day nearer your objective. We can send a messenger through to Spereshot from there, requesting that a boat and guide be made ready for you on the morrow. We could also glean news of Hugo's activities, being so much closer to Salwarpe. Is it agreed?'

'Yes,' said Benedict, looking askance at Reynold.

'Only if it is understood I am in command,' said Reynold.

Ursula jumped to her feet. 'I will settle this business for you if I may, Aylmer? I have your posy of flowers here. Reynold and Benedict shall each choose one. Whichever chooses my favourite shall wear my gage and be set in authority over the other. Is it agreed?'

Reynold laughed aloud. 'Of course. And I

choose the rose, the rose of love for the Lady of Love.'

Benedict frowned. He looked long and hard at Ursula, and then at the flowers she carried. He said. 'Honeysuckle. That is her colour.'

'Yes,' said Ursula. 'You have chosen wisely, Benedict. It is the honeysuckle, and you shall have overall command, under my grandfather.'

Before Reynold could object, she handed him the rose and closed his fingers over it. If he chose to interpret her gesture as a promise, then that was his affair. She was promising nothing, but she could still his mounting anger with a smile. He took his defeat gracefully. He even bowed to her, before turning and leaving the garden. When she looked round to give Benedict his flower, he also had disappeared.

'That was well done,' said Aylmer. 'Now, tell me—which of the flowers is really your favourite?'

'The rose,' she said, without hesitation. 'Naturally. But as you said from the beginning, Benedict is the best man for a siege. Also he seems to understand about grandfather, which is more than Reynold does. Now, may I come with you to the hunting-lodge, to see them off?'

CHAPTER FOUR

The sky began to cloud over during their canter through the forest and, as they drew up in the courtyard of the hunting-lodge, they were spattered with rain. Servants had been sent ahead of them, so that a fire was already warming the hall, and appetising aromas came from the kitchen at the rear.

Lady Editha dismounted somewhat stiffly, but was as eager as Ursula to enquire if there were any news. No, said the verdurer who lived there. Men had been set to watch the road from Spereshot, but no-one had ridden down from the north that day.

Aylmer took Ursula up into a solar above and behind the hall, and pointed out of a window to a gap in the trees. 'Can you see the jumble of hills beyond the forest's edge? There lies Spereshot, and beyond it . . .'

'The river and the marsh. I know my way from Spereshot, for we often ride that way when we hunt, and to see our neighbours.'

She thought of their recent wild ride from Salwarpe, pausing in Spereshot only long enough to gasp out the news to the lord of the manor and his wife, and collect a carrier pigeon or two, before they fled on and on, down the forest track to Aylmer and safety . . . in constant fear of pursuit . . .

She brushed her hand across her eyes and smiled at Aylmer.

He said, 'I will go send a messenger to Spereshot.'

She was grateful that he left her alone. Now that she was so much closer to home, her impatience mounted. She had had an important role to play at Aylmer's castle, but she had nothing to do now but wait, and smile . . . and smile . . . and tell Aylmer how grateful she was for what he was doing.

The business of hanging around waiting for someone else to do something was intolerable.

She was too restless to sit still for long, but wandered to and fro, up and down the stairs, pausing every now and then to peer through the lightly falling rain . . . up the road to Spereshot. So near, and yet so far away.

Back at the castle, all had been in a bustle, preparing for her wedding. In three days' time she was to be wed to Aylmer, and there would be another feast, with music and jugglers and acrobats and who knew what else? And meantime her grandfather would be sitting out a siege.

Time did not seem to move in the hunting-lodge. Salwarpe might be in another world. There was a placid air over the ancient half-timbered building, which communicated itself to everyone except Ursula. Even Lady Editha was content to sit back and do nothing. She was an excellent horsewoman and loved to hunt. Now she sat and yawned and talked to Reynold of stags and dogs. Presently Aylmer came to sit and play at chess with Reynold.

Benedict had vanished. Ursula found him in a byre, fashioning a harness which would carry a basket of pigeons on his back. He looked up from his task long enough to stare at her and then was busy again. One of the verdurer's children was holding some tools for Benedict and another, smaller one had curled up with a kitten and was fast asleep on Benedict's cloak.

Ursula struck one hand on the other and closed her eyes. She told herself that she must be patient. News would come sooner or later, and none the sooner for her chafing.

As it happened, she was not even looking out of the window when a horseman came riding down the forest road. The man was mud-spattered, and gasping with fatigue. He dragged his saddlebag off his horse and threw it on the table before Aylmer, scattering the chess pieces.

'You are bid . . . desist!' he said. 'My master sends you warning! Desist or it will be the worse for you!'

'Your master, fellow? Are you not a man from Spereshot?'

'Spereshot?' The man grimaced. 'Spereshot is aflame, my lord. Barns and all. Men dangle from the trees, and pigeons . . . roast.'

Reynold pulled on the thong that fastened the neck of the saddlebag, and upended it. Out tumbled a carrier pigeon, the shaft of an arrow through its body. It was dead. The cylinder on its leg was empty.

Lady Editha's rings scattered on the floor, but Ursula put her hands to her breast and pressed them there.

Reynold sprang to his feet, dagger in hand. Benedict, who as usual had come from nowhere, laid his hand on the messenger's arm and shouldered Reynold aside.

'Tell us what you know,' said Benedict.

'I know nothing,' said the man, his face glistening with fear. 'I saw nothing. I was thrashing corn in the barn when they came on us, and my master . . . Oh, God! I think he got away, though he was badly hurt, I know. But the mistress, and her little ones . . . he took them. Hugo de Frett. He took them away with him, and they were screaming . . .' He put his hands over his ears, and closed his eyes. Then he resumed. 'We were made to line up outside the barn, and he fired it with his own hand. Two of our men he strung up above the flames, alive. The manor house was already burning, and the other outbuildings. It was like hell. There was a man in your livery there, and he was writhing on the ground . . . but soon he lay still. He was luckier than some, for he died quickly. Hugo asked who could ride a good horse, and I said I could, and he said he would spare my cottage, if I rode to you with the pigeon before sunset . . . as you see . . .'

Benedict put his arm under the messenger's shoulders. The man sagged and fell. Now they saw that he was bleeding from a wound on his back.

Benedict caught him up. The man was still trying to talk. He said, 'My little girl . . .!' He caught his breath on a sob.

'Yes,' said Benedict. 'We understand. Have faith in God. It is the only way. Come, let me bind your wound.'

'No, let me do it,' said Ursula. 'None of this would have happened, but for us. You are needed to take counsel with my lord. So, let me do what I can.'

She led the messenger away to the kitchen, and bathed his wound and listened while he talked on and on, never ceasing . . . until finally she made him drink a sleeping-potion, and his eyes closed even as he said, 'My little girl . . .'

Ursula arrived back in the solar in time to hear Aylmer say, 'Then we are all agreed that the attempt must be abandoned for the time being? Ursula, my dear . . .'

'Why must the attempt be abandoned?' she said. 'Is the matter not more urgent now than before?'

'Without a guide or a boat—both of which we looked to find in Spereshot—we can go no further. We must send a strong letter of protest to Hugo de Frett, warning him that unless he withdraws, the end of the harvest will see the end of him.'

'By which time he will have his hands on our estates, and those of our friends in Spereshot, and since possession is nine tenths of the law . . .'

'I am not without influence, myself. Be sure the law will deal with him in due course.'

'How many more men must hang, how many more buildings must burn, before the law catches up with Hugo? Spereshot is not the only place on the river where one can obtain boats . . .'

'We realise that Benedict is going to make his way up river till he can cross it at the next bridge, and hire a boat and guide there. Or if not there—for it is far from here, and the local people may not wish to travel so far from their homes—then he can make his way back to the abbey, which is on the opposite bank of the river from Salwarpe. Surely the abbot will hire us a small boat and a guide.'

'That would take two days—three—maybe even four. I will guide Benedict and Reynold into Salwarpe. I know where there is a boat to be found on the marshes . . .'

Aylmer laughed. It was a mistake.

Ursula clenched her hands. 'Do you think I could not do it?'

'Why, that is no work for a maid, surely.'

'I am so recently become a maiden that I hardly know how to act when my people are attacked. Should I sit and weep all day? Should I retire to the chapel, and pray? Or should I strike a blow against my enemy, when his neck is bared before me?'

'Ursula, you have not considered . . .'

'I do not need to consider. It is clear what I must do. I know the tides, and I know the channel. I know the way up the hillside . . .'

'My dear, it is out of the question. For one thing, it is clear that your grandfather never received our message saying that Benedict was on the way . . .'

'All the more reason for me to give him the message, otherwise he may lose hope and surrender . . .'

'He may already have done so. Have you thought of that? An old man, faced with impossible odds . . .'

'You do not know him!' She threw up her head. 'He would never surrender!'

Aylmer sighed. It was the half angry, determined-to-be-patient sigh of a man sorely tried. 'A woman cannot understand . . .'

Ursula went white. 'To the devil with what you think women can understand! I tell you . . .

'Listen to me, Ursula!' It was not often that Aylmer raised his voice, but when he did, his servants quailed. Ursula did not quail, but she did hold her tongue.

'Listen to me, Ursula,' he repeated, this time more gently. 'If your grandfather did not receive our message—which he plainly did not—then even if you did by some outside chance elude Hugo's men and reach the marshes . . . even if you did find this boat of which you speak . . . and ran the hazard of the channel to reach the foot of the cliff . . . suppose you did all that, how do you suppose you are going to be greeted when you reach the postern gate? There will be no ropes, waiting for you. There will be sentries instead, ready to fire on any movement . . .'

'I . . . but Benedict was willing to . . .'

'He wishes to try, but he admits himself that he has small hope of succeeding. And do you think I would allow you to go, where even he is doubtful of success? My dear, be reasonable. Do you not think that all the boats on the river will have been commandeered by now? And a watch mounted on this famous channel of yours? Suppose the three of you were out on the river, and were captured by Hugo's men? Would not that be a fatal blow to our cause? Would I not have to abandon your grandfather, to ransom you? Would not your grandfather be forced to abandon Salwarpe, for the same reason?'

The Lady Editha gave a little cry and sank onto a bench. Ursula hesitated and then went to her, putting her arms round the older woman.

'There is only one thing,' said Benedict, speaking with his usual diffidence. 'All pigeons look alike, save to those who have trained them. But it seems to me that the pigeon we sent back to Spereshot had more white feathers on it than this one. I cannot be sure, of course. Could either of the ladies identify their pigeon?'

Both Ursula and Editha shook their heads.

'Then it is possible—only possible, of course—that Hugo is bluffing. Sir Henry may well have received our message, and know that we are coming. Hugo's men may have been on the look-out for a pigeon; very likely they were. But there is nothing to prove that this one is the one we sent.'

'Then how do you account for Spereshot being burned?'

'We did not keep our meeting secret the other day. He could have heard by a dozen different routes. Messengers have been passing freely from us to Spereshot. The ladies rode to Spereshot when they left Salwarpe. So Hugo looks hard at Spereshot and, when he hears that one of your men is there, he rides over to investigate. He could have learned the details of our plan from your messenger before he died, and not from the pigeon.'

'Either way he has burned Spereshot, and denied us the boat and guide we need.' Aylmer sighed. 'The man knows his business. We will return to the castle in the morning, and hold another meeting.'

Ursula said nothing, but her eyes were mutinous. Perhaps she would have accepted Aylmer's decision as final, if it had not been for the accident. In such case, it is unlikely that

Salwarpe would ever have been relieved.

*   *   *

The rain ceased, but a mist hung over the forest. The air smelt fresh, and there was a general stirring of greenery after the long drought.

'It will be another fine day tomorrow,' said Aylmer, looking out of the window at the evening sky. 'Providing this mist lifts. We should make good time on our journey back to the castle.'

Servants were bringing dishes in to lay on the tables for supper. Aylmer never travelled anywhere without his own cook and personal attendants, who tended to get in each other's way when in a confined space. A scullion collided with the butler, and a dish went flying. Aylmer stepped in the grease and fell, catching his side on a trestle-table.

At first it seemed the injury was slight, but Benedict looked grave as he helped Aylmer to a bench. Ursula took one look at Aylmer's contorted face and thrust Benedict aside. Her hands confirmed what Benedict's frown had already told her.

'Why, my lord! You have cracked a couple of ribs, it seems,' she said. 'You will not ride back to the castle as fast as you came here.'

Her eyes met Benedict's. The ribs were not cracked, but smashed. What an unlucky chance! And yet . . .

Benedict's eyes continued to hold hers, and seemed to be saying . . .

She rose to her feet, thinking hard. Had the idea leaped from his head into hers, or had it been there all along, waiting for an opportunity to surface?

If Aylmer were ill, and not able to oversee matters with his usual competence . . . If he were, for instance, to be given a sleeping-draught tonight . . . and oversleep. Surely he would need a sleeping-draught, for he was in pain. And then . . .?

Benedict gathered Aylmer into his arms and carried him up the stairs and into the solar. His strength was amazing. Of course, it was all in his arms and the upper part of his body, making him look top-heavy, except when he was on horseback.

Ursula continued to stand there, tapping her teeth. Then she realised that both Reynold and her aunt were staring at her; the one with bewilderment, and the other with something very like fear. Yes, Aunt Editha would guess what was in her niece's mind, and would be afraid, even as Aylmer had been afraid for her.

Ursula squared her shoulders and went to help Benedict make Aylmer comfortable.

Only, she was conscious that both men were watching her, and waiting . . .

At first she thought she would say nothing to Aylmer. It would be better to let him sleep, and then she could slip away at first light with Benedict and Reynold, and Aylmer be none the wiser till she was long gone.

Only, the look in Aylmer's eyes echoed the fear in her aunt's face. And Benedict seemed to expect her to seek Aylmer's permission for what she was about to do. Quite how it came about that she was aware of what Benedict expected of her, she did not know. He stood between her and the door, willing her to confess . . .

Confess? What an absurd word to use! She was merely going to do what lay in her power to save Salwarpe. Aylmer was not her lord and master—yet.

But presently she knelt by his bed, took his hand in hers and put it to her cheek.

She said, 'My lord, forgive me that I disobey you. I must go to Salwarpe. If I fail, then you are well rid of me. But if I succeed, then I will only be repaying my grandfather for his past care of me.'

Aylmer's fingers tightened around hers. He said, 'I knew you would go . . . I saw it in your face . . . and in Benedict's. Ursula, I am afraid . . .'

'So am I. But not as afraid as I would be if I stayed here, and did nothing. I know this is a bad beginning to our marriage . . . but would you have me break faith with my grandfather at such a time?'

'No. I love you the more for it. Only, I

wish we might have been wed before you put yourself into danger.'

Benedict said, 'Shall I send for the priest from the castle? He might be here some two hours after dawn, if he rides fast.'

Aylmer had closed his eyes, to hide his pain. Ursula bathed his forehead.

She said, 'I had thought to leave at dawn, but if you wish, I will stay . . . only, I want to be on the marshes at sunset, and any delay . . .'

Aylmer shook his head and then stiffened the muscles of his face. The slightest movement caused him agony. He opened his eyes and said, 'No, my love. Go at dawn. I would be a poor sort of bridegroom in this state, would I not? I did not think of wooing you like this. You shall go, and I shall stay behind to recover. And when it is all over I will come to Salwarpe and we will wed there, with your grandfather to give you away. Only, will you kiss me before you go, Ursula?'

She was near to tears. 'I don't want to hurt you . . .'

He smiled and gave her hand a tug. She kissed him, trying not to hurt him. He sighed and closed his eyes.

She stood up, feeling as if she had been dismissed. Benedict was ready with a sleeping-draught. He bent to Aylmer, giving him the potion with smooth efficiency.

He said, over his shoulder, 'Reynold and I will be ready at dawn. I will tell the servants to have your horse saddled. Go now and get some sleep.'

*   *   *

Aunt Editha cried. 'You cannot, must not go! You will be captured, for sure! Or that monster Benedict will do something terrible . . .'

'He is not a monster, and I think I would trust him further than I would trust Reynold . . .'

'If you would only let me come with you . . .'

'Impossible. Now, my dear, be sensible. You know you could never climb that cliff, and besides that, who is to nurse Aylmer if you come with me?'

'Ah, the poor man! How could you leave him in such straits?'

Ursula said nothing to that. In truth, when she thought of Aylmer, she did feel guilty. That kiss . . .

She had never kissed a man on the mouth before. It had been a strange experience, and she was not at all sure she wanted to repeat it too quickly. Of course she was going to be a good wife to Aylmer; that went without saying. But he seemed to want more than dutiful compliance from her, and she was not sure that she knew how to give it. When she had thought of being married to Aylmer, she had thought of his wooing her, of his putting his arm round her, and stealing a kiss . . . and then becoming bolder, perhaps . . . it was to have been a progression of love. She would have had time to become accustomed to his caresses that way, and then in due course she would no doubt have been able to return them.

She was—not exactly frightened—but certainly taken aback by the demands he was making on her. Of course she would have married him straight away if he had insisted on it, but she was rather glad that he had not done so. They would have time now, to adjust to their new roles.

* * *

Long before dawn the two women were up and about. Editha helped Ursula to coil her hair up into a net. Her skirts she kilted about her, as peasant women often did when they worked in the fields. Her long riding-boots would serve well enough, and overall she wore a serviceable wool cloak with a deep hood.

Benedict and Reynold were waiting for her by the stables. She mounted her horse and, with a lantern slung at her saddlebow, led them away from the lodge up the trail through the forest. She looked back only once. There was a light in Aylmer's room. She turned away from the sight as if it hurt her eyes.

She led them along the forest track, keeping well ahead, and relying on her ears to tell her if the others lagged behind . . . which they did not. Presently she could extinguish her lantern.

All the time she kept scanning the sky ahead. The mist had not cleared, and faint rustlings came from around and above as droplets formed and fell onto the earth beneath the trees. On either side of the track could be heard the mournful chirp of birds, disturbed in their passing; but ahead of them the sky was clear.

If there had been any great force of men moving on the track ahead of them, the sky above the trees ahead would have been aswirl with birds. But it was not.

At midday she led them off the track into the forest to the east, and sought for the stream which she knew ran parallel to the path. She could hear it even in this subdued, misty weather . . . yes, there it was.

She signed to the men that they should break their fast and rest awhile. They had spoken little to each other on the way there, and even now Benedict seemed as disinclined as Ursula to talk. She sat some way from them, with her back to a tree.

At last Reynold could bear it no longer. 'Shall we not pass the time of day with the maiden?'

Benedict said, 'If she wishes us to attend on her, she will no doubt say so.'

'You are so ungallant . . .'

'I am mindful of Aylmer.'

'Who is not here . . .'

'I am willing to be his left hand, even if his right is disabled.'

'A new part for you to play—that of protector of women!'

There was no reply, but it appeared Benedict had said enough to restrain Reynold, for the latter made no attempt to approach Ursula then, or during the afternoon's journey.

They did not return to the track, but followed the course of the stream, which gained strength as it ran north and then turned a little to the east. Once they came near the outskirts of the forest, and then Ursula held up her hand, and was still.

The smell of burning drifted downwind to them and once she thought she heard men shouting. They were within half a mile of Spereshot.

Now they went on with even more caution than before, picking their way to the north-east through dense thickets. They were following a second stream now. Not once did Ursula falter. She had hunted widely over this land and knew it well.

Dusk drew in early, but the light held till they came to a place where rushes began to thrust themselves up through the stream's surface.

Then and only then did Ursula dismount and turn, waiting for the two men to catch up with her.

'Your orders, lady?' said Benedict, also dismounting.

'You must obey me now as if you were children, and I your mother. If you wander from the path you will sink into the marsh, and there will be nothing I can do to help you. We are come to the edge of the estuary. The tide is coming in, as you will see in a moment. I wanted to arrive earlier, because no boats—except perhaps for a punt—can move on the marsh when the tide is out. But in this mist no one will see us.

'There are ridges of firm land in the marsh. One or two of these ridges lead to small islands which lie above the marsh even when the tide comes in and covers the rest of the estuary. On one of those islets lives a man, a fowler. He makes a living off the waterfowl and fish. He has a small shack in which we can rest till the moon rises. He also possesses a boat and a punt, one of which we will ask him to let us borrow.'

'Why ask? Why not take it by force?' said Reynold, his hand on his sword.

'Now that would be worse than useless,' said Ursula. 'The men hereabouts are a hardy lot, and resentful of foreigners. In this context you are both "foreigners". More, he is a freeman, and proud of it. If you get on the wrong side of him, he would sooner destroy his boats than allow you to borrow them.'

'How much should we pay him?' said

Benedict.

'He will do it for nothing, or he will not do it at all. Let me do the talking.' She held up her hand. 'Listen!'

They could hear the whirr of birds flying overhead, though in the misty conditions they could not see them.

'The birds are returning from the marshes on which they have spent the day. Come, follow closely where I lead. Keep your horses on a tight rein.'

She led them east, and then inland. Reynold began to protest, until he saw that they were skirting the mouth of yet another stream. They waded through the shallow stream some fifty yards inland, and then went on, always going east. Suddenly Ursula turned and walked out directly into the mist. Rushes loomed on either side of her, but the ground underfoot was firm, if springy.

Reynold slipped, and his foot splashed into water. He swore. Benedict said nothing, even when his eyes began to ache with the strain of keeping Ursula in sight. The mist was closing in. The dusk was deepening into night. Ursula's figure was sometimes a solid silhouette, and sometimes a dimly-seen wraith.

She stopped, waiting for them to catch up with her. Then she set off again, in a different direction.

Or was it a different direction? In that light it was almost impossible to tell which direction they were taking . . . time passed and surely they had been following a will-of-the-wisp for hours.

Then she paused again . . . and turned to the left, so sharply that Benedict's horse began to flounder, and he had to haul on the bridle, and coax it with muffled oaths, till it squelched out onto firmer ground, trembling . . .

A dog barked nearby.

She stopped.

She held out her hand to Benedict and looked over her shoulder at Reynold.

She said, 'We have arrived.'

They couldn't see anything. She stepped forward, and there before her a dark shape loomed out of the mist. It was a weather-beaten shack made of boards, tarred, and thatched with reeds. The lap of water was all about them.

'Ah . . . ee!' she said, between her teeth. Nearby a small boat lay, its bottom staves splintered. 'We may be too late!'

A light streamed out over them. A man was holding up a lantern, standing in the door of his cabin.

'Mistress, is it you?'

'Oh, Dickon!' Ursula ran to the man and clung to his arm. 'Oh, Dickon! We have to get back to the castle, and Hugo has sacked Spereshot, and I thought to borrow your boat . . .'

'Nay, nay! Sweetling, come within! How

cold your hands are . . . come and get warm . . . and your friends with you! Weep not! Did you think old Dickon would give Hugo best?'

He showed them where to stable the horses, in a lean-to at the back, and then drew them into his cabin, and barred the door. A fine-looking dog came to sniff and sneeze at Ursula's skirts Then—predictably—he sat at Benedict's feet to have his jaw scratched.

The cabin was barely furnished, but there was a fire, and a stew-pot simmered upon it. The aroma of stewed duck caused Ursula to swallow her tears. Dickon ladled broth and lumps of succulent meat into bowls and handed them round. His pottery was cracked but his cooking beyond reproach.

As she ate Ursula poured out their story while Dickon listened, one hand behind his right ear, and his face cracked into a hundred wrinkles.

'Nay, little mistress! We heard ye had escaped the net and we knew as you'd be back with help. I rowed into the town the day afore yesterday and spoke with the priest—poor man, fair doidered he was with all this trouble. Hugo had had the fisherfolk's boats drawn up onto the quay, and a set of his spoilers went over them, staving them in while the women wept and wailed around them.'

'What, all our boats? How are our fisherfolk to live?'

Dickon spat. 'The man's a fool. He didn't

even count them, or enquire as how many we had in the first place! Then today they rowed out here at high tide, and said as they knew I'd a boat, and where was it. So I showed them it, and they stoved it in, like the others, and I managed to squeeze out a tear or two, just as they like us to do. And then they went off, hugging theirselves, and I got the punt out of the water again, where I'd sunk it at the end of a rope, and it's drying out nicely.'

'You saved the punt? Oh, Dickon, how clever you are!'

'I thought as I'd best let them have the boat, seeing as they'd noticed me rowing around in it. They didn't know about the punt, and I wasn't about to tell them. Besides, I can go almost anywhere on the marshes in the punt, but the boat I can only use in the channels or when the tide's in. A' course, it'll only take me a day or so to mend the other.'

'So,' said Ursula, 'Hugo does know that we intended to get into Salwarpe by boat. He wouldn't have gone to all that trouble, smashing up the boats, otherwise. And that means grandfather probably doesn't know we're coming.'

Benedict leaned forward. 'Is Hugo keeping any sort of watch on the channel from the river which leads to the foot of the castle cliff?'

'Aye. He took the best of the Peasmarsh's boats, and it's sitting out there with a crew of landsmen in it, all holding their stomachs and wailing they're going to die. Aye, they're on guard, if you can call it that. At low tide they're more often on the mud than afloat, and at high tide they drag their anchor with the slightest of breezes. But it's true that they sit across the channel, a stone's throw from the foot of the cliff.'

'Then we're lost,' said Reynold. 'And what's more, we're trapped here, where Hugo can send to pick us up as he pleases.'

Ursula gave him an indignant look. 'Do you think Dickon would betray us? None saw us come, and none will see us leave. Dickon, can you get us to the bottom of the cliff?'

'Why, my little maid, we can but try. But have you thought as how the men in the boat will see you clear in the dawn, when you climb the cliff?'

'In the dawn!' Reynold swore. 'Are we to wait till then, to be picked off with crossbows as we climb a cliff to a place where the defenders will rain down arrows on us? If the people in the castle don't know we're coming, they're sure to mistake us for enemies . . .'

'We are in your hands, Master Dickon,' said Benedict, as quiet as usual. 'You will tell us what to do.'

The old man rubbed his chin and looked sideways at Reynold. He spat near that gallant knight's mailed foot, and then slapped his thighs.

'Aye. Ye'd best lay yourself down and rest

a while. You can't climb that cliff in the dark. No-one could. Not even the maid here.'

I'm afraid that's true,' said Ursula.

'There's another reason for waiting a while,' said Dickon. 'The tide's in now, which means that Hugo's boat can move about freely. They've eight strong men aboard, and if they set their minds to it they could overtake one heavy-laden punt afore you could spit out a Hail Mary. We'll wait till the tide's going out, when they can only move in the channel. We'll set out in the dark, afore dawn, going across the marshes. The punt-pole will take us where oars would not, sithee. I know every inch of the way. With luck they'll not see us or hear us till we get to the cliff.'

'Do we have to cross their path at all?'

'Aye. There's only one place you can land a boat and climb that hill, and that's where the channel comes in. We must try to reach that point before dawn, and wait there till sunrise. Sometimes the mist hangs about the estuary all morning, but I think there's a change coming in the weather . . . maybe it'll lift with the dawn. One thing. Ye'll have to travel without your armour. Three heavy men, a maid and a dog . . .' he shrugged. 'Ye'll have to sit as still as mice while the cat's watching . . . or else ye'll drown us all.'

Benedict took off his helmet, wriggled out of his chain mail tunic and unbuckled the heavy, padded jerkin beneath. He held up his sword in its scabbard, with a questioning lift of his eyebrows.

'I'd sooner ye didn't,' said Dickon.

Benedict threw that down, too.

Reynold's face was dark. 'Does a knight go into battle without armour? I shall retain my sword, even if you choose to disgrace your knighthood by throwing yours away.'

Benedict said, 'I thought it was our heads that were needed on the hill-top, not our swords.'

With a bad grace, Reynold also divested himself of his armour.

'I will take it back to the mainland and bury it where I can retrieve it later,' said Dickon. 'Mayhap I can even bring it out to ye another dark night, and leave it at the foot of the hill.'

'Will you not come up into the safety of the castle with us?' said Benedict. 'Surely you will be safer, there.'

'Nenni,' said Dickon. 'I be afeared of heights. The little lass knows.'

'Yes,' said Ursula, caressing the old man. 'I do know. But I wish you would try, just this once, Dickon. If Hugo finds out that you have tricked him, and been the means of Benedict's getting into Salwarpe . . . what then?'

'Why, then take to the punt and hide in the reeds till he be gone home again. Ye cannot tear Dickon from his roots, mistress. Now rest ye awhile. I will take the horses back to the mainland, with the armour. I have a cousin lives not far away to the east. I will have his lad bury the armour, and hide the horses on his farm. I will leave the dog with ye, and he will give warning should any man approach . . . though it is not likely any will venture on the marshes at this time of night. If any comes, ye must take to the punt and hide in the rushes till they be gone again.'

So saying, the old man pushed Ursula towards his bed and went out into the night.

CHAPTER FIVE

Ursula shivered, huddled next the dog in the prow of the punt. The night was at its darkest, but the whisper of the tide going out suggested that time was rapidly passing.

They waited in the reeds, hearing nothing but the suck and gurgle of water in the mud around them. They had to locate the guard boat before they could move out of the reeds.

The dog was pointing into the mist, the hairs on its neck bristling. The dog was well-trained, and would not bark when cautioned against doing so by Dickon, but obviously it scented danger.

Through the mist before them they received further news of the guard boat. The chink of mail, the creak of a timber . . . and now and then they caught the glimmer of light from a lanthorn swinging at the mast.

The punt also carried a lanthorn, but it was not lit.

Something brushed at Ursula's cheek. She looked up, to see the dim figure of Dickon stiffen to attention, too. The wind had changed with the coming of the dawn.

This meant that the mist would lift, and they be exposed to full view very shortly.

Ursula felt rather than saw Benedict turn his head, as if to ask Dickon what they should do. But Benedict did not speak, or even move his arm. For that Ursula was grateful. Any sudden movement, and they would be shipping water. If she rested her hand on the side of the punt, her fingers would be in the water.

There was a new, longer sucking sound. Dickon had withdrawn his pole from the mud, where he had been holding the punt steady . . . and was leaning forward to place it into the mud once more, further along . . . and withdrawing it, dripping . . . and then in again . . . tirelessly sending the punt forward . . .

Ursula's head swivelled. They were shooting across the channel under the very nose of the guardboat. They would pass within feet of it. And if the mist should lift at that point . . .!

Dripping pole and surge of punt . . . a drag, a pull and a lift . . . and still the mist was about them, but beginning to swirl here and there in ominous fashion . . . and to become lighter . . . surely that was not the lanthorn on the guard boat, but the sun rising?

Then the pole was set more surely into the mud, and the punt began to shoot along even faster as the channel became narrower and more shallow, approaching the bank . . . and the tide ran out fast, as it always did at this point, directly under the cliff . . .

And now they were brushing through the branches of a willow that grew at the base of the hill, and . . .

A shout from behind

Ursula looked back, to see the whole of the estuary laid out in shining colours with the lifting of the mist. The guard boat was close, far closer than she had thought it would be. It was close enough for a man with a crossbow to pick them off one by one. But you could not shoot with accuracy from a boat which was rocking. The foolish landsmen who manned the guardboat had all crowded to one side to peer at the punt and its occupants.

'Now I could wish for my chain-mail back again,' said Reynold.

Benedict stood with care and leaped for the shore. The dog jumped at his heels. Reynold lurched forward, steadied by Ursula.

Dickon was crouching in the punt, rigid with fear. His chin was on his shoulder, and his hands still clasped the punt-pole.

'You must come with us,' said Benedict, holding out his hand to Dickon. 'They will kill you, otherwise. You cannot get back into the rushes in time . . .'

'I cannot climb,' quavered Dickon. 'I cannot look down . . .'

Above them the cliff towered sheer. It was at first sight a mystery how anyone could climb it, unless they had ropes.

'Then this will be the first time,' said Benedict, splashing into the water to take the pole out of Dickon's hands and snatch the pigeons and the lanthorn from the prow. 'Come, or you will endanger the maiden.'

'Take my hand,' said Ursula, grabbing Dickon's arm. 'And don't look down!'

'The punt . . .' cried Dickon.

A bolt from a crossbow spanged into the water nearby and showered them with spray. Reynold started up a narrow track to the right, barely more than a cleft up the rock.

'No, this way!' cried Ursula. 'That is a blind alley.'

'My punt!' cried Dickon, in agony, as he was dragged away.

Benedict had secured the punt's rope to the bole of the willow. Now, using his great strength, he tipped one end of the punt under water, so that it slowly sank out of sight.

Ursula started aside as earth spat at her from the bank. An arrow had missed her by no more than six inches. Then she was hauling Dickon up and into a scrubby area, where the eyes of the marksmen on the boat could not pick them out.

Reynold was panting, his face mottled. Benedict breathed through his mouth and wiped a trickle of blood from the back of his hand. The climb was a steep one, but the path clear enough so far.

'There is some cover for the next few yards,' said Ursula. 'And then there is a scree. The slightest false step and you will end up at the foot of the cliff, so follow me, but do not try to move quickly . . .'

'A scree?' said Benedict. 'That means loose stones, doesn't it?' He grinned. 'Give me five minutes, and I'll delay those marksmen while you get across the scree.'

He crept off up the hill, leaving his basket of pigeons and the lanthorn behind. A moment later he reappeared, with an armful of fist-sized stones. He slid down the track again towards the water, and presently they heard a commotion out on the water, as Benedict began to chuck stones at the boat. The landsmen were alarmed, as well they might be—conceiving they had been lured into an ambush.

'. . . Now!' cried Ursula. She picked up the pigeons and, dragging Dickon, she set off across the treacherous scree. Dickon was quaking, and praying in snatches.

Reynold followed at her heels, the dog bounding ahead. Reynold slipped, and set off a stream of stones. They rolled down the steep face of the cliff until they dropped into the water. They were over the scree and clinging to some scrubby hawthorns.

'Which way now?' cried Reynold.

'To the right, and then back on your tracks, but . . .' She had been going to say that they ought to wait for Benedict, but Reynold was off. Dickon had his hands over his eyes. He was trembling too much to move of his own volition.

Then Benedict was with them, carrying the lanthorn and still smiling. He said to Ursula, 'Can you manage the pigeons?' Without waiting for an answer, he dragged Dickon to his feet, told him to keep his eyes closed if it made him feel any better, and swept on up the path.

Round a corner they climbed, back on their tracks, and then a large boulder gave them protection from below, and a moment in which to breathe and look around. Benedict looked round the boulder and down. He drew back, wiping his hand across his forehead. 'Christ!' he said. 'It's a long way down. I begin to see what Dickon means . . .'

'Not far now,' said Ursula, casting off her cloak. 'Another patch of scree, but out of their sight . . . then into the gully . . . Pray God the ropes are still there!'

Benedict snatched up her cloak. 'Do you need this any more?' She shook her head, making sure her skirts were well kilted. There were sounds from below as of the guard boat being rowed into the cliff. Reynold reappeared, eyes wide.

'We're trapped . . . it's a dead end!'

Benedict was lighting the candle in the lantern from his tinderbox, his hands steady. He seemed absorbed in his task. He wrenched out the sides of the lantern and wound the cloak round part of it till it caught fire.

'I'm coming,' said Ursula to Reynold. 'It's up the gully to the left. There should be some ropes dangling . . .'

'There's nothing, I tell you!'

'Gently,' said Benedict. 'There's plenty of time . . .'

He began to swing the lantern and cloak by one end of the material. The flames hissed as he swung . . . and then he stepped out beyond the boulder, and swung once more . . . and let his flaming missile go . . . falling out and down . . . onto the guard boat below.

Screams and shoutings . . . splashings . . . confusion . . .

'Now,' said Benedict, adding another smear of dirt to his forehead. 'Let's see what we can do to make ourselves heard up top.'

Ursula was standing within the gully, looking up. There were no ropes dangling, as there used to be. 'Someone must have seen the commotion from above,' she said, as Benedict came up, dragging Dickon with him. 'Surely they must guess who it is who comes this way!'

'Did you have a favourite tune that you used

to sing? Or whistle?'

Ursula clapped her hands. 'If only my mouth were not so dry . . .'

She began to whistle. Dickon had collapsed into a groaning heap at their feet, and the pigeons rustled and chirked in their basket. Reynold bit on his thumb-nail.

'It's not going to work,' he said.

'Stand forward!' cried a voice from above. 'Stand forward so that we can see you, and no tricks, mind!'

Ursula stepped forward. 'It is I, Ursula—with friends! Let down the ropes at once, I beseech thee, or we will all be lost!'

There was an oath from above, and then another voice broke in, giving orders.

'Our sergeant-at-arms,' said Ursula. 'They must have fetched him to see who was trying to break in through the postern . . . as if anyone would!'

'Why not? We came this way,' said Benedict. Was there a proper stair up the hill once?'

'I believe so,' said Ursula. 'Years ago . . . before I was born. But there was a landslip or something . . .'

Then at last a rope came slithering down the gully; knotted at intervals; it was possible, but not easy to climb. Ursula went first, to show them how to do it. There were about twelve feet of rope for her to climb, and then she was helped up onto a rocky platform outside the postern gate.

Benedict shouted that they should haul the rope up next, which they did; to the end of the rope Benedict had tied the pigeon's basket, and on top the basket balanced Dickon's dog, barking with excitement and terror.

Then Reynold, slipping and sweating . . .

And finally Benedict half climbed and half allowed himself to be drawn up, the rope wound round his chest, with Dickon over his shoulder. Dickon had fainted.

'Ah, he never could a-bear heights,' said the gatekeeper.

*   *   *

Amid an excited group of people, the newcomers were pushed and pulled through the gate into the interior of the castle. Some tried to touch Ursula, some to revive Dickon, and some to calm his excited dog.

Then the crowd parted to let through a tall man, wearing a golden surcoat over chain-mail.

Ursula clapped her hands over her mouth to stifle hysteria. She had left her grandfather an old man with white hair; an upright old man, it was true, but a man who generally took his time about things. When no company was expected, Sir Henry was accustomed to wear an old brown fustian gown, and shabby leather hunting-boots.

Now his hair and moustaches had been miraculously returned to their former gold, and his cheeks bore a freshness, a ruddiness, which was not natural, but which, at a distance, might pass for youth.

His eyes, only, were the same. Slightly weary, heavily lidded, they bore the same look of faded blue patience as had always been turned on her when she reappeared from childhood escapades in a dirty condition.

She straightened her dress and then went to him. She put both arms around him and rested her head on his shoulder. His mailed arm came up to hold her close. Her eyes were bright and tearless. Usually she ran to him and clasped her arms round his neck. But not now.

She felt old, and drained of her usual energy. She felt that she loved her grandfather very much—far more than she had ever realised.

She supposed she might be growing up at last.

'Child,' he said. And that was all. It was all she needed.

She stepped back, but retained his hand in hers. 'You did not know we were coming, and that my lord Aylmer is raising a force to relieve us?'

There was a murmur of pleased surprise around her. No, they had not known.

'We knew a pigeon had been despatched to us. It was shot down within sight of the walls.

And then Hugo sent a herald under a white flag of truce, to deliver a letter . . .'

'It was not Aylmer's letter, I'll be bound!'

'No, it said nothing about raising a force to relieve us. I took no heed of it, but . . .' The blue eyes blinked. 'I am pleased to see you, Ursula.'

She pressed his fingers, which trembled within hers. He was having to make an effort to hold himself straight. The strain of these last few days must have been tremendous . . . and heaven only knew what lying message Hugo had sent! In a little while she would enquire, but in the meantime there were other duties to perform.

Reynold de Cressi was bowing before her grandfather. Even as he bent his head, he sent Ursula a fleeting glance of complicity and amusement, which told her as clearly as if he had put it into words, that Reynold thought her grandfather a doddering old fool, so to ape youth.

'This, grandfather, is one of my lord Aylmer's most trusted knights. May I present to you Sir Reynold de Cressi, a knight renowned for his prowess in the tourney, and most humbly at your service.'

'You are most welcome, sir.' Did the old voice quaver? Perhaps. Reynold obviously thought it did, for he was not too careful about hiding a grin as he acknowledged Sir Henry's greeting.

Ursula looked round for Benedict. Needless to say, the man was showing signs of his rough passage up the gully. His black tunic was rumpled and stained. His hair was tousled, his face dirty, and there was an expression of terror on his face. He would back away from the introduction, if given half a chance.

Ursula did not give him that chance. She went to him, and took his hand in hers. He tried to tug away, muttering that his hands were dirty. She tightened her hold on him.

She pulled on his hand, drawing him towards her grandfather. Reluctantly, he went with her. She raised her voice so that all the crowd around them should hear her words.

'And this, grandfather, is the man whom my lord Aylmer has sent to act as your right hand, until such time as he shall be able to come with a strong force to relieve Salwarpe. This man will show us how to defend ourselves under attack. He is a man both strong and true, and I commend him to you all. He is . . .'

'Christian de Huste's son, as I live!' said Sir Henry, his eye brightening. 'You are young—Benedict! That is the name, is it not? Why, you are the very image of your father. I would have known you anywhere. Welcome, indeed!'

Something quivered in Benedict's face. He went down on one knee before Sir Henry and kissed the old man's hand.

Sir Henry's wrinkled claw rested on the

tousled black head and he repeated his words with emphasis. 'You are welcome, de Huste. For your father's sake, and for your own.'

Ursula had been expecting . . . she knew not what. She had not thought Benedict would be so unfeeling as to show amusement at the ancient knight's transformation, but she had feared there might be some moment of ungraciousness, due more to shyness than rudeness, which might have given offence.

But Benedict had done the right thing.

More, his gesture was noted not only by Sir Henry, but by the hundred odd men, women and children around them. A murmur of appreciation rose from their midst, and someone cheered. Ursula felt tears flooding her eyes.

* * *

Ursula had not really thought further than the moment of her return to Salwarpe. She had assumed that once she had cast herself into her grandfather's arms, all her troubles would be over. She had thought she could drop back into her old position in the castle, without responsibilities, except perhaps to tend the less serious of the cuts and bruises that befell the Salwarpe retainers. She had forgotten that the Lady Editha had been responsible for the smooth running of the domestic side of the castle, and that the Lady Editha was now far away.

Ursula stood straight and tall at her grandfather's side and felt the weight of her aunt's cares descend upon her own slim shoulders Her grandfather's hand was light as a leaf within hers. He was trembling with fatigue. In spite of the red on his cheeks, and the yellow on his hair, he was nothing but a tired old man.

She caught his arm within hers and, for the first time in her life, he leaned upon her. 'When did you last sleep?' she asked, quiet in his ear.

'I . . . not sure,' he said, in a dry whisper. 'Couldn't let them take the armour off. Not sure when needed, you see.'

'Benedict and I slept well enough last night. We will watch for you, if you will rest awhile.'

'Yes,' said Benedict. 'If you will give your permission, Sir Henry? If you will detail one of your men to accompany me, I would like to see everything that is to be seen. I would also like the services of a man who can write, and perhaps someone to draw me a map. And what workmen have you here in the castle? If you will give orders that I may see everything . . .'

'A sword I must have, and at once!' said Reynold. 'And armour! God's wounds, but I feel naked like this.'

'Certainly you shall have a sword,' said Ursula. 'Grandfather, go and take a rest. Benedict will come to you for orders later on.'

'Yes, yes,' said the old man. 'As you say, I must rest. Simon Joce!' A big man clad in armour appeared at his elbow. 'Simon, this is . . .' Sir Henry gestured towards the newcomers. 'See that they have everything they want. I will go rest awhile, now that my granddaughter is back.'

Sir Henry's valet and his squire stepped forward to take their master's arms, but he threw them off and, pulling himself upright, strode off to the keep with firm, unwavering tread

'That's right, my man,' said Reynold, claiming Simon Joce's attention. 'Take me to the armoury at once!'

Simon Joce looked at Benedict, looked back at Reynold and hesitated. Then he plucked a tall bowman from the throng with his eye and jerked his head towards Benedict. The bowman shrugged, rolled an eye in humorous fashion and bowed to Benedict, indicating that he was at the knight's service.

Ursula opened her mouth to protest. Simon Joce was her grandfather's sergeant and had charge of the men of the garrison. Simon ought by rights to go with Benedict. But Benedict was turning away, apparently well satisfied. Ursula bit her lip. How could Benedict expect to receive his due, when he was content always to take second place?

Well, it was done, and there were a thousand other affairs waiting to claim her attention. The Lady Editha's careworn face floated before Ursula's eyes. Ursula had sometimes wondered what Editha had found to do all day; Ursula was about to find out.

Voices were raised around her. Where were the newcomers to be lodged? And Dickon . . . oh, poor Dickon! What should be served at the evening meal? Three men had been injured in the fighting before the gates on the day Hugo came . . . would she be so good as to have a look at their injuries? And which of the Salwarpe men should be appointed to serve the newcomers? And which of the knights ought to sit at the right hand of Sir Henry at table? And God be praised, but what have you done with your gown, mistress?

This last came from the elderly tirewoman who had served the Ladies of Salwarpe for as long as Ursula could remember.

Ursula looked down at her gown, and laughed. She said, 'What can you find for me to wear tonight? And come to think of it, what can we find for the two knights to wear, for clothing have they none, other than what they have on their backs!'

* * *

Later, as she was crossing the garth from the infirmary, she caught sight of Simon Joce and sent a page to bring him to her in the garden.

'Well, Simon? It is in my mind that I should

speak to you about these two knights. You may say it is no concern of mine, but . . .'

'Nay, lady. The spirit of the old lord lives on in you. I am listening.'

She laced her fingers together. 'Then tell me what impression these men have made on you. I know you to be a good judge of character. For many years you have been set in charge of this garrison and your word here has been law. Now these two strangers come in from outside, and perhaps their coming is not welcome to you . . .?'

'Did the lame one really carry Dickon up the cliff?'

'Yes. And he delayed the guard boat, until we had time to reach the top.'

'Aye.' He sighed and shook his head. 'That other one. I can't be doing with him.'

Ursula had no difficulty in interpreting that. 'Yet Sir Reynold is a brave knight, and wishes to help us.'

'In his own way, perhaps. Yet I do not think his way is the old lord's way.'

'Authority is vested in Sir Benedict. Sir Reynold will be very useful too, no doubt.'

Simon looked doubtful. His nose twitched, as it did at all times when he was worried. 'That lame one. He wants to see inside the granaries. Told him "no". He didn't insist. He's got a man making lists of everything . . . horses, pigs, hens . . . men, women and children . . . pikes, swords, bows and arrows.

Just like a clerk.'

She seized on the important point he had been trying to convey to her. 'You told him "no". Is that because the granary is not as full as it is supposed to be?'

'Maybe. Maybe not. I haven't seen inside it myself. But he gave me such a look when I denied him entry. Went through me like a needle through wool. I thought—clerk or no clerk—you've put your finger on the weak spot before you're fairly within the walls.'

'I believe that my grandfather will trust Sir Benedict, as you should do. As I do. The man understands his business, and if he chooses to act like a clerk, then let us not denigrate clerks, but observe how useful they can be. How much grain is there left? Enough to last until Michaelmas?'

'I asked the old lord that, and he said "of course". Hmph! I doubt it, myself, or he'd not keep the place locked so tight. But I've not said so to anyone, mind.'

'I think you can take it that Sir Benedict has already guessed it. He is not a man who frightens easily, Simon.' Simon tugged at his ear, unconvinced. 'What is he doing now?'

'Looking over the ramparts at the countryside below. He stares and stares, then asks our friend the bowman how many trees there are in such and such a clump, and he has a man at his side, scratching away at making a map. An hour or more he's been on the west side, and hardly started. What sort of behaviour's that?'

'You are not impressed?'

Again Simon tugged at his ear. 'Did I say that, lady? I say to myself that I care nothing for clerks, and then I remember the way his eye went through me, and his dragging Dickon up the cliff, and I wonder why I go on thinking about him.'

Simon was called away.

Ursula sat on, twirling a spray of honeysuckle between her fingers.

'Yes,' she said at last. 'I wonder why I keep thinking about him, too.'

CHAPTER SIX

Benedict straightened up with a sigh. He rubbed his eyes. He had been staring at trees and mounds and water and rocks till he could hardly see straight. The sun was hot on his bare head, and his leg ached.

But . . .

'That's the third side done,' he said. 'Now there's only the marshes.' He looked up at the sky, which was beginning to grow dark. 'If the light holds.'

The dog panted at his side, tongue lolling.

Peter the Bowman, whose attitude had changed from veiled derision to respect during the course of that long day, also looked up at the sky, and then over at the marshes.

'Who looks at marshes?' he said.

'Dickon does,' said Benedict. 'Fetch him, will you?'

One of the growing group of men surrounding Benedict nodded and slipped away. The man who'd been making the maps looked up, frowning. 'Was that three humped rocks, about a stone's throw from the end of the elms? Or four?'

'Three,' said several voices at once. The clerk corrected his map.

'And you'll not forget that I want a map of the town and quayside, will you?' said Benedict.

'You shall have it early tomorrow,' said the clerk, 'If I have to sit up all night to do it.'

Benedict put his hand on the clerk's shoulder, and pressed it, smiling. Then he turned on the others. 'You're all familiar with the countryside as it is now. Tomorrow morning—maybe the morning after—maybe in a week's time, there may be some change in what you see. A tree may be missing here, a new track made over a meadow there. I want to know about it, as soon as you see it. You understand why, don't you?'

'Yes, my lord,' said Peter Bowman. 'A tree can be cut down for many purposes. Maybe only to feed fires, maybe not.'

'A new track may mean a cart is taking men

to cut down trees . . .'

'A fresh line of earth may mean a mine is being dug . . .'

'And what can we do about it?' said another man. 'Spit in the face of the wind? That's all we can do about it.'

Now that's where you're wrong,' said Benedict. 'Many people—particularly those who haven't sat through a siege before, think they can't do anything about what the enemy chooses to do to him. But they're wrong. There are all sorts of things that we can do. But we must have fair warning, so as to prepare our counter-attack. Oh, believe me! We will show Hugo such a bag of tricks as will break his heart, and cause him to curse the day he ever set foot on Salwarpe land!'

The men smiled, nudging one another. They liked what he said, and they liked the way he said it. They were all tall, well-built fair-headed men. Benedict thought it quite reasonable of them to expect nothing good from an ill-favoured dark lump of a creature like himself. Well, maybe they were right in thinking him not much of a man; but, God willing, he could show them how to defend themselves against the likes of Hugo de Frett.

Simon Joce wandered over, looking as if he had come that way by chance.

'Finished yet?' A nice blend of condescension and anxiety not to miss anything of importance.

'I'd like to get a general impression of the marshes before sunset.'

'Who'd choose to approach Salwarpe that way?'

'We did,' said Benedict and, though he had not intended to raise a laugh, the men about him chortled . . . Simon flushed. Benedict cursed himself. What good would it do to offend this man?

'A moment of your time?' Benedict laid his hand on Simon's shoulder and urged him along the ramparts to where they might overlook the flooded marshland, and the guard boat.

'That guard boat. Do you think it would be a good idea to sink it? I know it's out of arrow-shot from here, but if I made you a set of drawings could you find enough timber, and rope, and some craftsmen? And set up a catapult . . . about here?'

Simon's face went through a variety of expressions . . . unwilling respect fought with the distaste natural to one offered a tempting idea by a stranger . . . eagerness to fight won the day. 'Aye,' he said. 'It might be done, I suppose. If—I say if—we had any ammunition.'

'We're standing on it, man! This rock, the scree below . . . stones, man! Heavy, handy-sized stones. One or two of those, dropped neatly into the boat . . . farewell, boat! Eh?'

'Aye . . . well . . .!' Simon fought not to

smile. 'Perhaps,' he said, but his shoulders straightened as he strode away, and soon his voice was to be heard, issuing orders.

Dickon was brought up, cowering away from the ramparts. 'I only been up here in the castle twice afore in my life,' he said. 'Now don't ago making me look over the edge. I tell you, I can't!'

'No-one's asking you to do so,' said Benedict, hiding impatience. 'Here. I'll stand in front of you. Now look over my head. That shouldn't be difficult for a tall man like you.' There was an amused grin from the men nearest, but no loud laughter. Dickon looked, blinked and straightened to his full height. He could see the sky, no more.

'Now look over my out-stretched arm. No, no need to fear! I'm a good six foot from the wall itself, and it's breast-high hereabouts. There, now! What do you see?'

'The marshes in the distance. It's like being a bird, with the tide swelling in beneath you, and the mist all gone . . . What's that!'

He pointed to the middle distance.

'What? Where?' Men crowded around them, peering over the marshes.

'Smoke? In the marshes.'

Benedict said, 'Who was on the look-out here today?'

A man-at-arms shouldered his way through the throng. 'Not to say look-out, exactly. But I'm the gate-keeper here.'

'That smoke's where my cabin ought to be,' said Dickon, in a hoarse voice.

'Yes?' said Benedict, addressing the gate-keeper.

The man shrugged. 'I don't know. The guard boat went that way at high tide, surely, and I thought they'd lit a bonfire there later . . .'

'They fired my cabin,' said Dickon. 'They fired my cabin!'

'Well, they would, wouldn't they?' said Benedict, in a matter-of-fact tone. 'A good thing we hauled you up here.'

Dickon turned on him 'I said, "They fired my cabin!"'

'I know,' said Benedict. 'They fired your cabin, and broke up your boat. So what are you going to do about it?'

Dickon stepped to the ramparts, brushing Benedict's arm aside. He stared out over the marshes for a long time. He turned his head, looking at the line of the shore. Then he stared back at the wisp of smoke which marked where his cabin had been.

Benedict said, 'We are going to set up a catapult here, Dickon, to knock that guard boat out of the water. Peter Bowman, who is the best shot in the castle?'

'I am,' said Peter Bowman, without hesitation. 'And then Dickon Fowler.'

'Peter, there will be work a-plenty for you elsewhere. Will you cede the place of honour on this side to Dickon? Will you let him sink that boat?'

'That I will!' said Peter.

Dickon braced himself, put his hands on the stonework and looked over the edge. Then he stepped back, wiping his hand across his mouth. But his voice was firm as he said, 'Aye, I'll do that little thing for ye, my lord. And may God guide my hand!'

'Amen to that,' said Benedict.

* * *

Benedict was tired. He descended the steps from the ramparts, favouring his bad leg. Usually he had to swing his sword out of the way, when he was going down steps, but now there was an unaccustomed lightness at his hip . . . he felt strange without his sword. At the foot of the steps there was a small sheltered space where a bench had been set against the wall of the keep. It was full in the evening sun, and yet sheltered by a tangle of honeysuckle. He sank onto the bench to look over the papers he had taken from the clerk. It was good to sit down. He supposed he must have been on his feet for hours . . . someone had brought him a bite of food a while back . . . soon it would be time to wash and go into the hall for the evening meal. But at least there would be no formality here, no dancing, no women to hide smiles behind their hands at his awkward gait and general boorishness.

Not that the maiden would smile, of course. She was not like that. He had wondered, when he had heard that Aylmer was taking her as his second wife, whether his old friend was being wise. That tale about her birth had been widely circulated, thanks to Hugo. But then Benedict had met her, and she had been unexpectedly kind. And of course as soon as he'd seen her with Sir Henry he'd realised that she was certainly of the old man's blood.

Benedict yawned. He leaned back, letting the sun warm the strain from his face. So many problems . . . so little time . . . it was always the way in a siege. Plans must be made at once. That granary! Simon Joce . . . obviously not enough food there to last till Michaelmas, which meant . . . which meant . . .

He was too tired to think. He laid the papers down on the bench beside him and said to himself that one ought not to make decisions when one's mind was fatigued.

Not enough wood. The thought came into his mind and would not be driven out again. He had guessed there would be no store of wood, as soon as he had looked around. Stone-built walls and towers . . . the keep was built of stone, too. All that was to the good, in a way. In another way, not so good. There were some lathe and plaster buildings here and there, with thatched roofs . . . roomy barns, almost empty. Shacks here and there for carts, farm implements . . . a silent smithy . . . cook-houses, hen-coops, pig-styes . . .

But wood was needed for cooking and for a fire in the hall, and so the garrison had been burning their woodpile without thought of . . .

He rubbed his forehead. It would be best to think about something else for a while. But what?

He raised his eyes to the darkening sky and saw there the first star of evening. It had a soothing effect on him. The scent of honeysuckle was heavy and sweet. Had the maiden really preferred the honeysuckle to the rose? No. Aylmer's look of anxiety had betrayed her. So, she had said the honeysuckle was her favourite because she thought he, Benedict, ought to be set in authority over Reynold. Had Aylmer primed her to that trick? No, Aylmer did not think things through, always . . .

He frowned, thinking of another time when Aylmer had not thought things through. Then he shook his head and squared his shoulders. One could never throw off the past. One was like a snail, he thought, carrying the past about with one, like a shell on one's back.

Aylmer, lying in pain. That was a bad thought. And he could do nothing to help him.

Benedict sighed. He thought he must go and write a letter to Aylmer, using the cipher he had worked out with his old tutor before he left. If the pigeon were released when the ducks flew out to the marshes at dawn . . . that ought to confuse any archers of Hugo's waiting for carrier pigeons . . .

His eyes closed. A man coughed, nearby.

'My lord, I was sent to tell you. There is a bath made ready against your coming, and fresh clothing.'

A bath. Now who had had the brains to think of that? The maiden, of course. He felt a swell of gratitude to her. He opened his eyes and saw a youngish man in the plain dress of an under-servant, with a prominent Adam's apple. The man had such fair eyebrows and lashes that in certain lights they disappeared from sight. Benedict forced a smile. Smiles were important, in a besieged castle. The old lord knew that. Appearances were sometimes more important than reality. A gold surcoat and chain-mail could hide creaky joints, just as a bath and fresh clothing could bring Benedict to table smelling sweet, if not looking particularly beautiful. Looking beautiful he would leave to Reynold.

And come to think of it, what had Reynold been doing with himself all day?

He got to his feet slowly, annoyed to find his body unwilling to obey him. A night spent among the mists on the marshes had played havoc with his leg . . . but remember to smile, Benedict, and to speak loudly and cheerfully!

'What is your name, my good man?'

*   *   *

Benedict eased into his place at the table on the dais. He was seated between Sir Henry and the maiden; the place of honour. He looked about him. The hall was a relatively recent building, set at right angles to the much older, square keep. The windows of the hall were large and obviously the building had not been conceived with the idea of keeping out an attacking force. Benedict automatically began to plan how the hall could be made safe, if Hugo broke into the castle grounds.

The maiden was wearing a robe of pale green, embroidered at hem and neck with peach-coloured flowers . . . honeysuckle or rose? Did it matter? The robe was a trifle too big for her round the neck. Doubtless it was one of her aunt's, which she had borrowed for the occasion.

The base of the hall was crowded with trestle-tables, and the benches on either side of the trestles were filled with people. The whole community dined with their lord at nights and most of them would sleep on the trestles, and under them, afterwards. Food. Benedict noted that the food was well cooked and that there was plenty of it.

Minstrels? And tumblers? The Lord above! Sir Henry certainly knew how to set a feast! And yet, now Benedict came to think of it, was Sir Henry not wise to do so? The buzz of talk, the occasional laugh . . . the ready flow of ale . . . the music, the splendid dresses of Sir Henry and his granddaughter; were these not all part and parcel of Sir Henry's defence of Salwarpe? Morale in the castle was high. Benedict only had to close his eyes for a moment to hear that the buzz of voices spoke of men confident that they could defy Hugo with impunity. The old man had done well.

But Reynold was speaking and something in his tone roused Benedict to attention. There was a rasp to Reynold's voice which usually heralded one of his most bitter sarcasms. Benedict had been the object of Reynold's wit for so many years that he winced before the jibe was fairly out, even though it was not directed at him this time.

Reynold was calling their attention to the fact that Dickon the Fowler was being shown to a seat at the table next the dais. The high table on the dais itself was reserved for the Lord of Salwarpe, his family and guests of noble degree; a visiting priest or wealthy merchant might perhaps be invited to sit there also, but everyone else sat in the body of the hall. However, immediately to the right of the dais was a table where the most important members of the household sat. The steward was there, the sergeant of the guard, the chief huntsman, the Lord's body servants, and so on. Dickon was being seated there between Simon Joce and Peter Bowman. Reynold was expressing his surprise and amusement.

'. . . for the old man is certainly not accustomed to such surroundings, as can be seen!'

Benedict thought of Dickon's reception of them, of how he had spoken to them as equals, despite his poverty. Ursula was bending her head to hide a flush, and her hand was clenched around her knife.

Sir Henry put down his cup with deliberation, but before he could speak Benedict said, 'I assume Master Dickon is the maiden's foster-father?'

'And saviour,' said the old man, with emphasis. 'I will tell you the story, since it reflects on present events. You may have heard that Hugo de Frett claims Salwarpe for his own, saying my granddaughter is illegitimate. That tale is a lie, but I will tell you how it came to be put about.

'My son was a fool. It happens, sometimes . . .' The old man stared ahead with angry blue eyes. 'Yes, it happens, sometimes. He was my only son, and perhaps I was over-indulgent. He was brave. He was fond of the tourney. He was handsome, and welcome wherever he went, but he spent as freely as if he were a king's son, and he married a girl whose dowry was far less than her beauty.

'He was a friend of your father's, Benedict, though my lad was the younger by some five years or so. You will have heard the tale often enough of how your father took the Cross and went to the Holy Land, poor man, he was heart-broken when your mother died so young . . . I think he looked for death, and God knows he found it . . .'

'They say he died well,' said Benedict, crossing himself. 'I barely remember him.'

'No, you were just a child. My son had no heir when he left me to go on the same Crusade. I tried to dissuade him from going, but he would have it. What was more, he insisted on going in fine style, with a train of men behind him, and his wife to bear him company as far as Constantinople. He beggared me, that he might make a fine show, and he took the best of our men with him. Dickon the Fowler was a young man then, and among those chosen to accompany my son. Dickon had lived all his life till then on the marshes, and the day he came up here to join my son's company was the first time he had ever set foot inside the castle.

'Well, they rode away, my son and his beautiful young wife, with their men marching along behind them. And that was the last I saw of son, daughter-in-law, and nearly all our men. They died of this and that. Of heat and fever. Of thirst and Saracen blades. They never reached the Holy Land, any of them. But in Constantinople my son's wife bore him a child, a daughter who was christened Ursula. A fever—and my son was no more. Dickon the Fowler was almost the last of our men left by that time. He sold my son's few remaining jewels and his armour, and took passage in the next ship going west for his master's young widow, the babe, and what was left of our men. The widow died on the voyage. Dickon hired a woman to go along with them, to feed the babe. He sold the babe's costly wrappings, and wrapped her in homespun that she might pass as his child—for they were deathly afraid of robbers and pirates. And so he brought her home in the crook of his arm, with but three of my men plodding along at his heels.

'And that was the second time that he stepped within the castle, when he brought me my son's child, and only heir.'

'All honour be to him,' said Benedict.

'Indeed, yes,' said Sir Henry. 'I offered him a place in the castle. I offered to build him a fair stone house in the town below. But he would take nothing. He wanted nothing . . .'

'Except to have me visit him,' said Ursula. 'I am his child, even if he is not my father. He taught me the ways of the marshes. Do you wonder at it that I love him, and that I went to him when I was in trouble?'

'I do not,' said Benedict.

'Neither do I,' said Reynold. 'To have preserved such a rose . . . .! We should be forever grateful to him. And,' Here he dropped his voice, 'I see that you wear my roses on your gown tonight.'

'Are they roses?' said Ursula, in an indifferent tone. 'It is hard to tell. I thought they were honeysuckle, myself.'

Honeysuckle.

Benedict repressed a grin. So neat a thrust! So well-timed! Ah, but you have chosen well, Aylmer . . .'

Then he was staring ahead of him, food forgotten. He took a deep breath, and tried to hold on to it, but it slipped away from him, leaving him gasping for air. He fumbled for his goblet, and his fingers refused to obey him. The wine spilt on to the table and he watched it seep away, thinking how foolish he must look sitting there, watching spilt wine spread around . . .

'You are not well, Sir Benedict?' The old man was alarmed.

'I . . . yes, quite well.' He sat back in his chair and placed both hands on the arms, holding onto them to maintain his balance. Someone came forward to mop up the mess and refill his cup. 'I was merely thinking . . .'

Thinking about Ursula, who was betrothed to Aylmer.

'We must confer after the feast,' said the old man. 'But you eat nothing, Sir Benedict.'

'Thank you. I am not hungry.' Yet he knew he must force himself to eat, for what would happen to all these people—what would happen to Ursula—if he fell ill? He took a wing of chicken, tore it apart and then let the pieces lie on his platter.

Sir Henry was watching him. Benedict could feel the wise old eyes on him. Sir Henry had known Benedict's father and seemed to have remembered nothing but good about him. Some warmth crept into the desolation that was Benedict. The old man was waiting for him to recover, waiting with all the tact and kindliness that seemed to be innate in the de Thrave family.

Benedict took another deep breath. This time his lungs obeyed him. He reached for his cup, and his hand conveyed it to his mouth. He sipped the wine. It was a good wine, probably from Gascony.

'May I commend you on your choice of wine, Sir Henry? A brave wine.'

'For a brave man.'

Benedict looked sharply at Sir Henry. The wrinkled eyelids blinked, the lipless mouth smiled, the seamed neck bent in a gesture of homage. Benedict said to himself, 'Can he mean me?'

'A worthy son of a worthy father,' said Sir Henry, raising his goblet in a toast to Benedict.

Benedict did not know what to say. It would have been polite, of course, to turn the compliment aside with a laugh, or a deprecatory remark. But the old man had sounded as if he were making a statement of fact, rather than paying a compliment. Benedict bit his lip to hide a grin of nervous pleasure. He was not accustomed to praise. It was sweet. Undoubtedly it was doubly sweet because it had come so quickly on the discovery that he loved a woman whom he could never have . . . a woman who would never have given him a passing thought, even if she had been free and not betrothed to Aylmer.

And there grief had him by the throat again

He took another sip of wine, and set the cup aside as firmly as he thrust away his personal problems.

'Now, about the siege, Sir Henry. How do you see matters developing?'

CHAPTER SEVEN

Benedict was on his feet and groping for his tunic before his eyes were fairly open. It was the second morning after his arrival in Salwarpe. The thumping outside his door increased until his servant, Parkyn, managed to depress the latch and stagger in with an armful of armour.

'We are under attack?' said Benedict. 'Where is Simon Joce? And Sir Reynold?'

'Out there already, and the old lord is arming himself, too. They'll have the poor creatures inside and give Hugo a trouncing he'll not forget in a hurry!'

'Poor creatures?' Benedict pulled on his boots, dashed cold water over his head and reached for his belt.

'The Lady of Spereshot, with her two little ones. Shut in a great cage, she is. And the childer in another beside her. Crying out to us to release them. Out in the open. Put there at dawn, they say, for surely they were not there last evening.'

'What!' Benedict thrust Parkyn aside and leaped for the door. 'Simon! Peter Bowman! A moi!'

He had slept through the dawn. He had been busy with the carpenters yesterday, and then had worked late over his maps and drawings.

'Pray God I am not too late to stop them!'

He seized a scurrying man-at-arms and demanded to know where Sir Henry might be.

'Mounting his horse, surely!' The man took in Benedict's lack of armour and his eyes widened. 'Best hurry, my lord, if you don't want to miss the fun!'

'Fools!' Benedict spun the man away from him and looked around the garth. The place was ominously empty. Everybody must have gone to watch Sir Henry ride out with his men to rescue the captives. A page ran by and was halted by an outstretched hand.

'Where is Simon Joce? Who is in charge at the postern gate?'

'The postern?' The page looked blank.

'Everyone's gone to watch . . .'

'God in Heaven, but you deserve to be taken by Hugo!' said Benedict.

Parkyn appeared at his elbow, vainly trying to get his master to don a chain-mail tunic.

'Parkyn, is there a bell which we can ring to sound the alarm? Or a horn to blow?'

'A bell, surely. It is used when the priest comes up from the town . . . it is at the side of the round tower, overlooking the marshes.'

'Then go toll that bell, Parkyn. Toll it for all you are worth, and go on tolling till I send again!'

Benedict turned and ran towards the gatehouse, thrusting his way through the men who were crowding there. Simon Joce's burly figure was easy to pick out. Benedict caught at his shoulder.

'Simon Joce, until this morning I had formed a high opinion of you. What are you about? Think, man! Think! Will you let your master ride out without reconnaissance, while the postern gate is left unguarded?'

Simon's smile faded, but he blustered. 'Who comes by the postern . . .?'

'I did, Simon. And where I came, may not others come also?'

'How could they climb . . .?'

'We did, Simon. And suppose they have brought ropes with them, and grappling-irons to throw over the parapet . . .?'

Simon swallowed. 'But my lord Reynold

said . . .'

'I can imagine exactly what he said. He is a knight well accustomed to the tourney, and has no knowledge of siege warfare. Think, man! Take your time, they will not start without you, if I know your master! Think! The postern unguarded, all attention on the road below the gatehouse. The bait cunningly set out, the piece of cheese to tempt the mice out of its hole . . . and then . . .'

Voices were raised, calling Simon. Hands were laid to the windlass controlling the drawbridge, which was slowly creaking down. In a moment the way would be clear, the portcullis would be raised and Sir Henry and his men would sweep down the road into . . . what?

'It's a trap, isn't it?' said Benedict, his hands hard on Simon's arms.

Simon said, 'I . . . I will send to the postern at once, to see if there is aught moving. I do not think it possible . . .'

'And I will stop Sir Henry . . .'

Above their heads a sweet-sounding bell began to toll. Simon started and turned pale. Around them men ceased to look to the gatehouse and began to glance over their shoulders. The creaking of the windlass ceased and the drawbridge stayed where it was, half up and half down.

'Who has sounded the alarm?' said Simon.

'I did,' said Benedict. 'It might just save

us, if there is a force waiting to swarm up and attack the postern.' Benedict thrust Simon away from him. 'Go, take some of your men to the gate. Send for Dickon, and let him tell you if there is danger approaching from that quarter. I will stop Sir Henry committing suicide, if I may.'

The men around him were sullen, unwilling to believe that he might be right. They were only too anxious to break out of the castle and strike a blow against Hugo. They parted to let Simon through, but closed ranks behind him. Benedict clenched his fists. Would he have to throw some of them about, in order to reach Sir Henry?

A horseman in full armour pushed his way through the throng, and behind him came another.

'The tocsin!' said Sir Henry, hand over his eyes. 'Who has sounded the alarm?'

'I did,' said Benedict, stepping close to Sir Henry's horse. 'My lord, will you not dismount and talk a while? I fear a trap.'

'He fears!' sneered Reynold. 'Of course he fears! He sees death in every shadow! Why, he is not even armed! Let us to our work, my lord, and leave him to his pens and paper.'

'A trap?' said Sir Henry. He tugged at his yellow moustache.

'Yes, I know,' said Benedict. 'The trap was well baited, and any knight worth his salt would wish to ride out and be slaughtered, perhaps.'

'Fool! Dolt! There is no-one in sight of the cages! See for yourself!'

'I do not need to look,' said Benedict. 'I have no doubt I would see what you would see. The point is, would Peter Bowman see what I would see? Or would he see something different?'

'I understand you,' said Sir Henry. 'You are right. We gave the matter insufficient thought. There may not be a trap, of course. In which case . . .'

'I will gladly ride out with you. But not while the postern is left unguarded. I have had the alarm rung to deter anybody who thought to force the postern while our backs were conveniently turned . . .'

Sir Henry's jaw dropped. Then he said, 'Sir Benedict, if I move a step without your advice in future, may I never see another sun rise!' He dismounted and took Benedict's arm to assist him in climbing off the mounting-block. 'Pray God we are not too late. Men, dismount. Keep the horses walking about in readiness to leave, but bring the drawbridge up again. Send for Peter Bowman. Sir Reynold, we will take counsel together, if you please!'

* * *

Within a few minutes the alarm bell had ceased to toll, and within half an hour the castle had resumed its normal appearance, save for where the horses were kept waiting. High above the road, on the ramparts of the gatehouse tower, Sir Henry stood with his lieutenants, waiting for Peter Bowman to finish his survey of the countryside below.

Some hundred yards beneath, at a bend in the road, two wooden carts had been positioned. Crude woodwork had turned the carts into cages on wheels, and within them crouched the figures of a middle-aged woman in a wimple and torn but costly gown . . . and two children of perhaps twelve and fourteen years of age. All three clutched the bars of the cages and looked for help to the castle above. But still the portcullis remained down, and the drawbridge up.

Below the cages the countryside seemed asleep. The tops of the trees were barely disturbed in a breeze and there was a general air of peace and quiet.

'Nothing moves below,' said Peter at last. 'You said for me to take my time, and so I have. Nothing moves, anywhere. No men work in the fields below us, though they are moving around normally in the distance. No birds near here, though you can see they're flying around as usual over towards the forest. No birds . . . I don't like that, my lord. That's not natural. The men might be working in the distant fields for some good reason, but there's only one reason why the birds should have deserted us.

If there's no birds around, it means there's something else there as shouldn't be.'

'What?' said Reynold, striding up and down. 'If there's nothing to be seen, then there's no-one there. We sit here like children fearing we know not what, and all the time those poor creatures . . .'

'No birds?' said Benedict. 'What else?'

'There's something strange about the road there, just afore the turn. It's not the same colour all over. D'ye see?'

Benedict looked and said, 'Earth of a different colour has been strewn across the road. I see it, now that you point it out. They must have brought earth from somewhere else, and spread it there to hide . . . what?'

'Not a pit. It's not deep enough. It's not high enough for a barrier. But . . .'

'A rope!' Benedict slapped his thigh. 'A rope or chain across the road, lying flat on the ground and covered with loose earth. When the horses come galloping down the slope with their riders' eyes on the cages ahead, the rope is jerked up on either side . . . men could hide in that scrub to the side of the track, would they not? And the horses would be brought down, and the riders tumble off, and then . . .'

'It's those bushes there that trouble me,' said Peter, pointing to a thicket a little lower down the road. 'I can't remember a thicket being there, and yet it looks so natural. At least, it looks natural at first sight, and then

I look at the colour of it, and say to myself that it isn't natural for leaves to be turning, so early.'

'A thicket?' said Reynold, staring. 'Those poor creatures are waiting to be rescued, and you talk about the leaves turning early?'

But Benedict was consulting the maps he had caused to be made two days previously, and it did not seem that that thicket had been there before.

'A thicket need not be a real thicket,' he explained to Sir Henry. 'It could be a lot of bushes cut down from somewhere else, and brought here to act as protection for men stationed there. Who looks at a thicket? Who would think it might hide a force of archers, say? And if there are archers there, waiting to pick off any who come running out of the castle . . .'

'Hugo knows his business, it seems,' said Sir Henry. 'I wondered where he'd managed to mount guard on the road. I knew he must have done so, but since I could see nothing . . . yes, the man knows his business.'

'Well, so do I,' said Benedict, fingering his unshaven chin Now—what shall we do about it?'

'Do we have a choice?' demanded Reynold. 'Can you watch those poor creatures suffer and die out there? Think of their lot in the heat of the day, without food or water!'

'The art of siege warfare,' said Benedict,

'lies in not losing your temper. Hugo provokes us to action. He knows he has only four weeks to take Salwarpe. He knows you are a gallant knight, Reynold, skilled in combat. Be sure he will have questioned Aylmer's messenger before the man died at Spereshot. So he knows who and what we are. He sets a trap to draw us out and then . . . snip! He shears off our heads! Hmph!'

'But now that we know he has set a trap, can we not avoid it and still rescue the poor creatures?'

'Yes, there may be a way, but we will not take it yet awhile. Let us hear what Dickon has to say about the postern gate first.'

Dickon was brought to them, and with him came Ursula, looking anxious.

Dickon spoke in rapid bursts, appearing much excited. 'There's men there, Sir Henry. They'm ahiding in the willows down below at the water's edge. But I seed them. I knows how to look. The guard-boat's just come back from a trip to the harbour, and she's a-bringing in another load of them fool soldiers. They're no sort of good at hiding theirselves from sight. Slipping and splashing, and breaking branches. They've got climbing gear with them this time Ropes in coils, and twinkling bits of metal on the ends. Hooks, belike, to throw over the walls once they're up the cliff. And talk! How they jabber! If you listen hard enough, you can even hear them swearing!'

'How many?'

'Maybe forty in all. Maybe a few less. That's with the crew on the boat at present.'

'You've not let on you've seen them?'

'Nay, nay. For all they know we're all peering out over the road. May I go back now? I want . . .'

'To finish arming the catapult?' Benedict smiled. He rubbed his hands together. 'Forty men. A lot. How many fighting men can we muster? Not nearly enough. No, no. I know how many men you have, Simon. We do not have enough to repel an attack on two fronts at once. Hugo's men are mercenaries, remember, trained to war. Your men are badly trained, badly armed . . . oh, I know it is not your fault, but we must not expect too much of them at first. To fight on two fronts; no. One at a time, then.'

'First rescue the Lady of Spereshot, and her children,' said Reynold. 'We must ride out at once . . .'

'Even avoiding the trap of the rope across the road, you will be sure to lose men from the archers in the thicket,' said Benedict. 'Why waste men and horses, when we can perhaps lure them into thinking . . . a feint of some sort . . . but what sort? And on which side?'

'You mean,' said Ursula, 'that you want Hugo to think we are under attack and fully occupied on one side of the castle, in order to make him abandon his precautions . . .'

'And come out of hiding, where we can deal with him better. Yes, yes. But we only have so many men; to create the sort of effect we want we need . . . ah, I have it. If we can only make Hugo believe that the attack on the postern had been successful, and that his men were within the castle, in hand-to-hand combat with the defenders . . . would not his archers then rush out of the thicket and try to help their men, by trying to force the main entrance themselves? Eh? And the moment they come out of that scrub they would be fair targets for our own archers, and we could then send a group of men, preferably on foot, down the road to release the hostages.'

'On foot!' cried Reynold in disbelief.

'Why waste horses?' said Benedict. 'We may need to eat them, later.'

*   *   *

The sun rose higher, but still Benedict held his hand. An expectant hush lay over the castle. Benedict reflected that it was often thus at the start of the siege, when morale was high and there was yet plenty of food. The people of Salwarpe were looking on this as a sort of holiday. A mumming show, in which no-one was to be fatally injured. They were horrified and sorry for the woman and her children in the cages below, of course, but the Spereshot people were not Salwarpe folk. 'They' had not had the good sense to choose to live in a castle on a hill. 'They' did not have the old knight to look after them.

'Long may they think like that', thought Benedict, scurrying around the catapult and squinting along its beam.

The catapult—or trebuchet, to give it the name by which soldiers knew it—was a frame with a cross-bar on which was pivoted a long arm. The long arm ended in a sling, and this was at present winched down to the ground and held there with ropes. The sling was being loaded with lumps of rock. The shorter arm was at present high in the air. A basket hung from the shorter arm, also weighted with rocks, to act as counterpoise. When the long end was released, it would fly into the air and send a scatter of missiles over the castle wall, out and down.

'Are we not ready yet?' said Sir Henry, stamping around.

'One moment,' said Benedict, testing ropes. For the eighth time he peered over the parapet. The men below had still not yet begun to climb the cliff, but the willows shook and creaked with their presence below. No doubt the men who were to attack the postern had instructions to await a signal from Hugo, and that signal would probably not be given till the defenders were issuing out of the main gate to rescue the people from Spereshot.

A team of men adjusted the angle of the

trebuchet once more, at Benedict's command.

'We've had to alter the angle,' said Benedict, 'because the target's moved. We had been aiming to hit the boat when it was anchored in the channel, but now it's right beneath us, tied up to one of the willows. We'll have to aim for the scree, and that means shortening the range. Some stones may fall this side of the parapet, Simon. Best clear your men out of the way.'

'The scree?' cried Reynold. 'Are we playing games? We are under attack by mercenaries, and you fight back . . . at the scree!'

'Surely,' said Benedict, in his usual even tone. 'Once the scree is in motion, everything and everyone beneath it will perish.'

He stepped back, felt something soft beneath his foot, apologised and had one arm taken in a firm grip while someone lifted a mailed hauberk over his head. As the garment cleared his neck, soft hands began to pull it down around him.

'Lady, you should not!' he said, in a low voice.

'Really?' said Ursula. 'Then neither should you. If you put your head over that parapet once more without wearing a helmet, I will not be answerable for the consequences!'

And there also was Parkyn, waiting with a chain-mail hood, which Benedict accepted with a grunt of thanks.

But, 'No sword,' he said, thrusting that

aside. 'I don't need one for this. Now, are your women ready to play their part?'

'This hour past,' said Ursula. 'And Peter Bowman bids me tell you that he has done as you requested, though he would very much rather not be the one to cast the first stone.'

'Aye, it is a risk,' said Benedict. 'I do not like using fire, either.'

'Fire?' said Reynold, staring.

'Fire. Well, now!' said the old knight, caressing his moustaches. 'I think not, Benedict.'

'One fire arrow, sped into those yellowing bushes where the archers hide?' pleaded Benedict. 'I fear we may not be able to draw them out of hiding otherwise.'

'Fire!' said Ursula. 'There is no smoke without a fire, they say. Suppose we set fire to some oily rags and green branches within the castle, beside the gatehouse? Would not Hugo think the fires had been set by his men, who had successfully assailed us from the postern side?'

'Why, Ursula . . .' said Benedict. Then he crimsoned, realising he had addressed her by her Christian name. But the slip was soon covered up.

'What a ruse!' cried the old knight. 'It shall be. We will set alight to our false fires when you give us the word, Benedict!'

'We cannot start till this thing be set . . .'

But a quarter of an hour later he stood back

and announced that he could do no better. Teams of men stood by to winch down the sling end of the trebuchet as soon as it had been fired, so as to reload it. Dickon Fowler knelt by a spyhole which had been cut in the masonry of the wall, looking over the cliff and giving them a report of everything that happened below.

'They're all on shore now, save for a pair of scoundrels left in the boat. They've found my punt, damn them. But they're not moving up the cliff yet. What do you think the signal is for them? They can't see round the cliff into the harbour . . .'

'Signs of strife from above, I suppose,' said Benedict.

'So let's give them nothing to worry them, till we're ready . . .'

He left the postern to race over the sward to the gatehouse. A force of armed men, together with some carpenters, waited for him there. Here, as on the postern side, were a knot of women and children, with a multitude of pots and pans . . . and braziers filled with an assortment of rags and grass. Here Ursula stood, wearing a chain-mail tunic over her peach-coloured dress, and a round leather cap on her head.

With a muttered word to Sir Henry, Benedict swung up into the gatehouse and peered down into the valley. Nothing stirred. Only, one of the children was crying. The sun beat down on the heavy quiet of noon.

'So both sides wait,' said Benedict. He hesitated. Had he read the situation aright? One got involved in the business of preparation and then one wondered whether in fact one wasn't making a fuss about nothing. One might, easily, be making a complete and utter fool of oneself.

'Well,' thought Benedict, 'It wouldn't be for the first time.'

He gave the signal, and behind him Ursula thrust a burning pine knot into brazier after brazier, and the women began to beat on their pans with spoons and billets of wood, and to scream and shout. The noise was deafening.

Benedict grinned. Beside him Peter Bowman tested his bowstring. Peter was also grinning.

Sir Henry said, 'Now!'

The gatewarden gave the signal and the drawbridge began to fall.

At one side of the drawbridge, set in the left-hand gate tower, was a small postern. No mounted men could go that way, but a small company of men on foot could slip in or out without making a stir about it. Now this door was set ajar . . . though no man issued forth.

Benedict watched the yellowing thicket with eyes that stared till they ached.

'Look!' Peter Bowman was pointing not to the bushes, but to where the Lady of Spereshot and her children had turned their heads and were looking back down the slope. They could see what the men in the castle could not see. Hugo must have been arriving to oversee matters himself.

'Did that earth on the road twitch?' said Benedict.

'And . . . now!' said Sir Henry. 'Men to the portcullis!'

'If this doesn't lure them out . . .!' said Benedict, running his hands through his hair and thereby pushing back his mailed hood till it came to rest around his neck.

'Surely it will,' said Sir Henry. 'Do we not present a perfect picture of a garrison fighting with intruders in the very heart of the gatehouse?'

The portcullis rose halfway, hovered and returned to earth. Sir Henry's men filed into the area of the drawbridge which lay between the two sets of gatehouses, and began to make a lot of noise, and mock-wrestle with each other.

'There!' cried Peter, and lifted his bow to the arrow-slit. From the bushes below, from those yellowing, tell-tale bushes, a man had stepped, clad in full armour. Another man was rising from his hiding-place beside the road, holding one end of a heavy chain in his hand . . . and the chain went looping down into the earth at his feet and across the road . . .

And the woman and the children in the cages began to scream.

Benedict wiped a dirty hand across his forehead. 'I can never bear to hear women scream!' Then he grabbed Peter's arm. 'Not yet, I tell you!'

They were pantingly still . . . waiting . . . another man stepped out of the bushes. This man looked down the hill, presumably towards Hugo, for orders. The man with the chain threw down his end of it and shouted across the road to where another couple of men were emerging from hiding. They all looked up at the temptingly half open postern . . . and at the shouting, heaving mass of men inside the portcullis. And now the portcullis was slowly being winched up again, and then quickly lowered some feet . . .

'Not yet!' said Benedict, in a strangled whisper.

A stocky figure in a red and gold surcoat came into sight, loping up the road at the head of some more men, and together with the men from the thicket they all came charging up the hill with drawn swords, and levelled pikes . . .

Now!' said Benedict.

A flight of arrows came speeding down from the gatehouse and nearly every one seemed to find its mark. Hugo's men screamed and spun round, clutching at feathered shafts . . . and out of the postern gate at the side of the gatehouse issued a stream of purposeful men who avoided the road, to run straight down the bank. They made for the cages, the two carpenters in their midst. They did not look to left or right. They did not even seem to see Hugo and his men. Their task was not to engage the enemy in battle but to free the hostages.

Hugo's voice bellowed out, trying to rally his men, but even as they reformed and tried to run up the hill again, there came another flight of arrows, as deadly as the first. Men fell, shrieking. Some began to limp back down the hill. Hugo's attack turned into a rout.

And now another force of armed men issued from the castle, led by two men in full armour. These two lowered their visored heads and turned this way and that to see what went on around them. They made for the demoralised enemy and systematically began to slaughter those of the men who had fallen wounded. Hugo's voice was raised once more, this time in despairing shout . . .

Benedict had tarried only long enough to see the carpenters set to work on the carts, and then he had raced back across the garth, Ursula at his side, to where yet more women and more braziers were waiting for them. At a nod from him she set flame to braziers, and again the women screamed and beat on their pans.

'Just in time!' Dickon flapped his arms, dancing around like an old crow. 'They were getting anxious, like!'

While Benedict thrust the Salwarpe men

back from the wall, Dickon knelt to release the ropes holding down the long arm of the trebuchet.

There was a sweep of wind, and then a sharp thuck as the beam hit the cross-bar of the framework. And then missiles were falling far and wide, most of them over the wall, but not all . . . and from below came the screams of men who had no defence against the hail of rocks falling from above . . . and then there was a rumbling sound as the scree, hit full on, broke up and slipped down the cliff, carrying men and weapons with it.

And then there was silence from below.

Benedict held up his hand, listening.

The women ceased their caterwauling. Still there was silence. The sharp smell of burning rags hung in the air, the braziers still puffed out oily smoke, but the noise of battle had ceased. The women turned to one another to smile, to laugh and then to chatter.

'Simon!' Simon stepped forward. Dickon was kneeling at the spy-hole once more. He seemed to be praying.

'Take ropes and go down after them, Simon,' said Benedict. Grasping him by the arm, Benedict added, low down, 'Don't leave any of them alive. We can't afford to have them carry tales back, and we can't afford to feed them.'

Simon frowned, then nodded. He would obey. He led his men out through the postern.

They carried ropes, pikes and knives. Not one of the men who had landed at the foot of the cliff that morning would see the sun set.

They were shouting in the distance and the shouts were joyous. Someone came panting up to gasp out that Sir Henry was back with the Spereshot people, and that all was well . . . not one of our men lost and many of Hugo's men killed . . .

Benedict leaned against the trebuchet. Then he slid down till he was squatting on the timber framework. He put his head in his hands.

This was the bad time, when it was over, and not over. He would dream for nights to come of men lying helpless under the cliff and on the road, waiting to receive a fatal knife thrust . . .

Someone knelt beside him. It was Ursula and behind her was Parkyn. Both looked anxious. Ursula took a flask of wine from Parkyn and set it to Benedict's mouth.

He drank, his eyes on her. Her mouth was smeared with blood, where she had bitten her lip, a while back. He liked that about her, that she could feel, and yet control her fear. She was not one of those beauties who were afraid to frown or laugh, for fear of spoiling their looks. Their faces had the empty, unused look of stone heads carved for churches. This face of hers would wear well.

He would drink no more, or he would be the worse for it. He took the flask from her hand and set it to her own mouth. She drank.

She closed her eyes and tipped back her head, breathing deeply. So she felt the anticlimax, too. Ah, but she was of fighting blood, and worthy in every way of . . .

Of Aylmer.

For a moment he had forgotten that she was to marry Aylmer. The shock of remembering threw him back against the timber, sitting upright.

She smiled at him. It was the slow, bemused smile of one awakening from a dream.

He smiled back, but his was a guarded smile, hiding pain. He tore off his mailed hood and rose, balancing himself against the trebuchet. He turned away from Ursula, signing to Parkyn to remove his hauberk.

The girl stood, still looking at him. He could see her looking at him, out of the corner of his eye, but he made no sign that he saw her.

They were shouting to her to come, to attend to the Lady of Spereshot and her childer.

She crossed the garth with slow steps, her head bent.

Then, when she came abreast of the keep, she straightened up and called to someone to find her waiting-woman.

She would be all right now, thought Benedict.

He wasn't so sure about himself.

CHAPTER EIGHT

There was much to be done. Benedict soon followed Simon Joce and Dickon out of the postern gate onto the edge of the cliff, and so down the rope ladder they had left there. He did not return till the sun was sinking. Parkyn was waiting for him, with an order for him to present himself to Sir Henry in the latter's room on the third floor of the keep.

Benedict brushed some of the fresh dirt from his tunic and followed where Parkyn led him. The castle was full of bright faces. Here and there men and women danced round the braziers, which were still smouldering.

Well, it was good that they could rejoice.

Benedict found Sir Henry sitting in an old brown robe, with a towel about his head, reading. The room was crowded with books and manuscripts, hinting at Sir Henry's wide interests. The barber was setting his razors away and Sir Henry's valet was easing stockings onto his master's legs. Sir Henry lowered his book, inspected Benedict's ravaged appearance and signed that he should take some of the wine that had been set out on a table nearby. The barber unrolled the towel from Sir Henry's head and began to coax the stiffened, dyed locks into a neat roll of curls.

'You have been down the cliff?' said Sir

Henry. 'I heard you ordered all the survivors killed.'

'Yes.' Benedict's face tightened.

'Were there many?'

'A few.'

'Did you kill any yourself?'

'I . . . no. One leaped out at me, but Dickon saw to him. Dickon wants to go back to the ruin of his old cabin, tonight. His punt is unharmed. I told him, No. Not yet. He must help us repair the guard-boat first. A smashed prow and one oar gone . . . a hole through the bottom, some two planks wide. Bad, but mendable.'

'Now that is very good news.'

'Yes.' Benedict didn't sound as if he thought it good news.

Sir Henry tipped back his head to allow the barber to rub red stain on his cheeks and lips. Benedict stared at the floor.

A mirror was produced and Sir Henry pronounced himself pleased with his coiffure. His valet removed the worn brown robe, to reveal that the old man's figure was held straight in a long-bodied corset. Benedict did not smile. He had long since guessed as much.

'Your friend Sir Reynold is all smiles tonight,' said Sir Henry. 'He begs some armour of me, and I am happy to let him have whatever he chooses. Sir Reynold struts well, does he not? A fighting cock.'

'Yes. He is a brave man.'

'So thinks the Lady of Spereshot and her childer. My granddaughter grinds her teeth to hear Sir Reynold so highly praised. I must admit to feeling a trifle of . . . shall we say pique? . . . that he should steal our thunder so. What say you to that?'

'Nothing, my lord. He is a good man for attack, and you should use him thus. I do not know if you have heard, but I suggested to Simon that a foray might be made tonight to burn off all the scrub on the roadside, and as far round the slopes as possible.'

'I have heard. It is a good plan, and Sir Reynold will carry it out well, I have no doubt. As for you, my lad; I have a crow to pick with you. You went down that cliff today without armour on your back, or a squire at your side. Doubtless if Dickon had not been so sharp-eyed, we would be without our leader tonight. You will not do that again. I will place the largest and most able man in the castle at your disposal, and he will be your shadow from now on. You understand?'

Benedict licked his lips. He nodded. The old man was right, of course. Reynold was showy but expendable. Benedict was without price—at the moment.

'And when you come into the hall tonight for the feast—oh yes, of course there must be a feast, with dancing, and music—and not too much ale flowing, because of the night foray later on . . . but first we must have our hour of triumph! As I say, when you come in, you will be greeted with a spontaneous burst of applause. I have already given orders about that. The cheering should last till you are seated and my granddaughter has placed her wreath on your head.'

'What? But I . . .'

'Only, I can't remember which flower it is that you favour. Was it the rose? No, I think not.'

'I could never . . .'

'Honeysuckle! Some tale about her choosing between a rose and some honeysuckle.' He spoke direct to his valet. 'Make sure the Lady Ursula has a wreath of honeysuckle, and tell the tirewoman to ensure that my granddaughter's dress fits properly tonight. Everything must be magnificent.'

The valet held up the mirror once more and Sir Henry surveyed his person from head to foot. He was attired in a short and extremely stylish tunic, with dagged edges. It was liberally embroidered with gold. His stockings were parti-coloured, his shoes long-toed, and fastened with gold buttons.

'Damnably uncomfortable,' observed Sir Henry. 'But I suppose I can put up with it for a few hours.' He waved his servants away. 'Now go and prepare a bath for Sir Benedict. Shave him, cut and curl his hair and attire him as richly as our resources permit. And do something about his hands!'

Benedict looked at his hands, which boasted broken nails, scratches and the odd cut. 'I do not think . . .' he began.

'You do not think such things are important?' said Sir Henry. 'Now there I disagree with you.' The valet and the barber bowed themselves out.

Sir Henry's manner altered. He said, 'My dear boy, what is the matter? Is it because you had to order those poor creatures killed? You feel their deaths on your conscience? You should have left such an order to me, who am so much nearer my end.'

'No, it had to be done then, or not at all. We could not have taken them prisoner and killed them later on. I did not think there was enough food left in the castle to support a gaggle of prisoners, or I would not . . .'

'You were right!'

'. . . but then I found out that the guard-boat could be repaired, and that the punt was all right. This means Dickon can bring us fish and fowl from the marshes. Our food situation is therefore much eased. If I had known '. . . it was not necessary to kill them, after all.'

'We have enough food to last our present garrison fourteen days, at the present rate of consumption,' said Sir Henry.

Benedict thought that this was one of the times one's leg decided it had had enough. He felt for the edge of the bed and lowered himself onto it.

Fourteen days . . .!

Sir Henry fingered his waxed moustache. 'Hence this masquerade of youth. I wished to die—if I had to die—in style. No-one knows this but you and me. Simon Joce guesses, I believe. Possibly my steward does, too. But he is a close-mouthed fellow, and obeys orders. Everyone else believes there is a further store of grain in the back chamber under the keep. It is not so. The place is empty, and has been so since the last disastrous harvest.'

'But Aylmer cannot possibly arrive in under thirty days! Even with fish and fowl from the river, even if Hugo fails to mount another patrol boat in the channel . . . we cannot feed the garrison . . .'

'We must see if we cannot get some of the women and children away by boat. The problem is where . . . remembering the fate of Spereshot, none of our neighbours will be anxious to take them in. My mind turns to the abbey on the far side of the river. Now that we have transport, we must send to ask if they will take in our refugees.'

'Even when the guard-boat is repaired, it will take only a few people. There are nearly one hundred and thirty people here. Only a few of them are fighting men.'

'I know. We would not normally have so many people here in the castle, but when Hugo's men first came on us the gates were open, and many of the townsfolk and the country people from hereabouts fled to us. Could I turn them away? No. I knew from the beginning that we could not feed ourselves, let alone them, but I hoped. I hoped for a miracle, I suppose.'

'A miracle? And you got two men!'

'I'm hoping you're like the loaves and the fishes. Multiplying, you know. Now don't tell me I'm an unrealistic, day-dreaming old man. I prefer to think of myself as having faith. At my age, when the sword-arm loses its strength, it's tempting to think that faith can be a weapon, to take the place of the sword.'

Sir Henry picked up the book he'd been reading. 'There's something in this book . . . a distraction . . I suppose I ought to have been studying my missal, but . . . this makes me laugh. It's a book of ancient, heathenish tales. One of them's about things shooting from the head of a god. Ideas, I suppose. That's you. Open your head, and the ideas come out. You'll save us, I have no doubt on it.'

Benedict groped for words. He floundered between crude expressions of wrath and an explosion of laughter. He shook his head, throwing out his hands. He began to laugh, and went on laughing till he was weak.

'That's better,' said the old man. 'Either laughter or tears will do, but a man who commands others must be able to obtain relief from one or the other. Or he'll break apart. Now, off you go, and allow them to make you presentable for a change.'

'You,' said Benedict, with conviction, 'are an unscrupulous old man.'

'Am I not?' said Sir Henry, with pride.

Ursula tugged at the neck of her gown. Her woman had sewn it up so tightly that it chafed. More, her ribs were aching from being so closely laced. The gown was one of her aunt's, and the Lady Editha had grown so thin that it barely met around Ursula's more sturdy form.

The Lady of Spereshot was grumbling. She had been grumbling ever since they had extracted her and her children from the cages and brought them up into the castle, to be washed, re-clothed and made much of.

'. . . but Sir Reynold de Cressi is so gallant, is he not? I fail to see why we should have to wait for our meal until this uncouth Sir whatever-his-name-is condescends to join us. Sir Reynold tells us that we would have been out of the cages hours earlier, if it had been for that man's interference.'

'Or dead,' said Ursula. 'There was a trap set for us, remember.'

'Yes. Well. But could you not have countered it earlier? My poor little boy was so frightened . . .'

The 'poor little boy' was a stolid child. It seemed unlikely that anything short of a threat to deprive him of food would frighten him. The girl, on the other hand, though she had been roughly handled and was inclined to dissolve into tears, was doing her best to behave. She bit her lip at her mother's ungracious words and, catching Ursula's eye, looked distressed. Ursula put her arm round the girl's shoulders and held her close.

Everyone was gathered in the hall, waiting for Benedict. Everyone knew that they were supposed to cheer when he came down the stairs at the end of the hall, and crossed the floor to his seat at the high table. Ursula checked that her waiting-woman was standing nearby, with the wreath of honeysuckle for Benedict's head.

'He's going to hate it!' thought Ursula. 'He's going to wish he'd never come here. He'll blush and look at the floor, when he should respond with smiling civilities. He can't help it, Oh, it's cruel to make him go through this!'

Sir Henry wouldn't agree to altering the ceremony, in order to make things easier for Benedict. Sir Henry liked ceremonials. He believed, perhaps correctly, that they were of great value in raising the morale of the people, and instilled in them a reverence for authority. It had been difficult for Benedict to find someone to obey him that morning. No-one had thought it necessary to rouse him for the rescue party. But after tonight men would have no doubt that Benedict was chief in command under the Lord of Salwarpe.

Yes, it was all very necessary, thought Ursula. But extremely difficult for Benedict. If only she could run forward as he came to the foot of the stairs, and give him her hand! Then he would have somebody to help him walk through those waiting ranks of people to the dais.

But she could not go. Her grandfather's instructions were explicit. Even now, she had to begin to move the Lady of Spereshot and her children towards the dais. The children. Ursula stopped. She twitched a sprig of honeysuckle from the wreath and pressed it into the girl's hand. Bending forward, she whispered in her ear. Ursula gave the child a push towards the stairs.

'What?' said the Lady of Spereshot, on seeing her daughter leave them.

'She is to escort Sir Benedict to us,' said Ursula. 'A pretty gesture to her saviour, don't you think?'

Ursula felt her grandfather's eye on her and turned her head aside. She would not look at him. She did not wish to hear his words of censure. She would not allow Benedict to suffer unnecessarily, if she could help it. Sir Henry was whispering with the Lady of Spereshot, and now the good dame was smiling.

'Well, now,' said the Lady of Spereshot. 'I was not aware that Sir Benedict owned so many fine manors! And expectations, too, you say? Well, my little girl is not uncomely, and in a few years' time who knows?'

Ursula felt her mouth go dry. She had not thought . . . if she had considered for one moment, she would never have sent the girl . . . it was true that Benedict ought to marry again, and that in a few years' time the girl from Spereshot would be of marriageable age, but surely . . .

The idea was repugnant.

The girl was hardly a good match for Benedict. She was a scrawny, under-sized little thing, and her mother the sort whom one would avoid at all costs . . . and the brother! Save the mark! Benedict would never put up with him!

But the girl would have a dowry of sorts. And Benedict was not in need of a penny here or there, having married an heiress before and being already in possession of his father's estates.

Oh, but the idea of matching them was monstrous!

Ursula looked within herself and acknowledged the truth. The idea of Benedict's marrying the pale slip of a girl from Spereshot was monstrous because she, Ursula de Thrave, wanted him for herself.

No I don't!

Yes. Oh yes, you do. You want him, and have wanted him from the moment you saw him turn faint and sit down on the trebuchet this morning . . . No, before that. When he dragged Dickon up the cliff. Or even before, when he discarded his armour in Dickon's cabin. No, when he chose honeysuckle in the garden right at the beginning . . .

Oh, but this is ridiculous! The man is uncouth. Diffident if not downright rude in company. He is not even handsome, or straight in body. He limps. Hoppity, hop. It is enough to make one laugh. Or cry.

And there is Aylmer. You are to marry Aylmer, and you know very well that he is the sort of man you need.

Ah, but Benedict needs me more. And there is an end of it.

Someone was holding her arm. It was her grandfather. He said, 'Ursula? Are you sick? Benedict is coming down.'

She discovered that she was leaning against Sir Henry. She lifted her eyes to the collar of his tunic, but no higher, lest he read her mind. She smiled and smiled, and pushed him away, that she might stand on her own once more. There had to be no sign of weakness. There had to be no weakness at all.

The flight of stairs leading down from the keep into the banqueting-hall was wide and shallow. Benedict's legs came into view, first his good leg and then his bad. The girl from Spereshot was hesitating at the foot of the stairs, looking back at Ursula. Ursula nodded, and signed to the girl to press on. The girl, with a diffidence becoming in one of her years and position, held up the sprig of honeysuckle towards the dimly-seen figure on the stairs. Then Benedict was bending his head and taking the sprig from her. He stopped, to speak with the girl. And she . . . wonders would never cease . . .! She laughed, and put her hand in Benedict's as if she had known him all her life.

Ursula had forgotten how good he was with children and animals. The girl would seem but a child to him. He would see her shrink, and forget his own diffidence in caring for her.

They stepped into the body of the hall together, and Ursula caught her breath, for Benedict had been so polished and decked with good clothing that he was almost unrecognisable.

'Fine feathers,' said her grandfather, in her ear.

Ursula's mouth ached with smiling. She nodded, not taking her eyes from Benedict. She thought it was like the silver plate off which her grandfather ate. Now and then the plate became dulled and had to be polished back to splendour. The silver was still of value when it was dull, but when it was properly looked after it was hard to remember what it had looked like before.

Benedict's hair had been cut to a smooth bob and, though it had not been curled, it seemed to have a shining life it had not possessed before. He wore a black and silver supertunic of velvety fustian. It had been bought by Sir Henry some time ago but had proved too heavy for his slender frame. On Benedict it looked magnificent. His brown skin stood the test well. Every line of him seemed sharpened. For the first time Ursula realised that Benedict had considerable presence. If Aylmer were to stand beside him now, there might even be some doubt as to which was the more authoritative figure.

The girl gave a little skip as she walked beside Benedict. He was smiling, acknowledging the greetings of those around them.

Ursula started. Her grandfather had pinched her arm. She stepped forward, taking the wreath from her waiting-woman and presented it to Benedict. He was still smiling. Then she saw that his smile was as rigid as her own. She spoke a few words. He bowed, turning the wreath round and round, making it clear that he did not know what to do with it.

'Put it on your head,' hissed Ursula.

He shook his head, for a moment showing a flash of panic. Then he turned to the little maid at his side and placed the wreath on her head, instead.

'For me?' she cried, in delight. She put both hands to her head and settled the wreath more firmly upon it.

And now there came that burst of spontaneous applause which the Lord of Salwarpe had planned should occur when

Benedict first stepped into the hall. Why it had not come at the proper time was a moot point. Perhaps the garrison had been awestruck by the sight of Benedict in good clothes for a change. Perhaps they, too, had needed time to adjust their opinion of him.

However it was, the cheers this time were genuine. Benedict ducked his head, and turned to Sir Henry, with a disclaiming, modest gesture. This did him no disservice, either. Ursula rearranged the seating, so that Benedict should sit between the little maid from Spereshot and her mother. She herself sank into a chair between her grandfather and Sir Reynold.

'That was well done,' said Sir Henry in her ear. 'Now the little maid will win everyone to our side with her tales of Sir Benedict's chivalry. We could not have devised a better ambassadress for our cause than she will be, when she goes to the abbey.'

* * *

They feasted long and well. They danced. Everyone danced, even Sir Henry and Benedict. Sir Henry danced with his granddaughter because she, being betrothed to Aylmer, might not dance freely with the unmarried knights. Reynold danced with the Lady of Spereshot, who had taken a fancy to him, and Benedict helped the maid to walk through a measure before they both decided that they had had enough.

When the moon rose, Simon Joce slipped through the throng and whispered in Sir Henry's ear. Then the music was halted and the company's mood changed. Some prepared to bed down for the night in the hall. Some went to stand in watchful silence on the ramparts. Simon Joce passed from a man here to a man there, checking that all was in order, while Reynold was helped into his armour by the ladies of the household.

Benedict watched Simon for a while and then, being satisfied that the sergeant knew what he was about, left the ball and went to the gate-tower. He wore no armour, because he had no intention of going out with the assault party that night. He had other work to do; it was less obviously a soldier's work, but work that had to be done that night, and that none other than he could do.

He trod softly up the stairs. He felt, slow and heavy with an old sorrow, revived by this new love. Ursula had changed in her manner towards him. He could guess why. It was the usual thing for women to turn from him in disgust at some point . . . except that it had not seemed to be like that with her. She had altered the seating arrangements so that she might not sit beside him. It had hurt. It had been the sort of trick Idonia had played on him, time and again. And yet it had not been done for the same reason. He could have sworn that Ursula had sent him a glance of apology when she indicated where he was to sit. There had been something else . . . a plea for understanding? It had looked like it at the time, but . . .

No, no. It was simply that she had grown tired of him, as Idonia had done. There was nothing new in that, and he could bear it if only she did not turn from him to Reynold, as Idonia had done.

He came out onto the ramparts. Outlined against the moon were two figures, leaning against the wall. They were talking in low voices. One was Peter Bowman. The other Benedict did not recognise.

His ears were sharp, and they were careless.

Peter was saying, '. . . you really think he'll make a pig's eye of it? Surely, with Simon Joce behind him, even the Cock can't go far wrong.'

'I'd sooner it were Old Limpy in charge.'

'Aye; Simon would, and all. Likely the Cock will fire the bushes nearest the castle first, instead of getting as far down the hill as he can before the alarm is raised. He'd see a bogey in a hazel twig.'

'Doesn't the other one go with us tonight?'

Nah. He's got something more up his sleeve than his arm. Dickon says . . .'

Benedict's hands closed round the back of their necks and pushed their heads together down onto the stonework.

'And if Old Limpy hears you miscall Sir Reynold de Cressi once more, there'll be a public whipping! You hear?'

He released them, and they fell apart, muttering apologies.

'Don't apologise to me,' said Benedict, grim of voice. 'We'll have no tale-bearing and muttering about your betters in a siege, if you please. Sir Reynold is one of the bravest of knights and you'll not undermine his authority.'

'My lord, you should hear what he says of you, behind your back . . .'

Benedict laughed. 'So! What of it?'

'De Cressi is a fool!' said Peter's companion. This man had an odd habit of speech, as if his mouth were twisted, so that his voice came whistling through his teeth. 'But I'll not say so to any but you and Peter; and Dickon, of course. And Simon Joce. And Sir Henry, who is very well aware of it . . .'

'Save the mark!' cried Benedict, but softly, for fear he might rouse the enemy's watchman. 'What have we here? A man with no respect for his betters?'

'A man with every respect for his betters,' said the other, 'but none for fools.'

'My lord,' said Peter, nudging his companion into silence, 'they said you needed a squire. Sir Henry said as you must have a man at your back, wherever you go. Now that's not the same thing, it seems to me, as having a squire. My Lord de Cressi has chosen a squire from the oldest of the pages here in Salwarpe, and is having the lad fitted out with his own livery and a good horse, and all that. But what I said was that you'd prefer to choose a man who knew what he was about . . .'

'. . . and who doesn't talk too much, Peter Bowman!'

'Aye, there is that. Though sometimes it's good to know what goes on. So I said to Simon that Merle the Miller here would be best, and Simon agreed with me. Merle is from the town, but he's a good man, for all that. He was delivering flour when Hugo's men came, and so he was trapped here. I've asked Merle about serving you till the siege is over, and he said as he didn't have any great objection. So it's all settled.'

Benedict said nothing.

Peter began to fidget. The other man stood still, doing nothing, saying nothing. Only the whistle of his breath as it came and went betrayed that he was alive.

At last, 'Will you obey me,' said Benedict, 'whatever I tell you to do? And without arguing?'

'If I see my way clear,' said Merle.

There was another silence.

'No,' said Benedict at last. 'You are too valuable a man to be my bodyguard. The number of men who can think for themselves inside Salwarpe is small. Simon, Dickon, you and Peter here. And Sir Henry, of course.'

'And his granddaughter,' said Merle.

'Yes,' said Benedict. 'That is true. There are seven of us. Seven good minds and thirty able bodied men against . . .' He looked down the slope to where watchmen's fires flickered. 'Against how many? Two hundred mercenaries or a whole town of people. And twenty-nine days to go. I will have a council meeting tomorrow at noon, and will require you both to attend. In the meantime, I have something else to do, and I need a man at my back when I go down the cliff. I want a man who will react to my orders without argument, without thinking. I want someone who knows every nook and cranny of this place, and of the town below. He needn't be able to handle a boat, though it would help if he could. But his hand must live on his dagger. If you know of such a man, send him to my room in the keep in an hour's time.'

'I know of none such,' said Peter Bowman. 'Or none who would be of any use to you . . .'

'I know of one,' said Merle, and it seemed that he was enjoying a private joke. 'I will send him to you.'

Benedict considered whether he should press Merle to disclose the source of his amusement, but decided against it. Time was too short.

CHAPTER NINE

Benedict waited at the foot of the gatetower only long enough to see the file of men issue forth and creep down the hill. When the first of the fires were set in the bushes, he left the gatehouse and made his way back to the keep to write letters. There Parkyn had set a brazier of hot coals for him at the side of a writing-desk, with everything ready to hand. It was not long, however, before Dickon arrived and demanded speech with Benedict.

Dickon was angry. He stood with arms akimbo, glaring at Benedict.

'Yes,' said Benedict. 'I know just how you feel. You'd like to slide a knife into my ribs, but you aren't quite sure whether Sir Henry would back you up or no.'

Dickon thrust his hands within his belt and raised his shoulders to his ears 'I don't like being shut up in this place. Or any stone-built place. You said as you'd let me go when the tide went out. But they won't let me through the postern gate without the password.'

'That's war all over,' said Benedict. 'You do someone a favour, and they turn round and say it's not enough. You of all men should understand that.'

Dickon spat into the brazier. 'And if I refuse?'

'Then I'll let you go, without your punt. You'll have to swim back.'

'Can't swim.'

Benedict looked up from sealing his letter and smiled. 'Neither can I.'

Both men laughed and the laughter released the tension between them.

'What be it you want done?'

'In the first place, what I don't want is for you to go back to your place and be killed. As soon as Hugo's men see signs of life at your cabin site, they'll be over to deal with it. They know you helped us get into Salwarpe. They won't forget. You think you can hide in the reeds till they've gone. Maybe. And maybe not. Why take a risk, when if you wait till Hugo's been dealt with, you can demand what labour and materials you want from Sir Henry, to rebuild?'

'What be it you want?'

'More than you can perform. But for a start I want someone to take the Lady of Spereshot and her children over to the abbey on the far side of the estuary. I want them out of here tonight, before Hugo thinks up some way to stop them leaving. Once at the abbey, with letters which I shall give them, they can rouse the countryside against Hugo. And perhaps meet up with their lord and master, whom I believe escaped the burning of his manor. Will you do that?'

'Just because I saved a baby once . . .'

'Aye. Though these three will be more trouble to you than your present mistress ever was. The Lady of Spereshot is one who would raise Cain if she felt a speck of sand in her shoe, and the boy is a lump of dough. You'll find them worry enough, I'm thinking.'

'What's the point of it? What good will it do to rouse the countryside, when Hugo's hand is fast around the castle?'

'Food, Dickon. There's more people in the castle than usual, and less than enough to feed them on. I must have more grain, and there's not much point in asking Hugo for it, is there?'

'Hah! And am I to bring you back a sack of grain in my punt? 'Twould be enough to feed the chickens that peck around the granary door for a couple of days, maybe.'

'A sheep might be of more use, but a sack of flour would do. We have no mill here in the castle, so it would be a problem to deal with grain. But pay for it, Dickon. If I could only lay my hands on a half dozen punts, to bring in half a dozen sacks of flour at each tide . . .'

'No boat would risk coming to the castle, with Hugo sitting in the channel. But the abbot is one with an eye for a bargain, and it is well known his granaries are full. Even if they weren't full, he'd deny his own men, to sell flour to us at an inflated price. But he wouldn't sell unless he had cash. Promises—except those about sinners going to Hell—aren't in his line.'

'If I write a letter to the abbot, promising part cash, and giving him a draft on the merchant who buys my fleeces for the rest, do you think he would treat with us?'

Dickon fingered his chin. 'If you came with me . . .?

'I cannot leave here at the moment. Perhaps Sir Henry . . . no. Not he. Well, the first thing is to make contact with the abbot . . . and then . . .'

Someone pounded on the door. It opened and a white-faced youth was projected into the room. It looked as if he'd been thrown in, rather than entered of his own accord. The door slammed shut again. The youth picked himself up and backed away to the wall. His chin was on his shoulder, and his eyes everywhere. Benedict picked up the candle and took it over to the lad, who shrank from the light. His hand was on the dagger in his belt.

Benedict thought, Is this the lad Merle has picked out for me? Wherein lies the joke? The lad is terrified . . .

'What do you want with that one?' demanded Dickon. 'He'd steal the shirt off your back while you slept.'

The lad's eyes flickered at Dickon and returned to Benedict. He raised his right arm, as if expecting a blow. He looked as if he'd been fighting recently and got the worst of it.

'I wouldn't have him, my lord,' muttered

Parkyn. 'He's not one of ours. He's from the town. Lives off pickings, as you might say.'

'I didn't ask to come!' The lad was snivelling. 'That Merle pulled me up and kicked me up the stairs, and threw me through the door, and I wasn't doing nothing!'

'Let me throw him out,' said Parkyn, moving to grab the boy's arm.

At once the youth ducked. His knife seemed to jump into his hand, and his teeth came out over his lip, giving him a wolfish appearance. Parkyn stopped dead.

Benedict laughed. He appreciated the joke, but nevertheless . . . 'He couldn't be better. He's the man for me. Provided, my lad, that you don't try to cheat me, or to steal from me. Is it understood?'

'Would I do such a thing?' whined the boy.

'Oh, yes. I expect so,' said Benedict. 'That is, if you thought you could get away with it. You're to guard my back, do you understand? You'll sleep across the door here, have clean clothes when you need them, and eat with Parkyn. When the siege is over, I will pay you whatever you have been worth to me. Is it a bargain?'

The lad looked undecided. It was unlikely he had ever been promised wages for anything before.

'And now,' said Benedict. 'You must show me what you can do. I expect you know how to get into the armoury without rousing everyone.

Go and fetch me a leather-lined, quilted jacket such as foot-soldiers wear and a long knife. Oh yes, and a plain basinet. I don't want to be cumbered with heavy armour, so choose equipment which is plain, light and strong. The same for yourself. And be back here before I grow impatient.'

The lad hesitated, torn between the instinct to deny that he could break into the armoury in the middle of the night, and a cocky pride that he could display his talents without being punished for it. Finally he grinned, and vanished. One moment he was there, emitting an unsavoury smell, and the next he was gone.

'An excellent choice,' said Benedict. 'Now, these letters, Dickon . . .'

*   *   *

The sun was high overhead before Sir Reynold de Cressi made his way, with many a yawn, out of his chamber. He had heard something said about a council of war at noon, but he was in no mood to hurry himself. He swaggered up onto the ramparts to look with complacent eye on the devastation his little force had wreaked the night before. Charred and blackened grass, smoking stumps of bushes, were everywhere. The thicket in which Hugo had hidden his archers was now a tangle of twisted, leafless branches, wherein not even a bird could hide.

The cages which had held the Lady of

Spereshot and her children were now in the hands of the men of Salwarpe. Carpenters sawed at bars, while a horse and cart plied between the gatehouse and the turn of the road, taking down hides and a brazier and bringing back various pieces of timber which were no longer required. Peter Bowman and five others were on guard beside the carts, which were being turned into an outpost for the besieged garrison.

'A neat idea of mine, that,' said Reynold. 'That clerk Benedict would have wasted the carts . . .'

Then his face changed, for he had caught sight of a gown that he thought he recognised. Was that Lady Ursula going into the keep? He hurried down the steps from the ramparts and went after that flicker of colour. There would be plenty of time for dalliance, now that he had cleared the slopes around the castle, and what better object for dalliance than Ursula de Thrave? Particularly since she would not expect him to marry her . . . she being betrothed to Aylmer . . . most convenient . . . good omen for the future . . .

He hastened his steps.

* * *

Reynold was mistaken in thinking he had seen Ursula enter the keep, because she had been closeted with her grandfather a long time before Reynold emerged from his room. For a while they had talked of domestic affairs.

Then, when Benedict entered, she turned and smiled at him, holding out her hand in welcome. She had not intended to be so welcoming. Overnight she had reviewed her conduct and decided that it would be best to keep him at a distance. She had decided that it was only gratitude which made her feel so warmly towards him, and pity. It would be quite wrong to allow her emotions to get out of hand.

Only, when he came in wearing his black and silver, with his hair neatly combed . . . his eye had sought hers, and she had turned as a flower does to the sun, and smiled at him. Even as she did so, she thought: I ought not to . . .

The result was startling.

Benedict's face altered. The customary harsh lines of eye and lip vanished. It was like setting a torch to a beacon. He smiled. This was not the usual strained smile he kept for formal occasions, but a leaping-out of joy.

She thought: What have I done? And put her hand to her heart, to still its insistence.

He took a deep breath. She saw him take it. Then he steadied himself, and turned to Sir Henry with a formal greeting, but still with that smile on his lips.

'I fear,' said Benedict, 'that I have been presumptuous. Last night—and this morning, too—I have given certain orders to your men, without first consulting you.'

'My dear Benedict,' said Sir Henry, with an answering smile, 'you should try to say such things as if you really were sorry for what you had done.'

'Well, I am,' said Benedict, untruthfully. He tried to take the smile off his face and failed. He laughed.

Ursula marvelled. He had laughed! Not with amusement, but from joy. His eyes sought hers, and as she met their silvery glance she, too, took a deep breath, and held her head higher.

'Benedict,' said Sir Henry. 'Sit down. You are too energetic this morning. Here am I, a pitiable wreck of an old man, feeling all the worse for feasting and dancing till the small hours, while you come bouncing in as if you had had eight hours' sleep—which I know you cannot have done. Sit, lad! Sit here beside me, and tell me what terrible thing it is that you have done.'

So Benedict sat, and took his eyes off Ursula with an effort, and stumbled through a list of the orders he had given, with Sir Henry nodding approval.

'Yes, yes,' said Sir Henry. 'They call the lad The Weasel. A bastard born of fisherfolk from the harbour. He was outcast at an early age, for stealing. His mother was no better than she ought to have been, and died young as such women often do. For what you want, the lad might do well enough, if only he will obey you.'

'He is too afraid of Merle not to obey me at the moment, and perhaps he is a little tempted by the prospect of earning some money. And talking of money,' said Benedict, losing his smile. 'I did something else last night. I sent Dickon off . . .'

'Now that was well done,' said Sir Henry. The Lord of Spereshot is a good friend of ours, and glad I am to hear that he has survived the burning of his manor. But his wife . . .! I wish the abbot joy of her company.'

'It was not that,' said Benedict, showing signs of nervousness once more. 'I gave Dickon some money, to buy food.'

'Oh? Ah!' Sir Henry leaned back in his chair. He put his hand over his mouth, perhaps to hide a smile. 'I will, of course, repay you.'

Ursula shifted on her stool, and Benedict looked at her, and then away again.

'Of course you will,' said Benedict, looking down at his hands.

'You should have sent to me,' said Sir Henry, 'and I would have given you money.'

'The hour was late,' said Benedict. 'In my letter to the abbot, I offered to buy whatever grain or flour he had, and to pay for it partly in cash, and partly by a draft on the merchant who buys my fleeces every year.'

'Indeed! I could have given the abbot a similar assurance that he would receive payment.'

'Naturally,' said Benedict, being polite. 'We can settle the details when everything is quiet once more.'

Ursula said, 'The rents are due again at Michaelmas. We will repay you from them.'

'First we must get Hugo off your land.' Benedict looked around 'Where is Reynold? We must take counsel . . .'

'He was sent for, and told his servant to say he would be along soon. Is there any hurry? Surely we have only to sit out the siege, now.'

Benedict began to pace the room, hands clasped behind his back.

'There is much to be done. Not for Reynold, perhaps. Though somehow we must devise means to keep him out of mischief, or he will be wanting to ride down the hill to tilt at Hugo's archers . . . which would be disastrous. We must set every able-bodied man, woman and child to work. At once. No delay. If you have not lived through a siege, Sir Henry, you cannot realize how important it is to be prepared.

'Let us review the situation. Hugo knows he has only twenty-nine days before Aylmer comes. Hugo does not know that we have insufficient food. He thinks his assault on the castle from the cliff yesterday nearly succeeded. He will have noted the smoke from our braziers, and he will believe that his assault force managed to set alight various buildings within the castle, before they were finally overcome. Remember that none of the cliff force returned to the harbour. His guard-boat did not return, either. Yet he will find another boat, I think. At some time he will set another guard-boat out there, and then the channel will be blocked once more . . .'

'But the abbot will not send food to us, if he thinks the channel is blocked.'

'No, of course he won't. Any replacement boat must be dealt with. But let me continue. Hugo thinks us much weakened in every way, and therefore he will go on to the attack. A ram, certainly. A trebuchet; possibly. Fire arrows. Possibly a mine. Yes. I must have a dozen large bowls set about the ramparts, with water in them. Lady, will you arrange that?'

'Metal or pottery?' asked Ursula, trying to keep up with Benedict's rapid fire of ideas.

'Either, so long as they hold water. And your women must have a place prepared for casualties, in a stone-built room. Beds, water, bandages . . .'

'Casualties inside the castle?'

'Oh yes,' said Benedict. 'You would be surprised . . . no, I'll say no more Just be prepared for them. And the children—unless we can get some of them away to the abbey?—they must be kept out of the way and amused. They must not be allowed to run around, getting in the way of the carpenters and builders.'

'Carpenters and builders . . .?'

'But the older boys,' said Benedict, unaware of the interruption, 'must be given fishing-lines, and set to work at once. We need fish for tonight, and for salting down to eat later. We must take advantage of our access to the water, while there is no guard-boat in the channel. I had best set Merle to organise the boys, I think . . .'

'Ah, you have met Merle, have you? And did he spit in your face?'

'No. Or rather, he won't do so in future. But it would be best to keep him and Sir Reynold apart. One thing . . . the most important thing . . . it worries me that you have no smith operating in the castle. There is a forge, but it is silent. I have urgent need of a smith . . .'

'Then you must ask Hugo for him. He works below, in the town. His father used to work up here, but the son wanted to be nearer the ploughshares in the valley . . .'

Benedict rubbed the back of his neck. Frowning, he considered Sir Henry's statement for as long as it took to count ten. 'That's bad,' he said. 'Very bad. Well, how many of your men can turn carpenter?'

'The head carpenter is a good man, though somewhat slow. You must take his advice on that.'

'Very well. I need a set of semi-permanent ladders for the cliff, for a start. Boats or a raft. All the wooden buildings inside the castle must be torn down, and the timber put in storage under the keep. No thatched roofs must be allowed to remain, unless—I shall have to inspect them myself—if they can be covered with wetted hides . . . But that reminds me! I doubt you have many hides; here, have you? Then the remaining horses must be inspected and some must be slaughtered. Their flesh may be used for eating, the bones boiled for glue, and the hides . . . ah, the hides will be invaluable.'

Ursula said, 'You shall have my pony. There will be trouble, otherwise. I will lead him out, and you will slaughter him first.'

'My old war-horse, too,' said Sir Henry. 'He is past his prime, anyway.'

Benedict bit his lip. 'It is the worst, always. This business of slaughtering the animals. But we do not need to do it yet. Perhaps we will not need to do it at all. That is one of the problems with a siege. You never quite know what is going to be needed. But if you don't prepare well, then there is never enough time to take counter-measures, when the attacks come.' He examined the rug on the floor at his feet. 'You think me hard. I had a horse once, which I had gentled myself. But I swore when he was slaughtered that I would never again allow myself to grow fond of an animal in that way. A horse is only a horse. A dog is only a dog. If a man's life can be saved by killing that horse or that dog, then . . .' He nodded.

'Then that is what we have to do. You won't understand, yet. You will later, perhaps.'

'We are in your hands,' said Ursula.

'Yes, I am afraid you are. I have sat through two sieges, and done some besieging on my own account. It is never pretty work. There is nothing of chivalry and knighthood in it. Nothing like the old songs. The most important men in this castle at the moment—after me and Simon Joce—are Peter Bowman, Merle and your carpenter. And Dickon for communications. In fact, I would almost go so far as to say that if your carpenter is not a good craftsman, then we will be defeated.' He gave them a silvery glance. 'But I will have a boat ready and waiting at the foot of the cliff at all times, so that you may get away in safety, if the worst comes to the worst. That is why we can't afford to move the trebuchet to the other side—where I feel sure we are going to need it, and we have no more long timbers to make another like it—but we must keep the channel in the river clear at all costs.'

'You cannot think that we would leave!' said Ursula.

'Oh yes,' said Benedict. 'You will have to, if I say so. You are not your own mistress any more. I would be failing in my duty to Aylmer if I allowed you to be captured by Hugo. And now, if you please, since Reynold has not seen fit to honour us with his presence, I will go seek him out and learn what he intends to do with himself for the next twenty-nine days.'

So saying, he ducked his head at them and left.

There was a long silence.

Then Sir Henry said, 'I feel my age today, Ursula. That young man has a knack of presenting unpalatable facts in an unpalatable fashion. I wish I could pick holes in his arguments, but I cannot.'

She was leaning forward, her chin on her hand. She said, 'He will save us, I am sure.'

'Yes, I have no doubt of that. But at what a cost, Ursula! At what a cost!'

'Cost, grandfather? Ah, you mean the buildings which will have to be pulled down, and the horses which will have to be slaughtered? Well, they are not important, after all.'

'No, my dear. I wasn't thinking of the buildings, or the horses.'

He did not elaborate and she did not press him.

* * *

Ursula had smiled at him!

More, she had held out her hand and continued to smile! And he had been crass and insensitive in return. He could feel the blood rising in his neck now, as he thought how crudely he had put his demands . . .

What right had he to demand anything

of them, anyway? Had he not been sent to help them? Certainly he had not been sent to impose his will on them, and they so kindly to an awkward stranger.

But she had smiled.

He passed down the stairs into the hall and stood, smiling at those who went about their business there. He did not see them, or only as shadows. Ursula's face was before him all the time, and the sound of her voice in his ear.

She would find him out, of course. Perhaps at that very minute she and Sir Henry were discussing him, laughing at his awkwardness, and his effrontery . . . his impudence in believing that he knew better than they did!

Well, he did know more about sieges than they did, but he could have devised more tactful ways of letting them know the facts. If only he had been gifted with the social graces, as other men were. Think how much better Aylmer would have put the case . . . or even Reynold!

Which reminded him, where was Reynold? And Merle, and Peter Bowman? Had he not bidden them all to meet him at noon, and none of them had done so? He looked about him. He was standing in the garth outside the keep by now. The sky was clear above. The braziers had burned out and only the faintest of blue hazes showed above the wall, where Reynold and his men had burned off the scrub the previous night. But there was no sign of Reynold. Benedict was not to know this, but Reynold had gone chasing Ursula's tire-woman, who had a gown somewhat similar in colour to that of her mistress. Reynold had gone up into the keep by the outside stair as Benedict had descended through the hall. And so they had missed one another.

Benedict pinched his chin What next? A hundred things; but which first? He set off towards the gatehouse.

Idonia had smiled at him like that once, before she found him out for what he was. Benedict remembered how he and Reynold had ridden out with Aylmer to fetch Idonia from the convent in which she had been educated. She had allowed Benedict to throw her up into the saddle and had smiled down at him. Her hair was a smoky black, her skin white, and her eyes gleamed with mischief. She had shown her delight at being released from the convent in a dozen ways. He had ridden at her side all the way back, and she had smiled at everything he said, and had allowed him to dance with her that night in the hall.

Five weeks of smiles. He had been so much in love with her that he had hardly slept or eaten, or thought of anything else. He had known he was become the talk of the castle, and he had not cared. Reynold had been piqued, for Reynold had boasted that he would win Idonia for himself. Five weeks, and Aylmer had said that Idonia and Benedict might be formally betrothed. And so they were. They had walked in the garden and he had cut her a rose. She had pricked her finger on a thorn. That was the first time she stamped her foot at him and frowned.

But the frown had soon been smoothed away, and she had promised to ride out beside him the following day, when they were all to go hunting. And she had ridden by his side, and they had lagged somewhat behind the others on their return journey, and come back into the castle hand in hand . . .

And as they returned it had begun to rain. And it had rained and rained. And Idonia had become restless, and hasty of temper at being shut indoors when she wanted to ride out. They had quarrelled . . . a nothing . . . she had quickly been appeased with promises and kisses . . .

And then, the accident.

Benedict came out onto the roof of the gate-tower and looked about him. He had been seeking Peter Bowman, but that tall man was not there. Instead, a largish, clumsy-looking man with a twisted mouth turned from his scrutiny of the valley below and ducked his head at Benedict in an abrupt movement which might have passed for a salute . . . or which might not, if Benedict chose to ignore it.

'You are Merle? Tell me: where is Peter Bowman?'

Merle jerked his head towards the valley.

Benedict stepped to the parapet and looked down the road. Where two carts had stood yesterday, holding the hostages from Spereshot, a hide-covered outpost was being created. Peter Bowman was balancing on the topmost timber of one of the carts, clowning.

'You'll not be best pleased,' said Merle, with satisfaction. 'Told Peter so. Said you wouldn't like it.'

Benedict took his tongue between his teeth and said nothing. Merle folded his arms, leaning against the parapet.

'I'm to relieve him at dusk. Said you wouldn't like that, either. Got a bet on ft. I don't go, and Peter comes back. Stands to reason.'

Still Benedict held his tongue.

'Spit it out!' urged Merle. 'Or you'll bust! We told the Cock, moreover, that you wanted to speak with us come noon. He said for us not to go, as it couldn't be anything important. We'm all villeins, you see. Dirt beneath his lordship's feet.'

'That's enough,' said Benedict, with subdued violence. 'If Sir Reynold has given certain orders, then of course they must be obeyed. It is true that the outpost is . . . something of a surprise to me. Nevertheless . . .'

'Sticks in your craw, don't it?' Merle looked Benedict in the eye. 'I been a soldier, too. Twice to France with the old lord, when we was both young. I'm the miller down in the town, and I minds my own business, normally. But Peter's a friend of mine, and I don't want him sacrificed for nothing.'

'I daresay you'll win your bet. Thank you, Merle. And by the by, I do want that conference, as soon as possible. I will send you word, when and where.'

Benedict turned on his heel and caught sight of the Weasel whipping away down the stairs. The boy slid in and out of sight like a snake—or like the weasel after which he was named. Very aptly named.

Benedict raised his voice, that the Weasel might hear him. 'I have to thank you for something else, Merle. The boy you sent me. I think he'll be very useful.'

Merle guffawed with laughter and returned to watching the road below.

Benedict took a deep breath. He had hoped to avoid a show-down with Reynold. They had known each other too long, and disagreed about things so many times that it was unlikely the forthcoming interview would be pleasant. Well, he would try to handle Reynold with tact, but if tact were impossible . . . Benedict shrugged. There was always force.

CHAPTER TEN

'You sent for me?' Reynold swaggered in and took the only chair in Benedict's room.

Benedict was busy at the writing-desk. He jerked his head at Parkyn, who left the room.

'Yes. I will be with you in a moment.' He finished his letter, read it over and signed with a flourish.

Reynold yawned. 'A hard night's work. You should have been with us. You might have learned something for a change.'

Benedict said nothing to that, but pulled another sheet of paper to him and began another letter.

'Well?' said Reynold, becoming impatient. He glanced out of the window. 'If you have nothing to say, then I will leave you to your gloominess. I have something better to do with my time than sit here watching you make scratch marks on paper.'

'I was writing to Aylmer I thought you would like to see the letter. I want to get some of the children and nursing mothers away from here, if we can organise enough boats. I have told Aylmer that I am sending you back with the refugees. He'll understand. You can do no more here.'

Reynold sprang to his feet, hand on dagger. 'Now what maggot have you in that clownish head of yours?'

'Just that. There is no more of your sort of fighting to be done here. It is a matter of sitting it out. And supplies of food. And pulling down certain buildings, making machines and so on. All that sort of clerky nonsense that you find so distasteful. Therefore it will be best if you escort the women and children to safety.'

'You don't get rid of me as easily as that! Was I not appointed with you? Did I not win my place?'

'Under my command, yes. But you have done your part. I do not understand your reluctance to leave.'

'Am I not entitled to enjoy my reward for work well done?'

'Meaning?'

Reynold laughed and tapped his nose. 'Ah, but you are a backward lad, are you not? The ladies, my dear friend. The beauty and dignity of our lovely Lady Ursula. May I not bask awhile in her smiles? As you say, there is nothing more to be done, save to pass the time pleasantly till Aylmer relieves us. So . . .'

'Nothing more to be done? Well, that is a matter of opinion. But there is no more of your sort of work to be done. And that includes any plans you might happen to have for diversion with the Lady Ursula. You may remember that she is betrothed to Aylmer.'

'That doesn't stop you looking at her, does it? Eh? Did you think I hadn't noticed?'

Benedict said in an even tone, 'The Lady Ursula is indeed most kind and gentle. And worthy in every way to be Aylmer's wife.'

'Oh, you are thinking of him, are you, when you look at her?'

'Not always. Sometimes I think of all the other women and children in the castle. And sometimes I think about you. Reynold, I do not wish to quarrel with you. There is no stigma attached to your going with the women and children. They need protection on their journey, and you are the one best fitted to give it.'

'I will not go! What! Steal away at night like a felon, and leave all the fun to you?'

' "Fun" is not exactly the word I would have used to describe a siege.'

'You cannot order me to leave. Aylmer appointed me, and only he can bid me withdraw.'

Benedict weighed his words. 'Reynold, this is no time to revive ancient quarrels. If you will not go of your own accord . . . if you insist upon staying despite my advice . . . then you must acknowledge me as your superior officer. We can have no divided command. That way we waste men and resources. If you have suggestions to make, I will gladly listen to them, and where appropriate I will give orders that they be put into practice. But there must be no more over-riding of my orders, or redeploying of my men. And as for the outpost . . .'

'Ah! Now we come to it! I have done something to defend the castle which you had overlooked.'

'I am afraid that I cannot agree . . .'

'And what have you to say to that? Do you commend me? Oh, no! You find fault. Why? Because you had not thought of it yourself. You are eaten up with jealousy. Do you think I had not anticipated your reaction? Do you think I had not feared what you might say, if I took the scheme to you first? I knew you would not be able to stomach my having any glory . . .'

'Glory! The outpost is untenable!'

'What?' Reynold laughed. 'It is as safe as the keep itself!'

'It is out of bowshot from our walls, and you have sent one of the key men in the castle to man it! How will it be, if Hugo sweeps up that road at dusk today, and in the half-light, when bows and arrows are of little use, takes our men prisoner?'

'Why, are they not ready for an attack? And will they not repel it?'

'With what weapons? Five men—perhaps six—can hide themselves in those contraptions, and shoot through the slits in the hides. But not in the dark. Suppose Hugo sends fifty men at them! Then our men have no chance. They will be taken prisoner, or worse. You have not been in a siege, Reynold

. . .'

'Spare me! Have I not heard that tale time and again?'

'. . . and you do not know what happens to prisoners, if they have kin within the castle. Or friends. The prisoners are tortured, Reynold. Before the castle walls. Slowly, and with maximum effect, so that their cries will be heard by their kin and friends within. Then, when they are dead, their mangled bodies will be thrown within the castle walls by a trebuchet, and come to rest at our feet . . . at the feet of their kin . . .'

'That is not likely to . . .'

'How many children has Peter Bowman? Has he a wife here? And Merle?'

'How should I know?'

'You ought to know, Reynold. If you have sent them to their deaths, you ought to know '

'I have not sent them to their deaths. This is ridiculous. The outpost is as safe as if they were standing here in this room with us. It is your stupidity, your jealousy . . .'

Benedict turned away with an abrupt movement.

'. . . and if you think you will impress the Lady Ursula with this show of authority . . . this empty show . . . why, you are mistaken! I will make it my business to let her know exactly why you have taken up this extraordinary stand. And if you bring those men back against my orders . . .'

'They are to be brought back; the carts are to be dismantled, and hauled back into the castle by dusk. Or I will have you clapped in irons until such time as Aylmer comes to take you off my hands.'

'You . . .! I see how it is, you are bluffing! You would never have the nerve to . . .'

'No? You know me better than that, Reynold. You know I mean what I say.'

Reynold turned and walked out of the room.

* * *

An hour later Ursula stepped out of the keep into the heat of noon. She had resumed her old gown, and her hair was once more braided and covered with its silken sheath. She scanned the grounds. Everyone seemed to have some task to perform. A dozen or so men were sweating and straining to pull the thatch off the stabling here, and over there another group were clustered around the head carpenter, who was directing hammers and saws as if his life depended on the speed at which his men worked. As indeed it probably did.

Ursula shaded her eyes. There was a 'foreigner' working among the carpenters; a big man with a crop of short curly hair that gleamed blue and black in the sun. He was stripped to the waist, wielding a mighty mallet.

The men around him were all working with a will, as a team. It was a rare thing, thought Ursula, for her men of Salwarpe to accept a stranger like that.

She hesitated. She did not want to call him away from his work, and yet . . . her grandfather's words were still in her ears. 'Charm him, Ursula! You can get him to see reason, if anyone can!'

Yes, it would be easy to wind Benedict round her finger, but she did not wish to do it, particularly. It was like taking the coins out of a blind man's begging-bowl. Too easy by far. It implied a contempt for the man which she did not feel. He was so starved of affection that if she did but smile on him, press his arm and talk to him awhile he would do this thing for her. And that was not how it should be.

Parkyn was crossing the garth. She asked him to bring Benedict to her in the garden. Parkyn delivered the message, prevented his master from snatching up a tunic belonging to one of the carpenters, deftly pulled Benedict's own tunic around him, and twitched it straight. Then Benedict was coming towards her, running his fingers through his mop of hair in an ineffectual attempt to make himself look presentable.

'As if that matters,' thought Ursula. 'I like you as you are, Benedict . . .'

There was colour in her cheeks as she waited for him in the shade of the honeysuckle.

She clasped her hands together and seated herself on the bench. She told herself that she would not give him too warm a welcome, and felt her lips curve into a smile when he came up, bowing as awkwardly as the youngest of their pages.

He said, 'Reynold has been with you.' She nodded. He said, 'He wants you to intercede for him?'

'Yes. But that is not why I called you away from your work. Both my grandfather and I believe that your authority must be upheld. We have told Reynold so.'

'But . . .?'

'Yes. But.' She laughed to hide her uneasiness. 'I am supposed to charm you into giving in, but I will not.'

He was smiling. 'You could, if you wished.'

'I know. At least, I suppose I could if I . . . but that would be wrong. I know that I ought not to interfere. I asked grandfather to speak with you, but he said I would do it better. The truth is that we are worried what will happen if Reynold is discredited. Aylmer was insistent that you have a second-in-command to share the burden of the siege, and indeed we have no other man here fit to take Reynold's place, if only he would agree to work under you.'

'Which he will not do, I think.'

'It must be your decision. We see that very clearly. We cannot judge the wisdom or otherwise of maintaining the outpost. Only you can do that, and we are content to abide by your judgment. But what we felt was—both grandfather and I—that you might have been pushed into making a hasty decision by the bad feeling that exists between you two.'

He folded his arms and leaned against the wall of the keep, his eyes on the ground.

She watched him. There was no need for her to say any more. She knew he would give her argument full consideration She could gaze on him as long as she liked, because he was wholly occupied with his problem. His hair had been cut very short, but it was a becoming style to one whose head was so . . . not handsome, of course, but . . . perhaps 'noble' was the right word. The shape of his head was almost round. The features looked as if they had been carved with a blunt chisel, except for the nose, which had been given more delicate treatment.

He looked up at last, and she lowered her eyelids that he might not guess she had been studying him

He said, 'It might be so, though I do not think it was. I think my judgment was sound. Merle certainly thought so, and I would trust his mind in this, as you would trust mine. And yet—now that you have put the doubt in my mind, I do not know what to say.'

'No. I understand.' She had gained her point. She knew he would reconsider his decision now, and that if Reynold only came halfway to meet him there could be some sort of compromise. She ought to leave it at that, but she could not.

She said, 'This trouble between you. My lord Aylmer spoke of it to me once. Can you not forgive each other, after so many years?'

'Forgive him?' He looked startled. Then he looked puzzled. Then he laughed and, laughing, shook his head. 'Lady, it is not like that. Or not on my side, anyway. I do not hate him. At least, I don't think I do. You think our present dispute has its roots in Sir Reynold's admiration for my wife, years ago? Certainly that affair did not improve relations between us, but the roots of the trouble lie further back. They cannot be found in what we did or did not do, but in the sort of people we are. I cannot explain better than that.'

She would have probed further, but he pushed himself off the wall, and said he would go to the gatehouse. She walked beside him, but did not think he was aware of her, he was thinking so deeply. Merle was still gazing out over the ramparts.

Benedict sighed, shook his head and called for a bow and arrows. At once the Weasel, who had not appeared to be within earshot, dashed off for some, and returned panting, with not only a bow and a quiver full of arrows but also a half dozen men from the guard-room below, who wanted to know what the Weasel was doing, stealing their weapons.

'Peace!' said Benedict. And there was peace. Benedict said, 'Merle, what sort of shot are you? Send me an arrow downhill, in the direction of the outpost.'

'Middling fair. But I cannot shoot as far as that.' Merle took the bow, aimed and let an arrow fly. They all marked where it lay, about halfway between the wall and the outpost.

'Now I am but a poor shot,' said Benedict, taking the bow in his turn. 'Yet I daresay I am no worse than many . . .' He shot. His arrow fell short of Merle's.

Benedict looked at Merle, and then around at the intent faces of the men-at-arms. 'You see what must be done?'

'I still don't like it,' said Merle. 'And not only because I'm losing my wager.'

Benedict clapped him on the shoulder. 'I'll pay your wager for you. Have two draught horses harnessed up, ready for when Sir Reynold comes to give you the order. And Merle; let him work it out for himself, if he can.'

'Two horses only? Why not four?'

Bring one cart back to within the range of the arrows we shot. The men in that cart will then be able to provide cover for the men in the farther cart. Though I'd be happier if the farther cart were also moved back, say, a dozen paces. Otherwise, we might shoot down our own men, while they're running back up the hill.'

Merle grunted. 'If you say so. But I tell you I'm still not happy. I like stone walls around me when there's men like Hugo around.'

'So do I, but . . . well, reason tells me that an outpost is a good idea if it can be covered by protecting fire from somewhere else. Outposts can delay the enemy's advance, Merle. It is quite possible that they might save us an hour or two at a critical moment.'

Merle said, 'If you think it's worth while saving that one's face, my lord, then of course we'll do it. But for no other reason.'

'You insubordinate rogue!' Benedict aimed a blow at Merle's head. Merle ducked, grinning.

Ursula stepped aside to let Benedict canter down the stairs. He had passed her without noticing that she was there. She thought, Well, I have done it, and Reynold's face will be saved. I wish I could feel more comfortable about the part I have played. I did manipulate Benedict, although he does not realise it.

The men-at-arms were looking at her, and whispering among themselves. She heard her name mentioned, and then Reynold's. She realised they thought she had interfered for Reynold's sake. She ran down the stairs after Benedict, to hide her hot cheeks from their eyes.

After the evening meal Sir Henry de Thrave called a council meeting in his solar. Ursula was there, with Benedict and Reynold.

Also, seated some distance from the fire, were Simon Joce, Merle and Peter Bowman. Reynold, when his eye chanced to rest on one of the three villeins, would give them a look of offended surprise. But this did not prevent him making the most of his report to Sir Henry.

Reynold declared that he had strengthened his outposts, on his own initiative, by bringing one cart back to cover the other, in case of enemy attack. He had also, said Reynold—with a glare at Benedict—appointed new men to command these outposts, since it seemed that Peter Bowman and Merle the Miller were required not to fight in this siege but to act as clerks.

'Thank you, Sir Reynold,' said Sir Henry, with a sweet, meaningless smile. 'I think that is good news, is it not? An outpost . . . two outposts. Excellent. I would never have thought of it myself. Would you, Ursula?'

'No, indeed,' said Ursula. 'Sir Reynold must be given credit, where credit is due.'

Benedict's brows twitched. Ursula thought: Now is that laughter, or is he jealous because I have thrown a sop of praise to the Cock?

Sir Henry said, 'And now, Sir Benedict!'

Everyone stirred in their seats. The expressions of non-interest which had been worn by Simon, Peter and Merle since they arrived disappeared, to be replaced by watchfulness. Ursula thought: Holy Mother, defend us! They none of them believed a word that Reynold said. He's forfeited their respect, and they have given it to Benedict instead!

It was a sobering thought. The men of that coast were not given to easy loyalties, and were ever suspicious of strangers. Especially if the stranger were black-avised and swarthy. Yet the eyes now turned on Benedict bore identical expressions of trustfulness.

Benedict rubbed his head. Apparently he did not know where to begin,

Sir Henry helped him. 'I agree with you, Sir Benedict, that these trusted men of mine should know everything. About the food, as well.'

Benedict took a deep breath. He stood and went to lean against the stone hood over the hearth. 'Yes, it does not look good. We are going to have to do some hard thinking. I have a few ideas, but nothing worked out properly. Any suggestions . . .' He glanced at the three villeins. 'And I mean that. Any suggestions are welcome.'

Sir Reynold tilted back in his chair, looking bored. 'Oh, come now. Surely all we have to do is sit it out.'

Peter Bowman pulled on the lobe of his ear. 'They've cut down four or five trees, over Spereshot way. Only saw it when I came back up into the castle this evening.'

'Oaks?' said Benedict.

Too tough for them, I reckon. Beeches. Bad enough.'

'Yes. That means they've decided to make a ram, or a trebuchet. I'd make both, if I were Hugo. I've been trying to think what I'd do, if I were him. He's been quiet today. Too quiet. I wondered what he was up to. Now we know. He's going to make siege engines.'

'What can he do?' said Reynold, brows lifted. 'Pick at the front gate with a matchstick?'

'A giant matchstick,' said Benedict, nodding. 'With a well-protected ram, and enough men, I could get up that road and smash through the outer tower of the gatehouse in a few days . . .'

Reynold laughed. 'You'd be mad to try! You'd be met with a fire of arrows . . . you'd be cut to pieces . . .'

'And be met with fire of all kinds,' said Benedict. 'Yes, I would have to be prepared to lose twenty—maybe thirty—men. But what are twenty or thirty men to Hugo? Especially since he's sitting across a town full of free labour. I doubt he'd even bother to put any of his mercenaries in the front ranks. Once through the outer gatehouse wall, I'd raise the portcullis, because the mechanism for the portcullis is in the front pair of gatehouses. Then I'd be in the well between the two gatehouses, with the drawbridge up like a second gate in front of me. I'd have to bring in enough timber to make a staging of sorts across the well, and then I'd start picking away at one of the inner gatehouses. And despite everything the garrison could do to deal with individual men, I'd be through in about . . . ten to twelve days, I should think.'

There was silence in the room. Sir Henry put his hand on Ursula's. Reynold's chair fell to the floor as he jumped to his feet.

'Traitor! Even to think such a thing . . .!

'Given enough men, I could do it. So why should Hugo not do it?'

'You said you knew how to avoid . . .'

'There are things we can do. We have started on some of them already. We can man the ramparts of the gatehouse towers with archers, and with cauldrons of boiling oil to pour down on the enemy. We can try to set fire arrows into the shields they will carry to protect themselves . . . but if I were Hugo I would not bring my ram up the hill until I had a cradle to cover my men, and that cradle would be covered with hides which will repel all fire arrows . . . most missiles, in fact.'

'Then what can we do?'

'We can make grappling-irons, like big hooks. We swing them down from the ramparts and hope to catch the ram with them, and lift it up, and away . . . right into the castle, in fact. That might delay Hugo long enough to go and cut down another tree . . . say another couple of days. And making grappling-irons depends on our getting hold of a smith.'

'There is no hope, then,' said Sir Henry. 'We had best treat with the man, and obtain what terms we can.'

'Oh, I didn't say there was no hope.' Benedict pushed himself off the chimneybreast and began to stride up and down, hands clasped behind his back. 'Of course there are other things we can do to delay Hugo. Some of them we have already set in motion and others . . . when will Dickon be back? No matter. He could not go out again tonight, and the guard-boat will not be repaired until tomorrow . . . where was I?

'Food. Well, we have asked the abbot to sell us supplies sufficient to last out the twenty-eight days. I think he will agree to sell, but I do not think he will agree to transport the grain here. That is one problem. But there is a bigger one, and that is that we have no smith. And as a corollary to our having no smith, Hugo has one, and, what is more, he has an army of slaves below, which he can use against us.'

'My own men?' said Sir Henry. 'How could he force my own men to fight against me?'

'I daresay they won't wish to do so,' said Benedict. 'But they have little choice, do they? Hugo has only to take hostages: a child here, a young bride there . . . and the rest of the town will do his bidding. It will be they who have cut down the trees, and it will be they who shape the timbers and haul the ram up the road . . . to face fire from their kin within the walls here. Why should Hugo risk the lives of his mercenaries, when he has all those slaves at his command? What say you, Merle? Will your townsfolk do Hugo's bidding?'

Merle shifted on his bench. 'Hugo burned Spereshot. They'll mind that. I have kin still down there; a brother, and his wife and childer. My brother has a little girl, some three years old. If she were taken from him, he'd be beside himself. Aye, he'd work for Hugo, if that happened. As I would, in his place. I'm only thankful my wife died last year. At least I don't have to worry about her, now.'

Peter Bowman spoke up at that. 'I have friends down there, also. If they came up to the castle with the ram . . . I doubt I could fire my arrows to their hearts . . .'

'Strangely enough,' said Benedict, 'you would. You don't think you would now, because you are a kindly man. But when you remember that Hugo will set his yoke about your neck if your hand fails, when you think of what he could do to the women and children in this castle, then you will shoot straight. For if the men below become enslaved by the monster, yet the women and children here in the castle are still free, and you will fight for them, and for yourself.'

'Has the world gone mad?' cried Reynold. 'First you say Sir Henry's men will forget their duty to him, and next you say the men here will forget the love and duty they owe their families?'

'Yes,' said Benedict. 'That's what sieges are all about. There are no loyalties, except to self. The men, women, and children in this castle become your family. Those outside, however much loved before, must be thought of as the enemy. Only thus can we survive.'

'Never did I think to hear a knight declare that might should triumph over right,' said Reynold. 'You are a disgrace to your knightly vows!'

Benedict put up a hand, as if the candlelight had blinded him Then he was his calm self once more. 'Sir Reynold, be seated, if you please. We have not finished. In fact, we have merely started to set out the probable way this siege will develop. Now we must consider what we should do ourselves.'

Sir Henry said, 'How many days do you think we can last out, Benedict?'

'We have grain for fourteen—no, thirteen days. If we succeed in keeping the channel clear, we can take fish from the river, and fowl from the marshes. Also, if Dickon has luck with the abbot, we may expect at some point to receive fresh supplies. There are still difficulties, but I think that for the moment we can set that problem aside as in a fair way to being solved.

'Next, we must defend ourselves from Hugo's assault. The outposts will hold him off for an hour or two—not much more. The outer tower of the gatehouse must be stoutly defended. We will make and lower cradles—a sort of wooden shelving—from the ramparts and man them with archers to defend the approaches. We must defend the outer gate as if it were our last stand. But once he is through there and the portcullis is raised, we must defend the well between the two sets of gatehouses as if that were our last stand. He will be fighting in a confined space and there are tricks there which may stand us in good stead. Sir Reynold should have charge of the defence of the gatehouse. His swordsmanship is unequalled and, with Simon Joce at his elbow, I think he might keep Hugo out for . . . a minimum of four days and a maximum of ten.'

'And we have twenty-eight days to go.'

'Correct. So we must consider the alternatives.'

'There are no other alternatives,' said Sir Henry. 'Save surrender.'

'Oh, dear me, no!' said Benedict. 'We must redress the balance, that's all. He's got the one and only smith, and he's got the townsfolk. I think we'll have to see what we can do about that.'

With an air of having solved the problem, he sat down and signed to Parkyn to pour him a cup of wine.

CHAPTER ELEVEN

'I must be getting old,' said Sir Henry. 'Benedict, will you explain?'

Benedict scratched his poll. 'Well, we could evacuate the town . . .'

'What? How?'

'. . . though there might be difficulties . . .'

'Difficulties!'

'. . . I really can't tell you much more till I've been down there and talked to the mayor, or the reeve, or whoever you think would be best.'

'Go down there! How?'

'In the guard-boat, when it's mended, of course. Or in Dickon's punt. It depends on the tides and the weather. I'll manage it, somehow, never fear.'

Ursula looked at the half-amused and half-apprehensive looks which were being exchanged between Simon, Merle and Peter. They were taking Benedict seriously, even if Reynold wasn't.

'The man is out of his wits!' said Reynold.

'It's a good idea,' said Sir Henry. 'But I don't see how you're going to manage it.'

'Neither do I at the moment,' said Benedict. 'I have one or two notions, but . . . if we could only get the smith away, that would be something. And there are those boats which the fisherfolk sank before Hugo could get at them. Hugo doesn't know about them. Merle, will you come with me, and be my herald with the mayor?'

Peter Bowman laughed. 'He is mad, of course. But that's the sort of madness for me! I'd come with you, if it would do any good . . .'

'No, you get some sleep. And Simon, too. Oh, Simon; before you go. Keep a watch on the postern, and on our ladders. Dickon will be corning back that way, and we want someone on the foreshore to help him up the cliff. And Simon! That trebuchet must be kept loaded, and aimed at the channel night and day. If Hugo manages to get another boat out there, we're all lost. Merle, we're off as soon as Dickon gets back, provided you can drum up someone else to take the punt out . . .'

'The Weasel can manage a punt, I think!'

'What a blessing that boy is! Then I wish you goodnight, Sir Henry . . . Lady!'

'Utterly mad!' said Reynold, as the room began to empty. 'Is he to risk capture for the sake of a smith?'

'His ideas do tend to take the breath away at first,' said Sir Henry, 'But if he thinks we're likely to lose this fight without the smith, then it makes sense to go after the smith.'

'I suppose he'll get some sleep sometime,' said Ursula, but she spoke more to herself than to the room at large.

* * *

Benedict took Merle back to his own room, where Parkyn had ready some black, hooded capes to go over their clothing, and a dark lantern.

'Where is the Weasel?'

A sulky face and a hunched shoulder. 'I'll take you down there, my lord, but I won't take that . . . that pigs-meat, Merle!'

'And,' said Benedict. 'Because he kicked you out of your slumbers? Well, I have need of him, you see. He can talk on equal terms with the townsfolk, which you and I cannot do.'

The Weasel gave the impression of one flattening his ears. He seemed to slide rather than duck from under the hand Benedict held towards him.

'Let him take you down there, then. You don't need the punt, so you don't need me.'

'But I do. I need someone who can handle a punt. Otherwise I have to wait till the guard-boat is repaired, and every hour counts. So you see, I am relying on you . . .' Then Benedict's tone changed. 'What, lad! Is there another way out of the castle, save for the obvious ones? Is that what you are trying to say?'

The boy stuck out his tongue and retreated to the wall. 'Don't know nothing!' he declared.

'Another way?' Merle gasped. 'There couldn't be!'

Benedict considered the lad awhile. Then he

said, 'Come here. Here, where I can see you. What is your name? Your real name, I mean.'

The lad lifted his shoulders and let them drop. He didn't know.

'Were you never christened?'

The boy laughed and tossed his head. No, he'd never been christened.

'I'll have to give you a name, then. And when we can get to a priest again, I'll stand sponsor to bring you into the Church.'

Merle was incredulous. 'He'd have to confess all his sins, first, and be absolved. No priest would shrive that bag of rascality!'

'Oh yes, they would,' said Benedict. 'Especially if the lad here had helped save Salwarpe.'

The Weasel's eyes flickered and he kicked at a nearby stool. Then he nodded, once.

'Very well,' said Benedict. 'Now, what name would you like to be called?' The lad shrugged. 'Well, we must call you something. My father's name was Christian, but that is not appropriate yet, and to call you by my own name would be confusing.'

'Barnabas,' said the lad, twisting his arms behind his back. 'If you like it. And I don't care if you do or not.'

'Why Barnabas?' said Merle.

'My mother said she thought that was my father's name . . . though she couldn't be sure, a course.'

'Barnabas it is, then,' said Benedict. 'And

now, Barnabas. Tell me how many ways you know to get in and out of the castle, apart from the gatehouse and the postern on the cliff edge.'

'Two ways,' said Barnabas, giving Merle a sulky look. 'But I wouldn't have told, if you hadn't guessed, because they're my secret. How am I to get in and out, if you go telling on me? But I doubt you could take the best way . . . or anyone but me. It's up the cliff from the marsh, at the sea end. I keep a rope with an iron hook on the end of it in my boat, and if I fling it up sharpish here, and there, and then haul myself up . . . and right at the top there's a corner where the keep bellies out, and there's a crumbly bit of stone you can work round till you come to a straight stretch of wall above you. And if the sentry's not looking, you can throw the rope up, and climb over. But you have to be careful, because it swings out over the cliff, and there's nothing to hang on to. I been dropped into the marshes twice, when the rope slipped.'

Merle crossed himself.

'I don't think we'll go that way,' said Benedict. 'I've no head for climbing like that. What happened to your boat, Barnabas?'

'Hugo's men took it, and they laughed when they smashed it up. It wasn't much of a boat; all patched it was. But I could fish from it. When it was gone I knew I couldn't feed myself any longer, so I crept away and came up into the castle . . .'

'After the gates were closed? After Hugo came?'

'Yes. The bad men came, and pushed everyone into the church, and then they took out John Peasmarsh and his sons—he's the mayor—and they took out the smith, and some of the burghers, and two of the fisherfolk that own boats . . . they said they were going to look after them properly, but they put them in the jail, instead. Then they came back in and said as they would let the rest of us go, so long as we behaved ourselves.

'They let us out, all right. But when we got back to the quay, they were there, and they smashed and smashed . . . And so I came up here.'

'Yes . . .?' said Benedict, in a gentle voice.

'Up the hill from the town, by the back way. There's a track, sort of. Then . . .' He stopped a moment. He swallowed. 'You won't like it. The likes of you don't take such ways.'

'Let me be the judge of that. It's a sewer outlet, is it?'

The lad nodded. Merle swore. 'By all the saints! Who'd have thought it?'

'How bad is it, Barnabas?'

'Awful when there's lots of people in the castle. But I knew there'd be food here, and no-one'll give me food down in the town, and with my boat gone, I couldn't fish. So coming up here was better than staying down there.'

He shuffled his feet. 'A course, it's not easy to find. You get into it through one of the cellars under the keep, where the wall's broken away a bit in one corner. You have to wriggle and squirm, and then you drop down into the sewer, and there's not much light.'

'Surely there must be a grating!' said Merle. 'If Hugo and his men knew . . .!'

'Ah, but they don't. No-one knows but I. There's a grating, a course. And a mighty big grating it be! But I be small, and the brickwork be broken away like at one side, and so I slide through. And the other end it comes out in some bushes in a sort of little hollow, where a spring rises. The spring water takes the muck all away, so no-one notices where the sewer comes out . . . and the spring water's good for washing your legs, when you're through. Phew!' He held his nose.

'Why,' said Merle. 'I've lived here all my life, and I never knew a sewer came out above the town. I know that stream. It's foul. No-one uses it, even for washing. But we never thought . . . If we had thought, we'd have said the sewer from the castle must go out over the marshes.'

'The main one do,' said Barnabas. 'But the grating over that one is too stiff for me to shift. I know all the tunnels under the castle, you see. When people get in the habit of kicking you when they see you, you learn fast.'

Benedict began to laugh. 'Now, do I take my good clothes off, and risk being kicked when I get down into the town . . . or do I keep them on, and get them spoiled?'

Before leaving the castle, Benedict had a team of workmen roused to go down into the cellar. First they were to clear the entrance into the sewer, and then build a stout timber frame to support a new grating. This new grating would be padlocked, and a guard kept on it from now on. The gatekeeper of the postern overlooking the cliff was also warned that Benedict might be returning that way later on that night.

From Barnabas, Benedict had learned that Hugo had imposed a curfew on the village, and that a guard was kept on the causeway where the fishing-boats had been drawn up and put out of action. There was also a guard set about the jail which held the hostages. Apart from that, an hourly patrol had been deemed the only precaution necessary.

If the smith is in the jail,' said Merle. 'What's the point of going down there?'

'I doubt he stayed in the jail,' said Benedict. 'He'd be too useful. He'll be out by now. Maybe his wife or one of his children is standing hostage for him. We won't know till we get there. The point of this expedition is to find out exactly who is where, and why. Who do we ask, Merle?'

Merle scratched his chin. 'Old Mother Peasmarsh,' he said at length. 'She'm a holy terror. The mayor's her eldest son. She'd be mayor in his place, if they let women do the job. If she's not in jail, then she's the one to go to.'

The passage through the sewer was unpleasant but soon over. They washed their bare legs clean in the dell and resumed their shoes and hose. Then they set off down the hill by a winding track, bending low to duck under branches as indicated by Barnabas. The boy held a dark lantern, but they did not let its light beam forth, relying instead on the fitful shining of the moon. Clouds obscured much of the sky.

'Weather's changing,' whispered Merle. 'Lucky for us!'

They waited, crouched flat behind a convenient bank above the village, till Hugo's patrol had passed by, and then dropped down into the street. The houses were all dark, observing the curfew, but Barnabas led them with out faltering to a house somewhat larger than the rest. It was built partly of stone, with its upper story of wattle and daub.

Barnabas scratched on the door. Nothing happened. The house remained dark. Merle found a shuttered window and rapped in a certain fashion on it. Was that a chink of light within? They waited.

A voice hissed at them to be off. It came from the window.

Merle turned the lanthorn's light on his face for a couple of seconds.

The door was unbarred. It opened a crack and a hand drew them inside. All was dark, save for the glow of a banked-up fire. Then, when the door was safely barred again, Merle opened the lanthorn's sides, to reveal that they were standing in a large room, well furnished and with a tiled floor. There were benches round the long table, cupboards standing against the wall, and a locked chest at the foot of the stairwell. The fireplace was large and lined with baking ovens. There were bunches of herbs hanging from the ceiling, but no hams curing, as would be normal in such cases.

An elderly woman in a tangle of cloaks stood before them. Though she must have been disturbed from her sleep, her eyes were bright. The heads of two frightened servants peeped from round the door to the stairs. The woman went to the door and shut it, ensuring privacy.

Merle introduced Benedict and said that Sir Henry de Thrave sent his greetings to Mistress Peasmarsh.

'My son's in jail,' she said. 'And my grandson. And the bailiff. What do you want with an old woman that's long since done for?'

She was so obviously a force still to be reckoned with that both Benedict and Merle smiled.

'Well?' she said, her voice sharp. 'If you're caught here, do you know what will become of us all? If it's food you want, there's little we have left. Hugo's men have been through the village twice, looting everything they fancy. And we can't go fishing, without boats.'

'I did hear,' said Benedict, taking a seat unasked, 'that your people were clever enough to hide some boats by dipping them under water. I am certain you would not have let Hugo's landlubbers take away your livelihood without trying to save something for the future.'

'Boats!' She spat her contempt. 'Nasty, uncomfortable things! If you want our boats, if that's why you've come, then you can go searching for them yourself! Catch me having anything to do with boats! My family were all farming men. Why I had to go marrying a fisherman, I don't know. I can't do nothing for you, with my men in jail. You can tell Sir Henry we're all safe as long as we do what we're told. Hugo needs our men to get the harvest in, you see.'

'Ah, but what will happen to that harvest when it is gathered in?' said Benedict. 'Do you really think Hugo will allow you to keep any of it? Why should he? And as for leaving you alone, why did he take hostages, if he's going to leave you unharmed?'

To make sure we behave. You don't catch me putting a foot wrong, while they're in jail.'

'Suppose we got them out?'

She laughed. 'What, and have the rest of Hugo's men down on us, burning and raping and looting, like they did at Spereshot?'

'But suppose they thought your son and grandson were sickening of a fever . . . or what looked like a fever? And that the fever was spreading through the town, and people were dying of it? Suppose the fever reached the jail? Suppose you offered to nurse the sick all together, in a place set apart from the town . . . such as down on the quayside? Suppose you kept taking people out of their houses, looking very sick, and groaning as they went through the streets. And then kept them in the "fever" houses a day or two . . . so that Hugo's men could see they were really sick . . . and then you could tell Hugo that they had died.'

The old woman seated herself opposite Benedict. She said, 'Speak more plainly, young man. My hearing's not as good as it used to be.'

'I was only thinking . . .' Benedict gestured to the bunches of herbs that lay on the table and above his head. 'That nettles make an excellent soup, but they also inflict a rash on sensitive skins. That mustard makes people vomit. That perhaps symptoms of fever could be induced, in healthy people. You are short of food, you say. Doubtless there are one of two cases of sickness already in the town . . .'

The woman started and Benedict's manner became more assured.

'. . . And I suppose Hugo may know of these cases. And if he doesn't, you must be sure that he gets to hear of them. And tomorrow or the next day some of the sick people will die—or be reported to have died.'

'What good would that do?'

'It would explain why people kept disappearing from the town . . . whole families at a time would be stricken with fever . . . and "die". Only of course they wouldn't really die, and they wouldn't really be sick. They would only be "ill" long enough to give them an alibi, and then they would slip away from the town to safety, in the boats you have hidden away.'

'It is impossible!' she said, but her voice lacked conviction.

'Not if the priest helped you,' said Merle. 'He's a good man, and discreet. He could visit the sick daily, and then toll his bell for those who died . . . and bury the coffins . . .'

Mistress Peasmarsh said, 'The carpenter's a cousin of my daughter's husband. He'd do anything for money. So many coffins to be made . . . and filled with earth, no doubt. He'd be over the moon with pleasure! Ay, he'd play his part well enough. For cash.' She fixed her bright eyes on Benedict, who took a purse from his wallet and laid it, unopened, on the table.

'Well, young man? Suppose we did this? Where would our people go?'

'To the castle, of course. They would go round the hill in their boats, and climb up the cliff by ladders which we are having made.

They might not all stay in the castle, because we also have food problems . . . though these are in a fair way to being solved. But once in the castle they are out from under Hugo's hand.'

'Why should we leave our homes and set out in nasty smelly boats? Are we not safe here, while we obey Hugo?'

'Mistress, you know better than that.'

The old woman bowed her head. Presently she said, 'I know which herbs to use. The priest will gladly help us, and I can answer for the carpenter. You say you know how to get my folk out of the jail?'

'No doubt Hugo has decreed the town should feed its own people. No doubt you take pasties and ale to the jail for your menfolk. You will give them doctored food, and instructions as to how to act. Be cautious; no more than two or three must sicken in the jail at once. Then you will petition Hugo to let your men out, before they die. He will do so, for fear that the rest of the hostages may also be affected. For what use are dead hostages to him? So he will let out two or three . . . and take two or three more hostages in their stead. But these latter that he takes will be lesser men, because he took the best, before.'

'So not everyone can get away?'

Benedict hesitated. 'I can't answer that. Certainly you will be able to get your own menfolk out, and probably anyone else whom you consider important. Certainly we can take some ten or twenty folk away each night in our boats, if they are ready and waiting at the turn of the tide—after Hugo's patrol has been withdrawn . . . you must make sure that Hugo withdraws the guard from the quayside. Fear of infection should do the trick. When infection strikes a town, people flee. They will slip away in twos and threes, despite all that Hugo can do. They will melt into the forest, steal a horse and ride off . . . shoulder a bundle and walk . . . anything to escape. Some will not wish to leave their fields at harvest-time, but these are probably safe from Hugo for a while. The others . . . carpenters, the smith, fisherfolk . . . and all their families . . . they are very welcome in the castle. You must decide which families to approach, for there must be no tattling to Hugo. Once a man agrees to go, he must be taken to the fever-house at once, with all his family. I am giving you the power of life and death over this town, mistress.'

She shrank within her coverings. 'At my age, it is a terrible temptation. All the old scores I could pay off . . .!'

You would have me imperil my soul, master. Even with the priest to help me, how am I to say which man should live, and which die?'

'I will stay to help you,' said Merle. 'It is the only way. You cannot do this all by yourself. I know these people, and they know me. They will trust me.'

'If I do this thing,' said Mistress Peasmarsh, 'then I fear I will not go scatheless . . . I doubt I will be caught. And then I shall not die in my bed. Nor Merle, neither.'

'I realise there is a risk,' said Benedict, looking down at his hands. 'It is not for me, who am now about to go back into the safety of the castle, to say that you should or should not do this thing. You owe no allegiance to me. Only to your own people.'

'I think I can do it,' said Merle, clenching his fists. 'I think I can. But if I am caught—God have mercy—I do not think I could withstand torture.'

Benedict put his hand over his eyes. 'Merle, if you are put to the question, you must speak freely. I would not expect anything else.'

The old woman lifted her head. 'Merle will not betray you, master. I will give him a potion in a tiny bottle that he may wear on a chain about his neck. If he is questioned, he will say it is holy water from Glastonbury . . . and it will save him from the torture, if it should come to that.'

Merle stood up and trimmed the wick of the candle in the lantern. 'We'd best get started. Whose boat do we lift first? And how many people can we take away with us tonight . . .'

'They'll have to be fit,' said Benedict. 'They'll have to go back by the sewer, unless we can decoy the guard away from the quayside.'

'Oh, them!' The woman spat. 'They'll be fast asleep by this time! They took a barrel of my best home-brewed ale this morn, and I put a trifle of this and that into it to give them sweet dreams. I was planning to visit my granddaughter's on the quayside tonight, after curfew. She's been sickly these last few days, and kept her bed. Always the same, when she's pregnant, but I thought I'd go sit with her awhile.' She threw off her topmost cloak, to reveal herself fully dressed underneath. 'I would have had her with me all the time, but her husband's the smith, and they like to keep an eye on him. No visitors in the day-time, and so on. I told them, did they really think they could keep me from my own kith and kin?'

She began to gather various herbs and bundles of greenstuff, and put them into her wallet.

She said, 'I'll dose the smith tonight, and he'll be sick enough to worry Hugo tomorrow . . . and then in a couple of days' time, he'll be up with you. You'd best take his wife tonight, and her two little ones; you won't raise either of the sunken boats by yourself. They're round the other side of the harbour, in a little creek. We'd best waken one of my other grandsons, living next to her. He'll help you lift his boat, and you can take him off . . . and my granddaughter's husband's younger brother

. . .'

Merle was counting on his fingers. 'How many will that be?'

'You'd best take their lad, too,' said Mistress Peasmarsh. 'He'm only fifteen but he wields the hammer well enough. And that's what you came for, I take it. Isn't it?'

'Who?' said Benedict.

'Our apprentice smith,' said Merle. 'The smith's younger brother. He's not bad.'

Benedict seized Mistress Peasmarsh and embraced her. The old woman pretended to be flustered, but looked pleased. When they turned to go, Barnabas was there, holding out some coins and a silver-hilted knife.

'Is that you, Weasel?' cried the old woman. 'And what have you taken of mine, you thieving rascal?'

'Nothing,' said the boy, wincing as Benedict caught his arm. 'These were Master Merle's. It was only because he kicked me! Besides, I've not got to steal any more, 'cos of being baptised soon.'

'Very true, Barnabas,' said Benedict. 'And that includes the things you took from Sir Reynold earlier on this evening.'

'I didn't think you saw me. Well, maybe I will, and maybe I won't. But I swear I won't steal from you, ever.'

'If I weren't so near death myself,' said Mistress Peasmarsh, 'I'd take my broom to your back, Weasel!'

'Enough,' said Benedict. 'No one expects the lad to become a saint overnight. He is doing his best. What more can any of us do?'

'And God have mercy on our souls,' said Merle.

* * *

They roused the two households, managed to lift one of the sunken boats and transferred twelve men, women and children from the quayside to the foot of the castle cliff before dawn. The weather had indeed changed. Scuds of rain came and went and, when the sun finally managed to struggle through the early morning mist, it did not put up much of a showing.

Benedict was the last of the party to haul himself up the cliff and step out onto the sward. Then he had to steady himself against the boisterous greeting of the dog.

'Dickon must be back,' he said, making much of the animal. Benedict was tired and dirty. His hands were chafed where he had taken a spell at the oars. His eyes ached. Yet he smiled as he looked around him The men, women and children from the town were being taken care of, the trebuchet was in position and loaded and Ursula had come to greet him. More, at her back was Dickon, and behind him, smiling and nodding, was Peter Bowman.

Benedict straightened his back. 'Yes, Peter?

What is it?'

'Another two trees felled. Beeches.'

Benedict rubbed the back of his neck. Six or seven trees in all. Not only a ram, but also a trebuchet. The trebuchet would be brought up first, to hammer away at the gate-house. And the ram would be shod with iron in the meantime . . . except that the smith was now groaning and feverish on his bed, while the carpenter was knocking up coffins for his supposedly deceased wife and children . . . Would Hugo be able to replace the smith? Possibly, but not yet awhile . . . which meant no iron tip to the ram, which could only be to the good . . .

Benedict smiled. He'd give something to see Hugo's face when he learned that 'sickness' had broken out in the town, and that the smith was one of the first victims.

'Well, well. There is much to be done. We must have a better system of ladders up the cliff for a start. One broke on the last lap. The ladders must be attended to at once. And Peter, I will come with you. We must devise some system of padding to protect the gatehouse walls . . .'

Ursula said, 'You are not going anywhere, except to bed. Parkyn tells me you have slept barely four hours in the last two days. You are going to bed, and I am going to lock the door, and keep the key. If you are needed, they will have to come to me, and I will judge whether you are to be disturbed or no.'

Dickon was grinning, and so was Peter Bowman. So were many of the others who stood around. Ursula was smiling at him, too.

Benedict glanced at Barnabas. Barnabas was looking amused. Well, if Barnabas was amused at the thought of being locked in, it followed that Barnabas knew how to get out of the room without going through the door. Benedict hesitated. There was indeed much still to be done and he knew he could keep going for another twelve hours if necessary.

But was it necessary? Had he not done enough for the moment? It would take Hugo at least a day to build, and another day to bring up, a ram or a trebuchet—at the very least. Possibly as much as three or four days, depending upon whether he was going to waste time looking for another smith, or wait for the man in the town to recover. If he, Benedict, were to sleep now, he would be fresh and ready for when the attack came, later. Merle was doing well in the town. There would be alarm to spread about the fever, and hints that the guard might be safer, if withdrawn from the quay . . . coffins to be built, services read for the dead . . . more men to be sought out and dosed, their wives to be reassured and removed from their houses . . .

Ah, but it would be hard work, down in the town. And if the guard were removed from the quayside, and two more boats full of refugees arrived at the cliff stairs tomorrow morning, then there would be so many more mouths to feed, which meant . . .'

His mind went into a whirl, and then steadied.

He beckoned Ursula aside. It seemed only natural to urge her into the angle of the keep where the honeysuckle grew. The bench was warm beneath him as he sank onto it. 'Dickon is back? What news from the abbot? You will see that I am bringing the townsfolk here, and this means . . .

'It is our place to deal with the abbot,' she said. 'Did you think my grandfather and I could not do anything by ourselves? You will put the food problem out of your mind.'

Her eye was calm and she held herself well. He thought: Is she lying? I did not think the abbot would agree both to sell, and to transport, the grain. Yet if she says that she can deal with the matter . . . it is true that I am tired and could do with a few hours' sleep. But who will she send with money to the abbot? And when? Tonight, probably. I could go tonight. No, it would be best if I stayed, in case that trebuchet is brought up earlier than . . .

Ursula said, 'If you will let me have the letter you intended to send the abbot, authorising him to draw on your account with the wool merchant, I will see that it is sent to him.'

'Silver is better.' Fumbling, for he was

very tired, he unbuckled his leather belt and stripped off the lining. A shower of silver pieces fell onto the bench. 'The silver will convince, whereas the letter would only tempt him You shall have the letter as well, of course. It is already written.'

'Do we need to take everything you have?' Her face was troubled.

'Yes, I think so. After all, it is my fault that you have the townsfolk to feed now, as well as the garrison.'

'You should keep something back for yourself.'

He took two coins and put them into his wallet. He said, 'One thing. Was the honeysuckle really your favourite? What if I had guessed wrongly?'

'Whatever you chose would have become my favourite. You know that. But in fact the honeysuckle is one of my favourite flowers. It has always been so. My aunt has tried to get a garden growing here for years. She sets lilies, roses, peonies, fruit-trees. Few of them flourish in this barren spot. But the honeysuckle always seems to flower, every year. I had taken it for granted, till all this happened, but I think it will in truth be my favourite from now on.'

She spoke without coquetry, seemingly without intent to please. But it did please him. She was looking up at the honeysuckle, which was in full flower with bees humming around it

He jerked himself awake. 'The smith! The lad does not know what it is we need! I must speak to Simon . . .'

'You will do nothing of the kind. Simon has all your drawings. He and Peter Bowman will see that the lad sets to work at once. You are going straight to bed.'

She urged him off the bench and up the stairs into the keep. She saw that there was water and towels set ready for him. Then she locked him in with Parkyn and Barnabas, and took away the key.

CHAPTER TWELVE

Ursula hung the key to Benedict's room on a ribbon round her neck. She kept one hand over the key while she went about her work, settling in the refugees from the town and arranging about meals. Reynold invited her to go and walk with him, but she shook her head and hurried away.

The key seemed to become larger under her fingers as the day wore on. The key became warm, though the wind was chill. Now and then spots of rain fell. Stray gusts of wind began to strike at the walls. The water in the river was whipped into white flecks, and the gulls' cries became strident as they swooped low over the castle.

The key's warmth excited her. She had Benedict in her power while she held the key. As she caressed it, she thought of what it might be like to touch his hand, his arm . . . the hard line of his jaw . . . the crisp, short-cut hair at the nape of his neck . . .

The key represented power. She knew that she had power over him in more ways than one. Whatsoever she asked of him, he would perform. It was at once awesome and exciting to have so much influence over him. If she smiled at him, he smiled back. If she frowned, then he was cast down. If she showed him favour, he glowed.

If he had not been in a position of power himself, she would perhaps have been able to ignore him. But he was no expendable peasant. He was the man who was going to save Salwarpe, more or less single-handed. He was modest, he was courteous, he was . . .

'Benedict de Huste,' she murmured, 'Benedict . . .'

What did it matter that he limped, and was ugly? No, he was not ugly. He had the sort of features which made other men look insipid. There was so much strength there, so much . . .

'Goodness of heart,' she murmured. 'He has the face of a good man.'

'Talking to yourself, Ursula?' said her grandfather.

She covered her confusion with a smile.

'There is a very great deal to think about, especially if I am to leave at the next low tide with Dickon. We'll have to take the punt; the guard-boat is still not ready. You are sure you will be all right?'

'Oh yes,' sighed Sir Henry. 'You leave me in very good hands, you know. It's you I'm worried about. Are you sure you can manage the abbot?'

She nodded. She sat beside her grandfather and took the abbot's letter from his hand. Benedict had guessed correctly. The abbot's letter was full of shocked horror that his neighbours should have been subject to harassment . . . 'Harassment!' said Ursula, with a snort . . and naturally anything he could do to help . . . but though indeed he did have some grain which he might be willing to part with, at a price, he was not at all certain that he could risk supplying it without payment in advance, and he did not feel able to support or feed any extra mouths, if Sir Henry was thinking of sending the women and children out of the castle . . . and indeed the perilous passage would militate against such a course of action . . . and the blessing of . . . etc.

'He won't die a poor man, anyway,' said Sir Henry. 'Did you get the money out of Benedict?'

'Of course. There's more than enough there. He gave me everything he had, and the letter pledging further funds from his banker, the wool merchant.'

'He's a splendid example of true chivalry—luckily for us. You'll have to get Aylmer to give him a present when all this is settled. A costly present, mind! A loving cup or something of that nature.'

There was colour in her cheeks. 'He'd like a book better.' She fingered the key. She did not like playing the role of beggarmaid, even though Benedict had made it easy for her to do so. She was giving him nothing, while he was giving her everything he had.

'I don't like myself much,' she said. 'It's so ridiculously easy to make him do what we want.'

He patted her hand 'Yes, child. But there's the point. If he weren't such a chivalrous fool, he wouldn't do all this for nothing.'

'Sometimes I think . . . just occasionally . . . that he does realise I'm playing with him. And then . . . oh, you'll laugh!' I find myself being very anxious to reassure him. Really wanting him not to be hurt. He's so vulnerable, and he's a good man, I think. Don't you?'

'Not as great a man as Aylmer.'

'No. Of course not. Did you think I needed to be reminded of Aylmer?' She smiled at her grandfather with a sudden brilliance and then took the key off its ribbon. 'Keep him safe for me till I return.'

* * *

It was noon before Benedict awoke. As he came slowly to consciousness, he was aware of a sense of well-being such as he had not experienced in years. He lay still, eyes closed, to savour the moment. He was safe. No one was going to hurt him and he was not going to do anything stupid. The maiden had the key and no-one could get at him.

He listened. The sound he dreaded—the thud and crash of stones thrown from a trebuchet—was not to be heard. There were no cries of alarm outside. There was the clang of metal from the reopened forge . . . the hammering and sawing of the carpenters . . . the smell of freshly-baked bread.

He was hungry.

He opened his eyes and sat up. Barnabas and Parkyn were seated at the foot of his bed, eating hunks of bread and cheese and drinking ale while they played dice. The food and drink had not been in the room when Ursula had locked them in, so . . .'

Barnabas said, 'They forgot to put bars on the window. It's easy to get in and out. I put your share on one side.'

Benedict grinned. The two of them were looking shamefaced at being caught playing dice while their master slept. Barnabas had found a clean woollen tunic from somewhere—best not ask where—but it didn't look as if he'd washed or brushed his hair. Perhaps a word in Parkyn's ear about Barnabas's appearance might do the trick?

Parkyn said, 'No-one's come to the door. You can rest a while longer.'

Barnabas picked his nose. 'She's gone to the abbey for food.'

Ah. Benedict pulled up a pillow, punched it into a better shape and leaned back, munching bread and cheese. So she had gone, had she? He'd thought she would. The pattern had been laid down before, when she'd left Aylmer to come back to Salwarpe. As soon as he'd seen Dickon's dog, Benedict had known that someone would have to go to the abbey. That someone could not be him and therefore it would have to be the girl.

Typical.

She was right to go, of course, though it made him feel curiously empty to know that she was no longer in the castle. If only she had felt able to trust him—or Aylmer. Aylmer would have been hurt if she had gone without a word . . . and that word had only been spoken because he, Benedict, had seen to it that she confessed her intention. Aylmer had forgiven her, of course. Aylmer loved her. Well, who didn't?

Benedict thought about Aylmer. He remembered the first time he had seen the man who was to be his guardian. A big brown bear of a man, jumping down from his horse and sweeping the five-year-old orphan up into his arms. 'So you are Benedict? For your father's sake and for your own, I shall love you. I have no sons of my own as yet, Benedict When I have, you and I shall teach them how to go birds-nesting . . . eh?'

But Aylmer had had no sons, or daughters, either. His wife Joan had been a gentle, loving creature; not pretty, nor even very accomplished as noble women went, but she and Aylmer had fitted each other's corners well. She had taken Benedict to her heart as she took any stray animal or child . . . and he had mourned for her almost as deeply as Aylmer, when she died.

And now, Ursula. Ursula de Thrave of Salwarpe. Ursula of the long fair hair and quick intelligence. She had some of the same warmth as Aylmer's dead wife, but overlying it was a consciousness of her beauty, which Joan had never had. Joan had put her husband first in all things; Ursula put Salwarpe first. It was always as well to remember that, when dealing with her. Sometimes one forgot it, and thought she smiled at one because she liked one . . . but of course that was all nonsense. How could she like a limping, ugly, untidy creature like Benedict de Huste?

Now and again she had made him forget that he was awkward and lame. If she was kind to him, perhaps it was not only because he was the means whereby Salwarpe was to be saved . . . or was it only that? He couldn't be sure.

Idonia had never let him forget that he was awkward and lame. There had been other mornings when he had awoken and . . . he drew in his breath and closed his eyes. He lay rigid awhile, remembering. Then he made himself relax. It was all in the past. It was no good thinking about it. It hurt still, to remember it, but over the years he had trained himself not to think about it very often. He had achieved contentment working on his estates, building a new mill here, improving the water-meadows there. And he had won some sort of respect among his fellows, campaigning in France. Not that he had ever wished to take part in another siege!

If he could have got out of this one, he would have done so. He didn't like sieges. Very expensive, in more ways than one. It was clear that Sir Henry was a poor man and that he would never be able to reimburse Benedict the money advanced. Aylmer had offered to give Benedict some money, the night before they left the hunting-lodge, but Benedict had said there was plenty of time and that he had some with him . . .

Yes, Aylmer would repay him. Probably.

It was necessary to put one's problems into different slots and not take out one problem to look at it before the previous problem had been solved. The only difficulty was that you had to choose which problem was the most urgent. If you chose wrongly, then something was liable to get forgotten.

Those outposts. Reason told him that outposts were a good thing. Instinct told him they would lose some good men when Hugo came up the hill. Should the outposts be withdrawn, or did they have enough good archers to replace those they might lose? And how many men were they going to be able to get out of the town before Hugo discovered the deception practiced on him? And would Merle and Mistress Peasmarsh come out of this alive?

And Reynold. Benedict sighed. He could have done without Reynold, just at the moment.

Benedict had a nasty feeling that he had overlooked something, somewhere. What? Peter Bowman. No, he was all right. Dickon? Gone with Ursula, of a surety. Sir Henry? Trust that old fox to come through this in one piece. Merle? We've gone into that already. The trebuchet, the carpenters, the smith . . .

Benedict sat up with a sigh, shaking his head. Something was amiss, somewhere. He had better make a round of the castle, checking on everything. Someone rapped on the door and then put the key into the lock and turned it. Not Ursula, of course.

Reynold de Cressi. He had come to make trouble. Benedict saw that at once. Parkyn had a cauldron of water keeping 'warm on a brazier. As Benedict sat up, Parkyn took the cauldron from the coals and began to pour it into a tub.

Benedict brightened. He felt in need of a bath. That sewer last night . . . ugh! He thought: Must check that they sealed off the entrance to the sewer . . .

As Benedict stepped into the bath and Parkyn reached for the soap, Reynold kicked the door shut and stood with arms akimbo. 'Well, slugabed!'

'Reynold . . . any sign of the trebuchet yet?'

'Trebuchet? No. I doubt it's all a figment of your imagination. Your very fertile imagination.' Benedict was meant to wince at that thrust, but he was surrendering to the warm of the water. He smiled, instead. Parkyn rolled up his sleeves and attended to Benedict's feet.

'I came,' said Reynold. 'To demand the return of the knife and ring which your man stole from me. And to have him whipped.'

Barnabas shrank into a corner, his eyes flickering to the door.

Benedict brushed soap from his eyes—Parkyn was washing his hair—and said, 'I thought they had been returned to you already. My man Barnabas has forsworn petty theft. Hand the things over, Barnabas. My apologies, Reynold. It will not happen again.'

Parkyn's fingers were something less than gentle about Benedict's head. The man was more enthusiastic than skilful at his job. What had his old job been, anyway?

'It certainly will not happen again,' said Reynold. 'I will see he has such a whipping as . . .'

'No whipping,' said Benedict, standing up and allowing himself to be enfolded in a clean towel 'I need him in one piece.'

'How very like you to employ the scum of the castle!' said Reynold. 'A thief, and a clumsy, cack-handed ostler.'

An ostler? Was that what Parkyn had been? And was there so much difference between grooming a horse and grooming a man?

'They serve me well,' said Benedict, and was rewarded by grateful looks from both Parkyn and Barnabas. Well, he knew better than Reynold what sort of men they were. Badly-trained servants they might be, but then, who was Benedict to deserve anything better? Parkyn replaced the wet towel with another, dry one. Perhaps he was not so ill-trained, after all?

Benedict sat, while Parkyn prepared to shave his master. Usually Benedict shaved himself, shrugged on his own clothing and ran a comb through his hair—if he remembered. He had not had a personal body-servant since his father's valet had died . . . four years ago . . . five? Since just after he parted from Idonia.

'You spend long enough on your toilet,' said Reynold, with a sneer.

'I do not know when I shall have time to

do so again,' said Benedict. Barnabas was kneeling at his master's feet, rolling on a pair of hose. Barnabas's shoulders were hunched, and his elbows sharp with unspoken protest at Reynold's behaviour. Benedict closed his eyes, surrendering to Parkyn's hands. Perhaps the man was not so unskilful, after all. Perhaps he had merely needed encouragement, in order to display his talents.

Reynold still had something to say. 'When I think how poor a showing you make in the tourney, I wonder at it that you should have been put in command here! Of course the de Thraves knew no better . . .'

Parkyn's hands trembled. Barnabas was buckling on Benedict's boots, and his hands, too, had become unsteady about their task. Benedict thought: By the Rood, my servants want me to refute Reynold's charge, and I cannot do it.

'It is true that you are skilled in the tourney,' said Benedict. 'Very true. I believe you did well at York, recently?'

'You should have been there to see me! But then, you had other, pressing business on your estates, did you not? The building of a mill, or some such?' Reynold snorted. 'Understandable, seeing how often I have tumbled you in the dust!'

For once Benedict was moved to protest. 'The tourney is not everything. Wars are not fought according to the rules of the tourney, and I have seen something of war, you know.'

'The tourney is the only true training-ground for war. How else can a knight be sure of unseating his opponent in a charge?'

'The tourney is as much like war as a mumming play is to real life. The mummers pack their properties and jog on to the next town when they have finished their play, but in real life the war goes on, as this siege does. Let us talk of this no more, until you have come through a siege. Only then can you make comparisons.'

Parkyn handed Benedict a fine linen shirt, new-washed and smelling of herbs. Barnabas fastened Benedict's hose and drawers to his inner belt and saw to the brushing down of his black wool tunic. Then Parkyn combed through his master's hair and handed him a silver-backed mirror.

'You have done well indeed,' said Benedict, surprised to see how much they had managed to achieve with what was, basically, poor material. Both Parkyn and Barnabas beamed.

'If Idonia could only see you preening yourself!' said Reynold.

Benedict's brows twitched, but he said nothing. It was quite true that Idonia would have laughed if she could have seen her husband trying to make himself look presentable. Yet over the memory of Idonia's scornful face came another, of a girl with honey-coloured hair saying, 'Honeysuckle is my favourite'.

Once again Benedict was driven to protest. He said, 'Reynold, you have said much of my conduct in that old affair. Perhaps you are right to point the finger at me. Perhaps not. But let me ask you this—was your own conduct all that it should have been?'

Reynold's face took on an ugly look. He started to say something, then swung on his heel and departed.

Benedict took a pair of thick leather gloves from Parkyn and thrust them through the straps of the wallet that hung from his leather belt.

Parkyn said, 'My lord, if I do please you . . . it is true that I was once an ostler, but I have been learning the trade of barber and surgeon from Sir Henry's man, although I never thought to practise it, for he is not an old man. But he was kind enough to say I had some aptitude for it. Would you purchase me from Sir Henry, that I may continue to serve you in future?'

'And me!' said Barnabas, in a squeaky voice. He stood on one leg and twisted the other around it. Then, under Benedict's eye, Barnabas removed certain articles from about his person and placed them on the bed.

Parkyn gasped. 'My purse! And my Canterbury pilgrim's medal!'

'That's enough, Parkyn!' said Benedict. 'Barnabas has returned them to you, hasn't he? And by the by, I wouldn't play at games of chance with him, unless he assures you he hasn't loaded the dice.'

Barnabas looked shaken. He said, 'My lord, I would never . . .'

'Wouldn't you?' said Benedict. He laughed. 'Barnabas, it would serve you right if I allowed Parkyn to give you the beating which you so richly deserve. Unfortunately—or perhaps I should say fortunately for you—I need you. However, you shall strip, here and now. And Parkyn shall cleanse you as thoroughly as he has recently cleansed me. And then you will report to me again.'

'I don't hold with too much washing,' said Barnabas, sidling to the door. 'You can hit me, if you like! And I swear I will never steal again, once I am your servant.'

'Blackmail? Will you put it all on me? Nay, lad. Take your punishment like a man, prove yourself on your own ground, and I will consider your case when the siege is ended. And not before. Parkyn—special attention to his feet, please. And then take some rest yourself.'

* * *

Simon Joce met Benedict on the steps of the keep. Simon was looking grim.

'My lord, we have made up some large mattresses with rushes and the like, as you ordered. We have also found some rope, so that the mattresses may be lowered over the gatehouse wall to break the force of any stones thrown at it. But, my lord, they are covered with sacking only, and we have no more hides to spare. Sir Reynold took all our store of hides for his outposts.'

A sacking mattress could be set aflame with an arrow dipped in burning pitch, and Simon had had the sense to see it.

'I spoke with Sir Reynold,' said Simon, 'about removing some, if not all, of the hides from the outposts, but he would not hear of it.'

If they removed the hides from the outposts, then a flaming arrow lodged in the framework of the carts would set all ablaze. Reynold was right to refuse.

Benedict remembered Ursula saying that they should have her pony. She had tried not to show how much the animal had meant to her. And the old knight's war-horse. Were there no other animals fit to be slaughtered? Probably not. The pony and the war-horse were expendable.

'Slaughter the Lady Ursula's pony and Sir Henry's war-horse,' said Benedict. 'We have their permission. I trust these two horses will be sufficient.'

'Yes, my lord. I thought it might come to that, but the little lady will grieve.'

'Yes, Simon. I know. But she is not Sir Henry's granddaughter for nothing.'

Simon's face cleared and he went off—if not happily—at least content that he was doing the right thing.

Now what was it that had been troubling him? Benedict set off for the stairs that led to the ramparts, but was waylaid by a servant with a request to attend on Sir Henry in his chamber at once.

The old man was looking better. There was some natural colour in his cheeks, and his eyes were bright as he handed Benedict a slip of thin paper.

'My granddaughter sent this by pigeon. Luckily Hugo's men cannot intercept birds sent from the other side of the river, because they fly straight across the marshes. You see that the abbot has agreed to sell. There only remains the question of boats. He has few and is unwilling to let us hire them, but there is a fishing village nearby, and Ursula will charter enough, I dare say.'

'Yes, yes.' Benedict ruffled his hair. 'Flour, already ground in the abbot's mill That's not as good in some ways as sending us grain, although as we have no mill, we would have had to grind the grain by hand . . . but flour! If a sack falls into the water, it is spoiled. We must build a landing-stage, I think. And devise some kind of basket sling, or hoist, to bring the sacks up from the foot of the cliff. Men cannot bring them up on their backs. Oh, I suppose it might be possible, though tedious. No, I think we should have a hoist. I will speak to the carpenters straight away, and talk to the young smith . . . Simon says he is a handy lad, but . . .'

'We are saved, I think,' said Sir Henry. 'Perhaps prayers do bear fruit, now and then.'

Benedict thought of a certain time in his life when prayers had not availed him, and a sarcastic rejoinder was on the tip of his tongue. Then he shook his head at himself. What was he about, trying to shatter an old man's faith?

'Surely your granddaughter has saved the day.'

'With God. And a little more praying to do. It must be several days before the flour can be loaded from the abbot's store, and then—do they cross in the day-time, do you think? I doubt if chartered boats will agree to make the crossing at night. The tides are treacherous and the marshes all about us.'

'We will keep the channel clear.'

Then Benedict went down to speak to the carpenters, and the smith . . . and from them he went to the cliff . . . and when he came back up from the cliff, a sentry was waiting to speak with him. This man had been watching the quayside from that part of the ramparts which overlooked the town.

Hugo's men had set the fisherfolk to work on repairing two of the best boats, presumably so that they could once more command the channel from the river to the castle. The sentry reported that the men were working with reluctance, their chins on their shoulders . . . and that the mercenaries had whips out, to encourage the workmen.

Benedict thought about this latest problem. At all costs the channel had to be kept clear, or food supplies would not be able to come in. The trebuchet might well sink a stationary vessel, but if there were two of them, or if they were moving . . . he shook his head. Very doubtful. So, what else was there?

'A fire-ship,' he said. 'No, a raft. We put a couple of barrels of pitch aboard, well lashed down, and anchor it where the guard-boat used to be. Dead in the middle of the channel, where it widens to sweep into the river. Then if Hugo's men bring up their boats, we can send a flaming arrow to ignite the pitch, and that might keep them off for a while.'

The carpenters looked at one another. 'My lord, you asked for a better set of ladders for the cliff, and a hoist. Now you want a raft. We have some timber from the buildings we pulled down, but there are only a few of us, and . . .'

'You shall have every man, woman and child who is capable of helping and not hindering you,' said Benedict. And went back up into the keep to arrange this with Sir Henry.

And thence he went to the cellar to inspect the new grille that was being fitted into position . . . or rather the old ironwork was being replaced in a new, stronger timber frame, since the young smith had not yet had time to make a new grille.

While he was there he sent men down the sewer once more to check that the outlet into the dell was still concealed and no traces remained of their journey the previous night.

And then up to the ramparts to frown down on that same dell, which was a vivid spot of green among the burned-out brown of the slopes around it; and to wonder if it would be a good idea to set flames in the dell, too . . . and then to decide against it, for if fire were set there from within the sewer, then Hugo would begin to wonder how that had been achieved and perhaps to suspect the presence of an outlet from the castle and investigate it. And if it were set in flames by a party issuing from the gatehouse, then that same party would come under fire before they could get right round the hill to where the dell was situated, for surely Hugo would be on his guard now . . .

Peter Bowman was loitering nearby, looking anxious.

'No more trees cut down, Peter?'

'No. But he's too quiet for my liking, my lord. Not a sniff out of him since he set that trap with the carts and the family from Spereshot.'

'He has his own troubles. His smith's ill. You may have heard.'

'I have that.' Peter laughed, but was grave again at once. 'That was an idea worthy of you, my lord. But I ask myself; shall we lose Merle, in order to get ourselves a smith? And for every man capable of bearing arms whom we steal from under Hugo's nose, do we not bring up three or maybe four extra mouths to feed?'

'Tell me how we can get the men without taking their families as well, and I will put your plan into action straight away. Yet . . . I think men fight best with their loved ones at their shoulders. But I must confess to being on tenterhooks till we learn if our plan will work for a second night . . . and a third. I, too, ask myself how many of the townsfolk are worth as much as Merle's little finger. But, we need the smith. This boy that I collected last night is well enough in his way, but he makes a lot of noise in order to produce—practically nothing!'

'Like someone else we could mention,' said Peter.

Benedict understood well enough that Peter was referring to Reynold, but it would not be politic to smile. Instead Benedict said that he must be on his rounds; he had a feeling he had missed something, somewhere. But what?

CHAPTER THIRTEEN

Benedict was late for supper. As he took his place at the high table Reynold raised his voice, that Benedict might hear. Reynold was holding forth about the tourney he had attended recently. He looked somewhat more than half drunk. Benedict said nothing, but thought: If he's going to go to pieces now . . .

Reynold nudged Sir Henry. 'Here's the very man! Ask him how many times I've tumbled him off his horse in the lists!'

Sir Henry's eyebrows were a little raised, his tone a blend of amusement and disinterest. He said to Benedict, 'Sir Reynold is indeed a gifted raconteur.'

'Most amusing,' agreed Benedict. It was irritating that Reynold should seek to belittle him in front of everyone, but if Sir Henry were not going to take the matter seriously, then neither need he.

'Ask him!' insisted Reynold. 'Rolling in the dust, time and time again!'

'We were squires together in Aylmer's household,' explained Benedict, speaking direct to Sir Henry, and ignoring Reynold. 'We often used to break lances in the tiltyard. He is indeed my master in that art.'

'Ah?' said Sir Henry. 'Splendid!' His attention was obviously elsewhere.

Benedict grinned as he attacked his food. If Sir Henry were able to deflect Reynold's attempts to make mischief, then there was no need for Benedict to worry.

'Of course,' said Reynold, frowning into his cup, 'I haven't had a chance to see what he can do, recently. He might have improved. Doubt it. But he might.'

'True,' said Benedict, taking three lamb chops and signing to Parkyn that he wanted some more wine. 'But then, I haven't had as much practice as you, Reynold.'

'Skulking on your estates, instead of coming to tourneys.'

'Keeping busy,' said Benedict.

'The Burgundy campaign?' said Sir Henry, keeping the peace. 'I heard there was some fierce fighting at . . .'

'Tell you what we'll do,' said Reynold. 'We'll fit you up with some armour and a decent horse, and run a lance or two tomorrow. There's enough space before the keep.'

'Thank you, but no,' said Benedict. 'I have more important things to do.'

'Afraid? I'll let you have the best horse . . .'

'Not afraid,' said Benedict, speaking more sharply than usual. 'But this is neither the time nor the place for . . .'

'I challenge you!' Reynold had raised his voice. Almost everyone in the hall stopped talking and looked towards the high table.

Benedict put down his cup with care. He could feel the eyes of the garrison upon him. He grew cold with anger and also with something very like fear. He was not afraid of the failure itself. He knew that Reynold would unseat him, if they jousted. That went without saying. That wouldn't matter ordinarily, but it did matter now. Because if Reynold unseated

Benedict before the eyes of the garrison, then Reynold was not just unseating his old rival, but the commander of the garrison. And Benedict's authority would once more be brought into question.

Only, how to avoid the challenge?

'Come, now!' said Sir Henry. 'There's a fine challenge for you!' There was a note of derision in his voice. Sir Henry had taken sides, and it was not on Reynold's side that he had chosen to fight. 'A challenge between two such doughty knights would indeed be something worth seeing—if we were not in the midst of other, more serious business. Eh, Sir Benedict?'

Benedict tried to think. 'Indeed, Sir Henry. I fear that whether I won, or Sir Reynold, we might give each other such a buffeting as would lay one or the other of us out for a week.'

Sir Henry laughed and slapped the table. One or two of those around them also began to titter, following the old knight's lead.

'However,' said Benedict, beginning to breathe again, 'Sir Reynold has the germ of a good idea there. In the days to come there may be some couple of hours which we might devote to target practice, and to sports in general. To keep the garrison in fighting trim. We could run races, and jump, and wrestle and so on. What say you, Sir Henry; shall we get Reynold to organise such a training programme for us?'

It was the right touch. Smiles, quite natural expressions of amusement and interest, began to spread around the hall. Benedict took some more bread.

'You refuse my challenge?' Reynold was incredulous.

'Another time,' said Benedict, managing to smile as if he meant it.

'Certainly, certainly,' said Sir Henry. 'Another time.' And it was clear that he meant 'Don't make a fool of yourself, Reynold!'

*   *   *

Benedict slept late and woke with a start. Propped on one elbow, he listened to the noises of the castle. No trebuchet. No thudding at the wall. Bread being baked, men yawning, someone winding water up from the well nearby; the windlass creaked. Nothing new.

And yet . . . What was it he had missed?

Idonia's face came into his mind as he had last seen it. Face of stone, repudiating him. 'I swear you will be sorry . . .'

Sometimes when he thought of that moment bile rose in his throat and he choked. Now the memory was sore, but no longer as hurtful as it had been once. Sir Henry's championship of him last night . . . ah, but Sir Henry was a clever man. Benedict did not know whether the old knight had taken his side because it was politic to do so, or out of kindness. It had been a bad moment. Many of the bad moments in Benedict's life had been associated with Reynold.

As pages in Aylmer's household, they had disliked one another at first sight. Reynold was older, and quicker in every way. Reynold had a biting tongue and considered himself king of the pages. Benedict was slow and thoughtful, his co-ordination was not good and he was homesick. Such a combination made him a natural butt to Reynold. At length Benedict fell on his tormentor, and Reynold learned to his surprise that his victim could fight with teeth and nails and knees, even if not with knightly weapons. Thereafter Reynold treated Benedict with more circumspection, but when they were promoted to squires together it was one of the delights of Reynold's life to prove Benedict's inferiority with sword and lance, as often as he could.

But by this time Benedict had come to terms with what he could and could not do. He was secure in Aylmer's love, he was growing into a big-boned man and his courteous manners made him welcome in the company of the ladies. If Idonia had returned his love, Benedict would have matured into a well-balanced man.

Instead, something had been twisted and warped inside him, so that although one part of him had gone on developing the other had shrunk; the accident had crippled him in more ways than one.

He remembered how they had brought Idonia to him as he lay with his leg aflame, the day after the accident. And he had tried to lift himself, and to smile at her; to reassure her that he was not as badly injured as he appeared to be at first sight. He had been much scratched and bruised and he knew she did not like the sight of blood. She had taken one horrified look at his injuries and turned from him. And as she turned away, so Reynold had come in behind her; and she had gone to Reynold, smiling, and asked him to show her the trick he was teaching his dog.

To give him his due, Reynold had hesitated, glancing at Benedict. Then Idonia had pouted and shrugged, and said that she didn't think she could do anything for poor Benedict, and the sun was shining outside . . .

Aylmer had been sitting beside Benedict at the time. He had said, 'She is very young, Benedict. I will have a word with her.'

But whatever Aylmer said, it did no good. Idonia could never bear the sight of Benedict after that. He was so ugly now, she said; so awkward. If she had known he was going to ruin his looks . . .! She had avoided him while he convalesced, and he had known that during that time she was usually with Reynold. In the evenings he had to watch her dancing with

Reynold, in the day-times he had to watch her ride out beside him.

When she did meet him, painfully limping along on his crutch, she would turn aside with her hand over her mouth to stifle laughter. Reynold taught her to say things, slyly, about Benedict; hurtful things which she knew would be repeated to him. Aylmer had tried to protect Benedict, but what man could protect him from the wit of a spiteful girl?

Benedict had suffered, for he loved Idonia. He lost his self-confidence. He began to take himself at her evaluation of him. He would have released her from her vows of betrothal, but Aylmer had insisted that the marriage go through.

Why had Aylmer insisted? Looking back, Benedict thought of all the pain that had arisen from that insistence and wondered if Aylmer had been wise. If the match had been broken off, even though it would have meant a great deal of trouble for everybody, even though Benedict would have smarted for a while, yet surely he might have made another match, later on?

And she? Benedict sighed. Well, what would she have done? Married Reynold? Perhaps she might have wished to do so, but it had long been understood that Reynold was to marry a distant cousin. True, his bride was some years older than he, but there was a considerable inheritance involved, and

Reynold knew the value of a bird in the hand. He could not hope to gain Aylmer's consent to his marrying Idonia, if she broke her vows to marry Benedict. No, Idonia could not hope to marry Reynold, and so . . . over-persuaded perhaps by Aylmer . . . she had married Benedict. And made them both suffer for it.

For ten days she had held him off, making excuses, saying she could not be expected to enjoy the caresses of such an awkward creature, that he must woo her all over again . . . and then had laughed at his attempts to do so. He had been at that difficult stage, halfway between adolescence and manhood, when to be laughed at was doubly hurtful. He had been crude, even rough, perhaps. But he had tried every way he knew to show her that he loved her, and would be patient if only she . . . but she did not wish to listen. How well Benedict could remember the frustration, the humiliation, of that time! And then Aylmer had taken him aside and bid him show Idonia who was master. And he had done so, despite her raging. She had said he would regret it, and so he had.

Benedict turned over in bed and gulped. It was not an episode of which he was proud. He felt sick shame when he thought of it, even now.

Yet he had succeeded, in spite of what she said later.

Well. Perhaps he ought not to have forced

her. Only, what else?

If he had waited? But she had made it clear that he had lost her respect, because he had not exercised his rights . . . and then, when he did . . .

Benedict bit on his lip. She had waited till the whole court was assembled, and then gone on her knees to Aylmer to request that her marriage be annulled, on the grounds that Benedict was impotent. In front of everyone . . . of Reynold, sniggering behind his hand, of Joan looking distressed . . . and of Benedict, scarlet in the face, protesting . . . and feeling sick because he saw that his protests were unavailing.

Neither Joan nor Aylmer had believed Idonia, but it was plain that some way must be found of breaking the deadlock. Aylmer suggested that the couple separate for a few months. Idonia was very young . . . perhaps so much adulation had gone to her head, and so on. Joan had flatly refused to allow Idonia to stay on in her household: She would no longer be responsible for the girl, she said, because of her outrageous flirtations with Reynold.

Aylmer was to take a contingent of knights to fight in France, and it was decided that Benedict should be one of these knights. As for Idonia, she might take up her abode at one of Benedict's manors for the time being. Both agreed. Benedict took Idonia, with a train of servants, to a comfortable, well-furnished manor and left her there. She barely spoke to him on the journey and turned her back on him when he would have kissed her at parting.

And that was the last time he had seen her, for she had contracted a fever late that summer and died within the week.

Benedict had inherited her estates, which was all to the good. But the slander which she had perpetrated on him, the lie that he had not been able to consummate their marriage, that also had stayed with him.

Benedict opened his eyes and looked up at the ceiling. He didn't often think about Idonia, nowadays. Perhaps it was having Reynold at close quarters which brought her so much to mind. Yet the sting was leaving the old wounds. Sir Henry's kindness, Ursula's saying 'I choose honeysuckle'; even if both were due to diplomacy, even if they did not really like him for his own sake . . .

No, they both liked him. He was sure of that.

A strange thing, that he should find people to like him here in Salwarpe, so far from his own estates, even though Reynold was around to remind him how stupid and awkward he was.

Benedict thought: One can't get away from one's past, exactly. But as one grows older and has new experiences . . . perhaps the old wounds close up? I didn't think they ever would, but perhaps they can.

Someone came rapping on the door and he swung his legs out of bed.

*   *   *

Another evening in the hall, watching Reynold drink himself into a stupor. Another night of dreamless sleep. Another pleasurable awakening . . . no trebuchet, no cries of alarm, no Ursula. The smith had come, with another boat-load of refugees. Bravo, Merle! And now the forge produced more than just noise.

But.

His uneasiness grew. He frowned as he went about his work, overseeing the laying of the last planks on the jetty below the cliff, signalling to the men who were anchoring the fireboat in place . . . walking the ramparts with Peter Bowman, and talking of Merle. Below in the valley the church bell tolled for yet another family who were being 'interred' by the priest in the churchyard. How many coffins were being let down into the ground? Eight? There were unusual scurryings in the streets below and now and then they could hear the cries of mercenaries searching for and taking men to work on the quayside, or in the fields Or . . .

'That's where they're building the trebuchet,' said Peter, pointing to a space beyond the church. 'There's an open piece of ground there. You can't see it properly from here, because the church is in the way. But there's carts been hauling timber there, and the timber's not come out again, and there's men been driven with whips to that place . . . and they don't come out again, neither. So that's where they're building the trebuchet.'

'And no smith,' said Benedict, with a grin.

'Ah,' said Peter, also grinning. 'But if they catch Merle . . . he's a big chap and noticeable. They tell me he's hiding by day and moving by night. His brother and family have reported sick today . . . I saw them being helped out of the mill early this morning, and taken to the houses on the end of the quay. The mercenaries don't like working on the quay any more. Nervous, it makes them. And sharp with their whips. But they've nearly got those boats ready to sail.'

'We're ready for them,' said Benedict. 'The fever story is spreading better than I thought it would. Sir Henry says he'll give old Mother Peasmarsh a grant of land, if she comes through this. And Merle.'

'I hope I live to see it,' said Peter.

Benedict went up to the gatehouse. He had been avoiding it for some time, believing it best to allow Reynold his head there. He was not happy about Reynold. Drinking in the middle of the day? Benedict rubbed his head in perplexity. What the devil had got into the man?

Simon Joce joined him at the gatehouse. He was looking expectant. Benedict sighed. Was he going to have to do Reynold's work for him yet again? It looked like it.

'Have we any stone-masons? If not, we'll have to learn how, won't we?' The gatehouse was built in a hollow square, spanning a deep pit. Top and bottom of the square were the two sets of gatehouses, linked fore and aft by high walls with cat-walks above them. Between the outermost pair of towers was the portcullis, which dropped into a slot in the ground. The inner gatetowers supported the drawbridge, which, when it was in the 'up' position, formed a second door, barring the way to any who had got through the portcullis.

Except that you didn't need to break through the portcullis or the drawbridge; if you were wise you broke into one of the outer gatehouse towers, inside which was the mechanism that operated the portcullis. A narrow postern was situated at the bottom of one of the outer towers.

'Wall that up for a start,' said Benedict. 'And fast!'

He waved his hand at the stone walls which linked the two sets of towers. 'Bad design,' he said. Both sets of towers had stairs within their walls, leading from ground floor to ramparts. You could run up the stairs within the first tower, run across the catwalk overlooking the pit into which the drawbridge was meant to sink, and then run down the inner tower steps.

'We must either break down the catwalks,'

said Benedict, 'Or build walls blocking off the ramparts, and preventing access to the catwalks. If they force the first tower, well and good. But we needn't give them easy access to the inner towers.'

'If we do that,' said Simon, 'we'll have to keep the drawbridge lowered, or our men won't be able to get into the front towers at all.'

'That's right. Put extra men on duty, ready to bring the drawbridge up at a moment's notice. I doubt they'll be needed yet awhile, but it's as well to be prepared. If only I could think of a way to bring a trebuchet into use on this side . . .'

Both Simon and Benedict shook their heads. The castle wall was so high at that point, and the gate-towers so extensive in area, that no trebuchet could be brought near enough the inner walls to throw stones over it.

'We might make two smaller ones, to mount on top of the gatehouse towers,' said Benedict. 'But there's so little room up there that they couldn't be very big, and if they aren't big they won't have much power. I'll speak to the carpenters about it.'

'Sir Benedict, do I ask Sir Reynold, before I start these alterations?'

Benedict hesitated. He'd passed Reynold, drinking in the hall, some time back. Then he nodded. 'Ask him, but make sure he's asked in such a way that he does it.'

'The men at the outposts will have to come back under the portcullis every time we change the guard. I'll have to put extra men on duty at the portcullis, as well as on the drawbridge, if we wall up the postern.'

Benedict nodded and left Simon conferring with his men. What was it he had not done? He went in search of Sir Henry, who was wandering towards the garden.

Sir Henry took Benedict's arm. 'Smile, my lad. Always smile when things are going badly.'

Benedict took one look at Sir Henry's elaborate gold coiffure and wide grin, and stretched his own mouth in a smile. Things must indeed have been bad.

'We are short of food?' he guessed.

'Appallingly,' said Sir Henry, smiling and bowing as they passed a group of carpenters. 'You eat enough for three, my boy. You ought to know.'

'I thought the food would be here on the next tide.' They had daily news of the troubles Ursula was having, getting the ships loaded and away.

'Certainly. But I have just been told that Hugo's men have two boats in the water, and are loading them with men.' Here he stopped to pat a small boy on the head. 'There'll be a certain amount of sabotage, naturally. One of the refugees has a son who swore he'd left a seam uncaulked. Perhaps the boats will not be able to set sail this afternoon. But it's going to be a close-run thing.'

'A fight at sea. Not precisely my strong point. Never had to do it, before.'

'My men have, of course. That's a point in our favour. But I don't like to think of my granddaughter in the middle of one. Sit down, boy. It wasn't about that I wanted to speak with you . . .'

Benedict snapped his fingers. 'Merle has been found out!'

'He has been taken hostage in exchange for two others who "fell sick" and have been released by Hugo. I doubt Hugo knows what Merle was doing, but took him merely as being a man of substance. Still, it is a blow. Both the Peasmarsh men have arrived here. They really have been ill, incidentally. Conditions in the jail are not, I gather, quite what one would wish. But it wasn't about that I wished to speak, either.'

'Reynold.' Benedict sat beside Sir Henry and folded his arms.

'You must be more careful with him, my boy. Poor Reynold lacks your self-confidence. He is so afraid he will fail when it comes to the crunch.'

Benedict's jaw dropped.

'Hadn't it occurred to you? He's never been in a siege before, has he? You keep telling him it's different from the tourney, and of course it is different, but . . .'

Benedict began to laugh. Then he sobered.

Sir Henry was looking at him with a mixture of amusement and concern.

'You really think he's afraid?' said Benedict. Sir Henry nodded. Benedict rubbed his head. 'Well! And here was I coming to you to ask you to help me with him. And something else. I've missed something, Sir Henry. I don't know what. I've been over and over it, time and again. Can you spare the time to go over it with me once again?'

A page came out, bearing cold meats and some ale for them to drink. It was pleasant to sit there in the sun and share one's troubles. The page poured out some ale for Benedict and set it on the bench beside him Benedict made as it to lift the cup, and then stopped, hand in the air.

The surface of the ale had been disturbed by an intrusive fly.

'What a fool I've been!' cried Benedict.

Food forgotten, he snatched up the cup and raced to the nearest stairs. Up onto the ramparts he went, crying for Peter Bowman, for Barnabas, for Simon Joce. To the astonishment of the sentries he set the cup down on the flagstones by the outer wall and crouched above it, watching the surface of the liquid as if his life depended on it.

'Here, my lord!' Here came Barnabas, with Peter Bowman loping along behind him.

'Bowls. I asked for bowls of water to be set about the ramparts. Quickly! Run!' Barnabas ran.

'What the devil . . .' This was Simon Joce.

'Look at the liquid, man! Look closely. Did it tremble? No, perhaps not. I thought for a moment . . . Not here, at any rate.' He stood up and looked around him A dozen or so men had collected to stare at his antics. He pushed through them, to set the cup down twenty paces further on and once more crouch down beside it.

Parkyn and Barnabas ran up with two more bowls. Then Sir Henry was there, too.

'Benedict, what . . .?'

'Mines, Sir Henry. A standing bowl of water will show if anything is moving under the surface. Deep down, where we can't feel movement normally. There are tunnels and caves beneath this castle, are there not? We know of two, but what if there are more than two? What if Hugo has learned of one, and . . . see!'

The surface of the water was shuddering.

'Magic!' whispered one man, and crossed himself.

'Not magic,' said Benedict. 'But picks and shovels attacking the rock beneath us. Picks, mostly. Set those bowls down further on, Parkyn . . . and over there, Barnabas. Let's see if we can discover exactly where they are working . . .'

The bowls were set and men craned their necks over each one.

'Yes . . . here!' cried a dozen voices at once.

'Not much movement,' reported Simon, from the far end.

'Set more bowls here, and here!' said Benedict, pacing out distances. 'And further over, just in case they've got two mines going. We needn't worry about the cliff side, or the gatehouse . . . just this steep hill overlooking the town.'

'But the townsfolk, the refugees, would have told us if anything were going on,' protested Sir Henry.

'Would they know? Ask them. And ask them about the existence of any other tunnels. Barnabas, where are you? Ah, there you are. Are there any tunnels they could reach from this side?'

'N-no,' said Barnabas. 'Not to say "tunnels". There's the Dead Man's Cave, a course. But that doesn't lead anywhere much.'

Several men rushed to the ramparts and looked over. 'There!' cried one. 'Look, there!'

Peter Bowman held his hands over his eyes and scanned the ground below, where the furthest flung of the houses were situated at the bottom of the cliff.

'There's men been using that track,' he said, pointing to a dusty space between two houses. The track disappeared into some bushes, and then an outcrop of rock cut off the view. 'That's where the entrance to the Dead Man's Cave lies, and it's right beneath us. No, a trifle to the left.'

'And the sewer is a dozen yards or so to the right,' said Benedict, also peering over the edge. 'See where the dell lies? They can't know about the outlet from the sewer. The track up to the dell doesn't look as if it's been used recently.'

Sir Henry sent for some of the refugees from the town and questioned them. No, they had never heard of any tunnel up into the castle. No, they thought the sewers from the castle all went out the other side, into the marshes. Yes, Hugo's men had been asking about tunnels and caves and sewers and the like, and it was true that one of the younger ne'er-do-wells, who had been accustomed to spending a lot of time birds-nesting, had recently disappeared from his home and been seen in Hugo's camp, eating with the mercenaries. And yes, about twenty of their men had been taken from field-work and now lived in those two houses down at the bottom of the cliff there, under close guard. They were driven into the cave every morning, with picks and shovels. It was thought they were constructing extra stabling for Hugo's horses, or some such. Daft-like. Wasn't there stabling and plenty to be had, already?

'I think we can take it,' said Benedict, 'that Hugo knows there is a sewer outlet somewhere about here, but he's not sure where. He thinks he can get into it through Dead Man's Cave.

Now why?'

Several men smiled. 'Because of the stench, that's why! They call it Dead Man's Cave because way back a vagrant died there, and wasn't found for weeks . . . Phew! But the smell's still there. They reckon it's some seepage from the castle sewers, that gets into the water as it trickles through a fault in the rock at the back of the cave.'

'And if Hugo follows that trail of water by widening the fault into a tunnel he'll come eventually to our sewer. And when he arrives at our sewer he'll come up into the castle that way. Humph! We'll have to see what we can do about that.'

He measured distances with his eye. 'Well, he's got some way to go yet. Set basins of water all along here, at intervals of two or three feet. I want to know how fast he's going. And if the picks stop at any time let me know at once.'

'Why should we bother, if they stop?' asked one.

'Because,' said Benedict. 'We have no map to show us the course of our sewer. It may bend inwards a little—I rather think it does. If the picks stop, it will mean Hugo's broken through. Where is Simon Joce?'

'Here,' said that stalwart.

Benedict drew him aside. 'You heard.' We might have learned of this days ago. Why were my orders disobeyed . . . or need I ask?'

'Sir Reynold fell over one of the basins

early one morning, while you were otherwise engaged. He ordered them taken away.'

'I thought as much.' Benedict's hands clenched into fists. 'It is time we had a reckoning, he and I!'

'One moment,' said Sir Henry. He took Benedict's arm and urged him towards the stairs. 'We have not finished our meal. Come back to the garden. Yes, I know you want to wring Reynold's neck, but I think we had best talk about it first.'

CHAPTER FOURTEEN

Sir Henry seated Benedict and sent Barnabas for more bread and ale.

'You think I am being an interfering old man,' said Sir Henry, exercising charm. 'But I take a great interest in you, young Benedict, and I don't want to see you making a mistake.'

'Have I not good cause to break him?'

'Oh, certainly. He has behaved very badly.' Sir Henry spoke of Reynold's behaviour as one might refer, with indulgence, to the misdeeds of a naughty boy.

'Has he not done his best to undermine my authority in every way? Has he not spoken slightingly of me to your men?'

'The stupid fellow!' Sir Henry shook his head at Reynold's folly. 'He went about it quite the wrong way. My men of Salwarpe like to make up their own minds about people, and Reynold's silly talk merely made them dislike him the more, without diminishing in any way the respect they have come to feel for you.'

Benedict's jaw dropped. Respect? For him?

'Oh, dear me, yes,' said Sir Henry. 'I don't say they'd willingly die for you. They wouldn't willingly lay down their lives for anyone. Not even for me or Ursula. But if you asked for a party of volunteers to follow you down into the sewer to fight Hugo's men, in all that filth—which I suppose is what it will come to in the end—why, you'd get your quota. They wouldn't enjoy it, of course. They'd grumble and swear. But they'd do it, for you.'

'But wouldn't they rather follow Reynold?'

'No, he hasn't the knack of commanding men. He can only shout and bluster and order men to be whipped. Doesn't do any good around here. It might go down all right on his own estates, but not here. Also, those of my men who've seen service abroad have been watching Reynold. They say he's no care for men's lives. Every time they look at those outposts, they shake their heads. Soon Reynold won't be able to get anyone to go out there, to man them.'

Benedict put his head in his hands. 'I knew there was some criticism of him, but I didn't think it had gone that far.'

'I know you didn't. You came here with a

preconceived idea of Reynold, and unless you modify it you'll destroy him. Not that he'd be much loss. I agree with Simon Joce and Merle that we could do without Reynold easily. But there are some small remnants of manhood in Reynold that you might like to save. He could be useful about the place when the attack comes.'

Benedict stared at the ground. Barnabas brought more food and ale and then sank out of sight. Benedict ate and drank without seeming to realise what he was doing.

'There is bad blood between you, I believe,' said Sir Henry, when all the food had gone. 'Will you tell me about it?'

Benedict's hand jerked. 'I . . . he tried to make love to my wife. But that's not it, really. We have never liked one another.'

'Yet I suppose you rubbed along well enough till he trespassed on your territory. I must say, I'm surprised he's still alive, if he made love to your wife.'

'I wanted to challenge him, but Aylmer stopped me. Reynold is my superior in the tourney, but I'd have killed him, even so. Only . . .' He stopped.

'I have heard something of the affair. It was more her fault than his.'

Benedict flushed. 'Yes,' he said, in a dull tone. 'It was more her fault than his. And he never got any further than flirting.'

'Have you ever talked to him about it?'

Benedict looked at Sir Henry as if he thought the old man mad. 'Obviously not,' said Sir Henry. 'Well, why don't you do so now?'

'What good would that do? She's dead.'

'A good thing, too.' He went on, apparently unaware of Benedict's indrawn breath. 'After all, you wouldn't have wanted children by her.'

There was a long pause. 'You know, I never thought of that. No, I don't think I would have wanted children by her. Not now. I did at the time, of course. I thought that if I could only get her pregnant she would settle down.'

'I heard something about that, too. She said you didn't make it. You said you had. Did you?'

Benedict had gone a sickly white. 'Yes. I am sure of it. It was very hurried, but I . . . I swear I did. Only, afterwards, I began to wonder, because she was so very insistent, you see . . .'

'Dear me! What a very naughty little girl she was!'

Benedict hadn't thought it possible he could laugh about Idonia. But now he did. At first the laughter hurt, and then it eased him.

When he had done laughing, Sir Henry said, 'I do trust that you took a woman to bed with you immediately afterwards; two or three women in fact. To take the taste away.'

'Not till I got to France. That was all right. I mean, I was all right. But the bad taste remained. Especially when I heard she'd died.'

'Someone told me she was running away to

meet her lover when she caught a chill, and died.'

'Nothing so romantic. I questioned her servants closely, as you can imagine. They said she used to ride out in a certain direction every day, and linger on a hill-top, looking to the north, but that no-one ever came. They say she got wet that night by accident. She had not intended anything but wilfulness. She went out on the moat in a punt to gather water-irises. The gardener had said he would get her some on the morrow, but she wanted them there and then. At once. And so . . .' He spread his hands. 'She couldn't bear to be kept waiting for anything. She wanted me at first, and was all impatience till my looks were marred, and then she did not want me any more. She could not bear the sight of anyone ill, or deformed.'

'Perhaps she would have learned wisdom in time.'

'I think probably not. The nuns at the convent looked grave when they spoke of her to Aylmer, bidding him be very careful about choosing a husband for her. Aylmer thought I would be best for her. If it hadn't been for the accident . . . no, I must try to think clearly. If it had not been that accident, it would have been something else. The moment her will was crossed, she was unmanageable.'

'It was your ill fortune to love an unprincipled girl. If she had not died, you would have found her out, and ceased to love her.'

'She wanted an annulment. I refused. All these years I have thought I was right to refuse. But, perhaps . . . if I had let her go, she might not have died.'

'To misquote you, "If it hadn't been water-flags, it would have been a horse too spirited for her," or some other dangerous toy. You did not cause her death.'

'I am not so sure about that.'

'Be sure. And neither did Reynold. Presumably you have held it against him all these years. No wonder he is afraid of you.'

'Afraid of me? Reynold?'

'Perhaps he wasn't when you first came here. But he is now. That is why he drinks. He can't face you, and he can't face the duties you have laid upon him. And so I say, destroy him if you like, but remember that he is a much weaker man than you; it is easy to squash a fly under your heel, but difficult to raise a sinful man up from the dust. Or even to forgive him the wrong he has done you. Yet you can do it. You are a bigger man than he, in every way. You have power over him, in more ways than one. Use your power wisely.'

'Or? Is there a threat behind your advice?'

'No. No threat.'

'No warning, even?'

Sir Henry laughed. 'You have an over-tender conscience, young Benedict. I like that in you. But you must learn to look forward now, instead of grieving over the past.'

'I do. I have. My estates, my new house on the Downs . . . the mill I am building . . . I take great pleasure in all these things, I assure you.'

'And you had a great inheritance to look forward to, did you not? Are you not Aylmer's heir?'

'He said I was to be his heir, but of course when he marries Ursula . . . if he has children. . . .' He shook his head, as if to clear it. 'It is good that he should find happiness in a second marriage. He brought me up, you know. I have always thought of him as my father, for that is what he has been to me.'

'Perhaps that is as well,' said the old man, in a soft voice. Then, in his normal tone, 'Look how you gobbled up that bread! For all you know, it may be the last we have in the castle!'

'Then I will teach you to suck nectar from the honeysuckle, instead. Did you not know that you can take nectar from the trumpets of these flowers? That is, if the bees have not been there before you. Aylmer taught me that.' He got to his feet, rubbing his bad leg to ease it. 'Well, I must be about my business, I suppose. I'd best sober Reynold up, before I talk to him. When is high tide? I must be at the quayside by then.'

Ursula was expected to return that evening on the high tide.

Sir Henry also got to his feet and, equally openly, rubbed at the small of his back. He yawned. 'The sun has made me sleepy. I'll go take a rest. And Benedict—God go with you!'

'And with you.' Benedict put his hand on the old man's shoulder for a moment, then turned and limped away.

The old man looked after Benedict for a while. He said to himself. 'I wish you had indeed been Aylmer's son. The sooner you are married again, the better I'll be pleased.'

* * *

Benedict found Reynold splashing in a tub of cold and dirty water. The contents of a basin on the floor proved that Reynold had recently been sick. His squire lay on the trestle-bed, snoring. There was no other servant present.

'I know, I know,' said Reynold, hauling himself out of the tub and reaching for a towel which was already sodden. 'I'm leaving when the boats return to the abbey.'

He snatched up a soiled shirt and pulled it over his head.

'Why?' said Benedict. 'I haven't asked you to go. In fact . . .'

'I know you haven't. You've been very forbearing. I think that's the right word. Simon Joce used a harsher term. I'll give Aylmer all the news, when I see him. He'll understand. After all, it's not as if we ever get on well together, is it?'

He sought for hose and shoes, turned his

squire's inert body over, and finally located the things for which he was looking under the bed.

Benedict sat down on the big bed—which was unmade. He rubbed his head.

He said, 'Reynold, it is true that you and I have had our differences over the years, but . . .'

'Say no more. Just let me get out of here. You said you couldn't order me to withdraw. Well, I'm saving you the trouble.'

'What if I ask you to stay?'

'That's not likely.' He began to throw bedclothes about, looking for . . . ah, his belt.

Benedict studied Reynold. The man was sober enough now. He was neither sweating with fear, nor was he blustering as he had done recently. He was angry with himself. There was still plenty of energy in his movements. Yet there was a pickety, sparrow-boned look about him, which made Benedict think of what Sir Henry had just been saying . . . 'You are a bigger man than he is, in every way.'

'No need to look at me like that,' said Reynold, tying up his hose. 'I don't want your pity.'

'Pity?' Benedict shook his head. 'Reynold, sit down and listen to me.'

After a moment's hesitation Reynold cleared dirty clothing off a stool and sat.

Benedict said, 'Reynold, if you think you have been at fault in your dealings with me, then I must confess the same to you. I have not taken you into my confidence as we went along, as I ought to have done. Because I knew more of siege warfare than you, I thought it best to take the major decisions by myself, and leave you in charge of the area I thought best suited to your talents; that is, the gatehouse. Now in this I was wrong . . .'

Benedict was looking at Reynold, but the latter had turned his head away. His neck was red, though, so presumably he was listening.

'Yes, I see now that I was wrong,' said Benedict. 'You are a brave man, you have brains and energy, and you could have carried some of the burden for me, just as Aylmer planned that you should. I thought it would seem a waste of time to you, to construct jetties and build stone walls and dicker with fisherfolk. It is hard for a fighting man to stand by while clerks scratch their heads counting bags of flour and calculating tides. But at any moment now Hugo will strike. He will not just strike at the gatehouse, but also through a tunnel he is driving under the castle, and possibly also on the cliff-front as well. In two hours' time this peaceful scene may be turned to one of fiery chaos, with arrows impaling women or children, with men screaming and tumbling from the ramparts, with horrors such as you have never known in the tourney. Will you not stay to do your part?'

Reynold's head was still averted. He shrugged. 'Everyone knows that you want me out of the place.'

'They know more than I do, then. You are needed at the gatehouse now. At this very minute. Who will give the orders there, if I am on the quayside when Hugo's trebuchet throws its first stone?'

Benedict rubbed his leg, rose to his feet and picked up the steel-and-leather jerkin Reynold had been lent by Sir Henry. Without a word Reynold put it on. Benedict helped him with the buckles.

Reynold said, 'After all, we got on well enough when we were young.'

'Of course,' lied Benedict.

'I want you to know that I did not write to her, after. She wrote to me, but I did not reply. It didn't seem fair, somehow, when you were in France. And it never went further than a flirtation, you know.'

'I know,' said Benedict, forcing a smile.

'Yes, I've often thought of telling you that, about there being nothing in it, and that I didn't write to her. They said she was running away to meet me. That's not true. Is it?'

'No, you need not feel guilty about that. She wanted to gather some flowers at the edge of the moat. She fell in. And so . . . a chill.'

I'm glad about that. I mean . . .'

'Yes,' said Benedict, stony-faced. 'It does make it easier, doesn't it?'

'I've wanted to say I was sorry about . . . you know! But somehow the right time never . . .

you understand?'

'Of course!'

Reynold clasped Benedict around the shoulders with an abrupt movement, and as suddenly released him. Then he stalked out of the room.

There was a rustle and Barnabas rose from behind the bed.

'See if his hand-mirror's around, Barnabas.'

Barnabas handed his master the mirror. Benedict sighed.

'I could have sworn I'd have grey hairs by now . . .'

* * *

Ursula de Thrave lay curled up in the prow of the boat. Beneath her was the cargo that was to bring fresh hope to the besieged garrison. She lay on her back, looking up at the darkening sky and trying not to think. She was so tired that when she tried to make plans her mind went round and round . . . Benedict—Aylmer—Benedict—her grandfather—Benedict.

She had always liked to watch the great arc of sky above her, while she lay cradled in a boat. True, Dickon was not steering today. But Dickon was sitting with his dog beside the helmsman and theirs was the leading boat of the convoy of seven, so she was in safe hands.

She had volunteered to leave the castle in

search of food because she had felt it wisest to put some distance between her and Benedict. A few days away, concentrating on more important issues, would do her good. And they had indeed been a hard four days, bargaining, brow-beating, cajoling—she felt a dozen years older than when she had fled from Salwarpe the first time with her aunt by her side.

She touched the wallet at her belt. Inside lay letters from Aylmer and her aunt; letters addressed to her, to her grandfather and to Benedict. The one from Aylmer to her was particularly touching. He had written the first few words himself, but had been forced by pain to surrender the quill to a secretary, that it might be completed. He wrote that notwithstanding his injury—which was proving more tiresome than he had expected—the muster of weapons and men would take place on Michaelmas Day as planned. Salwarpe could look to be relieved either the following day at dusk, or at any rate within forty-eight hours thereafter.

There were other messages, too, in that letter from Aylmer, messages from a man very much in love with his promised wife. Ursula had found it difficult to write back in the same vein.

She could barely remember now what Aylmer looked like. He was a big man, she knew, and in every way worthy of her love. As for Benedict . . . she moved uneasily within the shelter of her cloak . . . well, she would have to be careful, that was all.

It was only natural that she should admire Benedict, at the moment. At such close quarters admiration might well breed something stronger, and when she saw him again—especially if she remembered to contrast his awkwardness with Reynold's grace—why, there was nothing to worry about! Nothing at all!

Her grandfather had known that she was in danger of losing her head over Benedict. He hadn't said anything. Much better not to put it into words, when a few days' absence and the exercise of common sense might serve to scotch this ill-timed fancy of hers.

I wish I were not going back to Salwarpe, she thought. No, I don't. I couldn't be happy anywhere else at the moment. But I won't be happy when I do get back, will I? Not if he's going to go on looking at me in that intense way. His eyes are strange, so beautiful . . . and his hands are beautiful, too . . . though I doubt he has ever thought of any part of himself as being beautiful, and would laugh if I said so.

I will laugh at him. Yes, I will. I will laugh and laugh, privately, just to myself. This folly of mine cannot withstand laughter. Every time he limps across my sight, I will say 'Hoppity-hop!' to myself, and laugh . . . so!

She gritted her teeth. 'I can do it,' she whispered. 'I can! I can!'

A hoarse cry from Dickon brought her to her knees. The sun was sinking behind the hill on which the castle stood. The battlements were black against the yellow sky, and over the rippling waters crept an evening mist.

A pinpoint of light showed at the foot of the cliff, which was otherwise featureless, deep in shadow. The light must have been a lanthorn at the foot of the cliff, showing where they must aim to take the boats in . . . and unload in the dark . . . it was going to be a terrible task, unloading the precious sacks of flour and humping them up the cliff, but she would think about how to do that when she got there.

Dickon was pointing to where a small brown fishing-boat was bearing down on them.

'Peasmarsh, come out to greet us! And since he's swept past that raft that's moored in the middle of the channel, it must be safe to go in.'

One of Ursula's problems had been to persuade the local fishermen that it would be safe to venture into waters patrolled by Hugo's men. She had had to offer extra money to persuade them to come this far and she knew they would turn tail and run for safety even now, if Hugo's men contested their passage.

Now John Peasmarsh was being hauled aboard and his boat pushing off once more. John looked thin and tired, but was smiling.

'Lady, you are more than welcome. I am told we eat the last of our own flour this evening. Tell your boatman to make straight for the light at the foot of the cliff, and we'll do the rest.'

Dickon's dog barked once, twice, and then growled.

'Ah, that'll be Hugo's boats,' said John, rubbing his hands and peering into the mist. 'One . . . yes, two of 'em, manned by fools as don't know nothing of our ways. Yes, lady: tell your helmsman to fear nothing. He's to go straight in.'

The owner of the boat was unhappy. 'I'm not a-taking my boat anywhere, if Hugo's men are out.'

'Don't fret about them none,' said John, his smile widening into a grin. 'They be taken care of. Dost think we been sitting on our hands this last week?' He chuckled. 'Na, Hugo doesn't get the better of us that easy.'

'I assure you it is quite safe,' said Ursula, hoping her voice would not betray her fear. With some reluctance the captain of the boat hailed the rest of the fleet and relayed John's orders.

Ursula pulled John down beside her. She did not want to broadcast any bad news he might have to give her, and there could hardly be any good news to tell . . . could there? 'Tell me, John. What news?'

John slapped his knee. 'The Lame One—there's a bit of Old Nicholas for ye! My gran swears he's the devil incarnate! Got me out of jail, and my dad with me. The old man will be out here soon, you'll see. A-raring to go is father, sharpening his knives and tightening his belt and swearing fit to bring the parson down on us! Hugo thinks we'm all dead and buried, ye see. Tell your helmsman to take the port side of the raft . . . that's it. No need to get too close, seeing as it's a trifle dangerous at the moment.

'Hola!' The shout echoed over the waters from Hugo's leading boat. 'Drop anchor, or we'll make you sorry for it!'

'Mercenaries!' John Peasmarsh spat over the side. 'Hugo's got a crowd of mercenaries there. Not so many of his own people with him, because of its being harvest time. So he hires these ruffians, who don't give a damn for God or Devil, and he brings them here with promises of plunder and I know not what. But I'll tell ye one thing—they know damn all about handling boats!'

As if to refute John's statement, Hugo's leading boat now shot forward and managed to manouevre itself between the first of the relief ships and the cliff face.

'We're going to board you!' cried the voice of authority from Hugo's boat. 'Stand by! We want to see what cargo you bring us!'

Ursula felt for her knife, but John cackled with mirth. He pointed towards the castle.

Two pale shapes had detached themselves from the foot of the cliff and were floating over the water towards them. Their flapping sails were white and so were the faces and forms of those who manned the boats . . . even the boats themselves showed white in the gloom.

''Tis the ghost-ships, surely!' shouted John. He nudged Dickon. 'Go on, man! Shout that 'tis the ghost ships coming to haunt Hugo and his men!'

'Ghost-ships!' screamed Ursula, understanding at last what was required of her. 'Help! They are come to drown us!'

Hugo's men ceased rowing, to crane round in their seats. Their sails flapped in the calm water at the base of the cliff. They began to take up the cry . . . 'But he's dead . . . And that one, too! And the boat—surely it is a ghost-ship!'

John seized the helmsman's arm. 'Straighten her up, man. Go on, keep well to port of the raft, and slip through that gap there . . . and then straight on to the light.'

'But the ghosts . . .' The man jibbered with fear.

'No ghosts, you fool! Only my father and some more of the Salwarpe fisherfolk, all pale with flour and whitewash. Only, ye see, Hugo and his men thought as us lot were all dead with the fever . . .' And he chuckled again.

Ursula looked. 'Will the others follow?' They seemed to her to be hanging back.

'They will in a minute . . .'

Hugo's leading boat was rocking as the crew

left their posts to look at the 'ghost-ships'. Some shouted that it was indeed a crew of ghosts, come to exact vengeance, and others shouted to their fellows not to be fools.

'Take it gently,' said John to the helmsman. 'Or let Dickon take over. We can slip quietly past those fools, while they're aruging amongst themselves.'

'Halt!' cried the voice of authority from Hugo's first boat . . . but even as he cried out the prow of Ursula's boat slid past him

'Dowse our lanthorn!' hissed John. 'And make for the signal lamp at the foot of the cliff.'

Dickon fell on the lanthorn and dowsed it. Their crew were open-mouthed, one or two were praying.

A streak of light came from nowhere and vanished.

Someone in Hugo's leading boat was shouting his men down, bidding them get back to their oars, ordering those who had weapons to make themselves ready.

'They've drifted nicely,' said John.

There was a terrifying blast of sound and air, which buffeted Ursula and rocked their boat.

And then . . .

'Fire!'

The shriek came from Hugo's second boat, which had drifted up against the harmless-seeming raft, anchored in mid-channel. The raft burst apart, scattering fiery embers, throwing them into the air . . . some of the embers fell harmlessly into the water, but the rest fell into the boats that Hugo's men manned.

'Hold her steady,' said John, as if he had noticed nothing unusual. 'And now, sharp to starboard.'

Screams came from the two enemy boats. Ursula looked back. The second boat in the convoy was following her in, and behind her the third . . . and yes, they were all coming in, now that they saw Hugo's men were otherwise occupied.

The 'ghost' ships were circling the burning boats, disposing of the men who floundered overboard. None would be left alive to tell the tale. Hugo would look for the return of his boats and their crews in vain.

'Look, mistress!'

Something was happening to the dark cliff face above her. A light was travelling down it in broad, sweeping zigzags. And as the light came down, it left duplicates of itself at every stage, revealing . . .

'There's a stairway up the cliff!'

'That's not all,' said John, with grim satisfaction. 'Look!'

Lights were now flickering along the base of the cliff, lighting up every detail of willow and scrub, and even . . . Glory be! Even out into the water!

A small but sturdy jetty had been built at the base of the cliff and even now men were running along it with more lighted torches, hands outstretched to catch the ropes which Dickon was ready to throw up.

Among these men moved a man in black and silver, a man at whose bidding chaos turned to order, a man who took her outstretched hands in his, and drew her up onto the jetty and safety.

And she looked into his eyes, and knew herself lost.

CHAPTER FIFTEEN

Hugo's men pulled and pushed a large trebuchet up from the town at dawn the following morning, and by noon the odd stone was being hurled up the slope towards the castle. None did any damage, for Hugo's men seemed to be having difficulty in adjusting their cumbersome machine to the correct range.

Benedict made his rounds. He paused to talk with Reynold for a few minutes, but did not go up onto the gatehouse as usual. Reynold was looking careworn. He had given up his room in the keep to the latest band of refugees that had been brought in from the town overnight, and was now sleeping in one of the gatehouse towers.

The castle was filling up. Benedict's stratagem was working better than he could ever have hoped. Not only did refugees leave the creek beyond the town by boat each night, but it was reported that many families living near the mill and on the arable lands had sought refuge in the forest, for fear of the contagion. Some of Hugo's men had also reported sick; it was not known whether this was as a result of their eating some contaminated fish, or to drinking water from the stream that rose in the dell. Either way, dysentery had struck Hugo's host, and this could only be good news for the garrison.

All this should have pleased Ursula, but she did not look happy when she sought out her grandfather in his chamber. There he sat, being pomaded and curled against what the day might bring.

'Grandfather, I must speak with you. I cannot get anyone to tell me what my duties are now to be. The townsfolk have organised themselves into groups, taking orders only from the Peasmarsh men. The womenfolk occupy themselves with the children and the cooking. There are seemingly no orders for me to give in the kitchens, since the women there tell me they know just what is to be done. They say I am to take a rest. But I cannot!'

She was close to tears. She did not want to cry. What was there to cry about? She said in a fierce voice, 'No-one seems to need me any more.'

'He finds it hard to delegate authority,' said Sir Henry, waving away his mirror with a satisfied nod. 'But he is learning. Yes, I will wear my armour today. Ursula, he said you were looking tired, and so you are. Why don't you take a rest? There will be plenty for you to do later, you know.'

'Why didn't he tell me himself?' She brushed something from her cheek—surely not a tear? 'He must realise I want to do everything possible for Salwarpe.'

'You have played your part for the moment, my dear. It would be as well now if you found something to do, out of his way.'

If she were wise, she would accept his advice, and say nothing more.

'Why?' she said. 'Why should I keep out of his way?'

'Because he is a very busy man,' said Sir Henry, holding himself rigid as he was laced into his corset. 'If you were to distract him . . .'

'You talk as if I were some foolish young girl, wanting him to flirt with me when he should be attending to his duties.'

'And are you not? Leave him alone, Ursula. You are strong. You will recover your equilibrium as soon as this is over. As for him, he has not yet realised that his feeling for you is any different from the love he bore Aylmer's first wife, Joan. It would be best, perhaps, if he did not make any discoveries in that direction. If he did, his love for Aylmer and his love for you might tear him apart.'

'So you think he does not love me? No, I dare say he does not. Why should he, indeed? Especially when I hardly see him Oh, I am being so wicked!' She hid her face in her hands. Then, when Sir Henry would have put his arms round her, she jumped to her feet and ran away.

* * *

Benedict was conferring with some workmen when Reynold came up, demanding speech in private with him. Reynold was wiping the back of his hand across his mouth. Benedict was about to put Reynold off, when he saw that his old rival was a bad colour.

'The t-trebuchet,' said Reynold, stammering. 'They got the range.'

'So? It was to be expected. Cheer up, man! The gatehouse walls cannot be breached in a day.'

'Not the gatehouse. They got the first outpost with one of their big stones. All the men were killed, or so badly injured that they could not even crawl back up the hill.'

Benedict grasped Reynold's shoulder and turned him away from the nearby workmen. 'You are not going to be sick. Do you hear? Breathe deeply. That's it. Turn to face the wall, and then walk towards it. Try to smile. Let no-one see that you are disturbed by this set-back.'

'Set-back?' Reynold wiped the back of his hand across his mouth again. 'I should have listened to you. You said . . .'

'That was in the past. On balance we decided—did we not?—that the outposts were a good thing. We knew men might be lost when they came under attack. We gambled. We lost. Have you withdrawn the other outpost?'

'Yes, I . . . straight away. You see, the trebuchet was out of bow-shot, so the archers could not even . . . they shot into the air, knowing they could not reach their target. And then . . . oh, God!'

'Very well. Did we lose anyone of importance?'

Reynold's mouth worked. He could not say the name, but his eyes implored Benedict's understanding. Benedict stiffened.

'Not Peter Bowman?' Reynold nodded. 'Dead, or just injured?'

'I don't know I didn't even know he'd gone down there, till it was all over. They were short of people, and Peter Bowman said he'd make up the number, if everyone else were afraid . . . but I don't know if he's dead or not.'

Benedict thought a while. 'Is the drawbridge now up, and the portcullis down?' Reynold nodded. 'So we can't sally forth to see if he's alive or dead.'

'I thought of that,' said Reynold, swallowing. 'My first thought was to go out myself, to see. But though I looked hard—and got other men with better sight to look—there was no movement from the cart. Only, we could hear someone crying. And then that stopped, too. Some of the men did say they would go and have a look, but in the end I said "No." I thought they might be killed as well. I thought . . . I gambled. It was probably the wrong decision to take.'

'No,' said Benedict. 'You were right. We can't afford to lose more good men, and it would only be good men who would volunteer to go out there, under the nose of the enemy. Well, it's done now. You will forget about Peter Bowman, Reynold. And that's an order. Now go back to your post, and see that your men are well fed at the next meal, but don't drink too much. And Reynold—don't expose yourself unnecessarily, on the ramparts.'

'No. I suppose you are right. Dickon brought me back my own armour. See? I thought he said he'd brought yours back as well? Didn't he?'

'I believe he did say something about it. I don't need it yet. Off with you.'

* * *

Twenty days, and the trebuchet had the range

of the left-hand gate-tower. Reynold ordered the mattress to be hung out over the wall, to lessen the impact of the boulders which were being hurled against it. Two elderly men and one child died of dysentery, which had been brought up into the castle with the refugees from the town.

Eighteen days. At dawn the boats came back from a trip to the town, so heavily laden that it was only by the grace of God and a calm sea that none had sunk. As the men, women and children wearily stumbled out onto the jetty and were helped up the stairs, Benedict looked in vain for one particular face. There could not be many people of importance now left in the town, and surely . . .

John Peasmarsh and his father were helping a gaunt creature to his feet. His arms were round their necks, for he could not walk unaided.

Merle.

Benedict could hardly believe that this shivering, rake-thin creature was the thick-set man he had left in the town, barely ten days earlier. There were tears in Benedict's eyes as he helped carry Merle along the jetty, and those tears did him no disservice, for many had accounted Merle as good as dead. The sick man was carried up the stairs in a litter and delivered into the hands of Ursula.

Seventeen days, and the boats went into the town at night, only to return almost empty.

The place was deserted, they said, except for Hugo's camp, the jail, and the houses in which he had billeted the miners. Cats and dogs still roamed the streets, but doors and shutters hung open, giving access to empty houses. The valuables and the food had been taken out either by the people who fled to the woods, or those who had withdrawn to the castle. The church bell had ceased to toll some days previously when the priest had been taken to the jail. The carpenter was nowhere to be seen; it was thought by some that he had fled to the woods, but others said he had been taken away by Hugo's men to help make siege machines.

Merle, when he could speak, told the same story of desertion. Salwarpe was become a ghost town. The only Salwarpe men still working were the few mining in Dead Man's Cave, and those who were sent out under guard to bring in the harvest. All these slept in houses commandeered by Hugo's men and had no contact with their families or other townsfolk. It was not known how many had died of dysentery in Hugo's camp, but under his orders a common grave had been dug, and corpses were thrown into it each morning.

Merle said that Mother Peasmarsh had been taken to the jail as hostage in Merle's place, when he had been judged too weak to survive. It had taken him the whole of one day to crawl through the deserted streets to the creek, where John had scooped him up and taken him off.

No, said Merle; Hugo did not suspect the trick which had been played on him, since so many of his own men had sickened and died of dysentery. The mercenaries had begun to talk of the siege as unlucky, but they had no intention of going home till they had sacked the castle. Hugo had said he would hang the Lord of Salwarpe over the walls of his own castle in an iron cage, till the birds had picked the flesh from his bones. And as for the Lady Ursula . . . but there Merle's voice broke and Ursula bade him rest.

*   *   *

Sixteen days. The range of Hugo's trebuchet was altered. It began to hurl boulders higher, over the gate-tower and into the grounds of the castle.

'Waste of boulders,' said Benedict, getting workmen to cordon off a space where it was not safe to walk. 'But we'll use them ourselves, perhaps. I have an idea . . . it will break Hugo's heart!'

The workmen laughed. They were delighted at the thought of breaking Hugo's heart, and they didn't mind how hard the work, or how dirty, that Benedict might set for them to do, provided only that they might make Hugo pay for turning them out of their homes.

Benedict went to Sir Henry, whom he found

sitting under the honeysuckle. The blossoms were now past their best, but the garden was still the quietest spot in the castle.

'Sir Henry, Hugo is throwing stones over the castle wall near the gatehouse. I told the men it was a waste of boulders, but of course it wasn't.'

'No, my boy? Tell me what it means.'

'I think, although I cannot be sure . . . it might mean he wants to keep us away from that section of the wall.'

'He can't be mining below the gatehouse as well.'

'No. I was thinking . . . a surprise attack at night . . . ladders thrown against the wall by the gatehouse . . . at a spot previously cleared of men by stones thrown seemingly too high to do any good. Do you think I can be right?'

Sir Henry patted his back hair into place. 'My dear boy! Action at last! Tonight or tomorrow night, do you think?'

'I have no idea. I might be quite wrong, of course. But I think we must divide our fighting men into three companies, and have one on watch all the time, another sleeping, and another standing by. And the watch on the walls must be doubled at night.'

Nothing happened that night.

When Benedict passed through the infirmary on his rounds next morning, he looked about him in such a distracted manner that Ursula left her charges to follow him. He made his way to the garden, but Sir Henry was not there.

He paused, biting his lip.

Ursula put her hand on his arm and spoke his name. He started.

'Forgive me, lady. I did not hear you. I was looking for your grandfather.'

'You are worried about something? Tell me.'

'It is nothing. At least . . . you do realise, don't you, that I have never actually commanded a garrison during a siege before? Suppose I have done it all wrong? Suppose . . .' He threw his arms wide. 'Suppose I fail?'

'Then I take it that we all die. What do you think you have done wrong?'

'I am not sure. I can't think of anything, but from now on, if I have forgotten anything, it will be too late to make amends.'

'Hush.' She held out her hands. 'Hush, now.' He put his hands in hers.

'You are quite safe,' she said. 'I have you fast.'

They stood there holding hands and looking into each other's eyes, till a bird came fluttering down to perch on the bench. The bees filled the air with their heavy drone and still they did not move. His eyes flickered silver and grey. She began to smile.

Then there came a sudden clamour; it was not close by, but came from the gate-tower.

She caught her breath. He withdrew his

hands.

'They have set their ladders against the wall at last,' said Benedict. 'Poor fools! Little do they know that we've been waiting for them.'

Then, without any sign of the panic which had lately afflicted him, he went out of the garden and back to his duties.

* * *

With grappling-irons and pikes, with long poles and with boulders tumbled from above, the scaling ladders were displaced or knocked over, carrying their burdens of soldiery with them. And still the ladders were put up, and still Hugo's men came on. Benedict directed the defence for a while and then, when he thought Reynold had mastered the trick of it, left his second-in-command and hastened down to the cellars below the keep.

Not before time.

Hugo's picks had ceased a short while before, and Simon Joce was looking anxious as he went down on his belly to peer through the grating into the sewer below. Benedict wriggled into place beside Simon and took his turn at listening and looking. Then both men withdrew, taking care to make no noise that might betray their presence to the miners below.

They climbed back into the next cellar and bolted and barred the door before signing for the lanthorn to be opened. A dozen men had been stationed there, with knives and drawn swords.

'All is well,' said Benedict, speaking in a hushed voice. 'They have broken through the fault into the sewer, and are clearing the debris. They have no idea that they can be seen and heard from above. They have lanthorns and are moving about freely. They have discovered the barrier that we made with boulders, blocking the outlet to the dell, and they think it is a natural rock-fall, just as we planned that they should. Their leader was shouting back down the tunnel, telling someone to hurry up the men-at-arms.'

'Are any of the Salwarpe men down in the tunnel?'

'Yes,' said Benedict. 'There are men there who are stripped to the waist, and who are doing all the hard work, clearing and enlarging the way into the sewer from the tunnel. They must be Salwarpe men.'

There was a strained silence. Someone muttered that it was hard, surely, to fight your own kin.

'That is why we are waiting,' said Benedict. 'I am hoping that Hugo will send all his slave labour back down the tunnel before he gives the signal for the mercenaries to attack us from inside. I am hoping he will think the Salwarpe men might give the alarm, if they were allowed to stay in the sewer.'

'And if he doesn't?'

'Then we must go ahead with our plan,' said Benedict, in a firm voice. 'Better that a few of the Salwarpe men should die, than that the castle should fall. Simon, set up a candle, marked with the hours. We will give them one hour to clear the debris and send the slaves back. But if they strike before that time, then . . .' He shrugged.

Simon nodded, and so did most of the others.

Fifteen minutes . . . half an hour . . . men were set to report progress, sitting in darkness above the grating. Now and then a man would slip down to take his fellow's place, and word would be carried back up to Benedict and Simon, waiting above.

'They are trying to shift the boulders between them and the dell . . . they say they will bring more men up shortly . . .'

'They have found the timbers we have built up into a wall at this end, to contain the sewage! They discussed the timbers amongst themselves, and said the structure must be very old . . . it was lucky we used the weathered timbers from the stabling, or they might have guessed . . .'

'The Salwarpe men have been sent back!'

'Hasten!' whispered another man, beckoning from the doorway. 'They are filing into the sewer now . . . twenty of them, maybe more . . . all armed, wearing helmets and carrying swords!'

'Let us go!' said Benedict. The lanthorns were shuttered once more and a long file of Salwarpe men groped their way after Benedict and Simon down into the lower cellar, to wait above the grating. Benedict and Simon took long, well-honed knives and wriggled into position. Far above them another assault was being mounted on the walls. Benedict sent up a grim prayer for the defenders and then put his face to the grating.

Someone down in the sewer was hushing his men, bidding them creep forward with care, less they alarm the unsuspecting garrison.

Benedict was momentarily blinded by a flash of light. The captain below was playing his lanthorn up at the roof above the timber dam. Then the light passed on . . . the man had not spotted the two faces peering down on him through the grating above. But the lanthorn was now illumining the cellar through the grating.

Benedict turned his head to meet Simon's grin. Simon raised his eyebrows. Benedict nodded. The two men put their right hands and forearms through the grating and began to saw at a rope. The rope was taut, for it held back the crude wooden damn which Benedict had caused to be built across the sewer, beneath the grating. The damn was holding back many gallons of sewage, which had built up over the last few days till it now ran some foot or so only below the roof of the sewer. Here and there it trickled through the baulks of timber to run away down hill. The stink was overpowering, but it was worth a little discomfort to take the smile off Hugo's face.

A scrabbling sound, and a helmeted head appeared in silhouette over the top of the timber baulk . . . and another . . .

'Christ's sake!' gasped the first man, on seeing the pool of sewage before him. 'We can't get through this!'

'Let me see!' said an authoritative voice. There was more scrabbling, and a third head appeared above the baulks of timber. Simon and Benedict sawed on their ropes.

Then Simon's rope parted, and so did Benedict's. The plank and timber damn shuddered and groaned. The men-at-arms below cried out, not understanding at first the full horror of the fate that was about to overtake them, but uneasy because the dam was wavering above them.

And then the weight of the sewage was added to the weight of the men who had been climbing on the timber, and the whole structure gave way with a screech. The heavy timbers overwhelmed the men who stood closest to the dam, while tons of sewage fell solidly on those who stood behind. Timbers and sewage alike pushed along the tunnel until they met the rock barrier which Benedict had caused to be created blocking the outlet to the dell. And then the whole lot washed back, knocking over any one who had managed to get to his feet . . . and finding no outlet but this, poured into the newly-made tunnel, carrying bodies, timber and planking with it.

The screams of the mercenaries were stifled. They floundered and drowned, trapped with broken limbs, their lanthorns extinguished.

Simon and Benedict knelt above the grating, appalled at the horror they had unleashed. Finally all was silent. The sewage had found a new channel and, instead of going out to the dell, now ran down hill through the mine and thence into Dead Man's Cave. Dead men were once more to be taken out of the cave, and in such a horrific state were these corpses that the place was avoided for years after.

All was quiet, save for the occasional sucking and tumbling of a plank or a piece of timber resettling itself.

Benedict peered down. Still he could hear nothing moving below. He motioned for a lanthorn to be opened and brought forward. He hooked it onto the grille and looked down again. Sewage glistened on the walls. Bodies and timber alike were unrecognisable beneath the sludge.

Simon Joce was staring as if he couldn't believe his eyes.

Benedict wriggled back into the cellar and stood. Simon followed him. Both men did some breathing exercises.

‘Do we go in and finish them off?’ said one of Simon’s men.

‘I doubt there’s any need,’ said Benedict. ‘But yes. Of course someone must go down there to make sure.’

* * *

Fourteen days. Three separate waves of ladder attacks had been mounted against the wall by the gatehouse and been beaten off. Reynold was looking fine-drawn and had become sparing of speech.

The last of the mattresses which had been taking the impact of the stones thrown by the trebuchet burst. A fire-arrow set it alight, and then . . .

‘Do we make more?’ said Reynold.

‘Yes,’ said Benedict. ‘But it means slaughtering some more horses. Ask Sir Henry which ones.’

‘And what happens then?’ said Reynold. He cleared his throat. ‘The first mattress lasted three days, but the other two . . .’

‘Yes, the first was well made, when we had plenty of time to do it. Also, the trebuchet did not have our range properly. The others did not last so long, but that was only to be expected. Oh, I know what you wish to say. Although we have an almost unlimited supply of rushes—so long as the channel is kept clear—yet our supply of horses is beginning to fail us, and some damage is still being done to the walls. I know. But keep on with the work, Reynold. Time is on our side. And I think it best that you and Simon rest, one off and one on.'

* * *

That night a great tree-trunk shod with an iron point was brought up from the town and began to pick away at the weakened gatehouse wall. The ram was mounted on a cart, driven backwards and forwards by dozens of sweating men under the direction of an overseer with a whip. The men themselves were protected by a well-built timber roof, attached to the cart on which the ram was mounted. This timber roof was covered with hides and therefore the archers shot at it in vain.

Now Benedict woke not only to the sound of the trebuchet at work—for this had transferred its attentions to another section of wall near the gatehouse—but also to the boom of the ram. Now the garrison began to collect in knots, not to talk, but because being in groups comforted them in their fear. All looked in the same direction, towards the gatehouse.

Now Hugo began to toss the decaying corpses of the archers who had been killed at the first outpost into the castle, by means of the trebuchet. A grown man's nerves will break when the head of an old friend is suddenly tossed onto the sward at his feet. Peter Bowman's head had been horribly crushed by the time it was given burial within the castle walls.

*   *   *

Thirteen days. That night Benedict went out in the boats with the Peasmarsh men and landed in a deserted town. There were no soldiers lodged in the quayside buildings, nor anyone to patrol the streets. Guided by Barnabas, Benedict reconnoitred the market-square, which was deserted, save where a heavy guard still watched over the jail. There were also guards over the two houses near the entrance to Dead Man's Cave, and a strong contingent around the church and the houses nearby, which were all well inland. Hugo's watch-fires were counted and his soldierly precautions against surprise attack observed.

'The man knows what he is at,' said Benedict. 'And he's got himself another smith from somewhere. All the same . . .'

Later that morning Benedict called a conference in Sir Henry's chamber.

Reynold could not sit still, but wandered around near the window, from which he could catch a glimpse of the gatehouse. Hugo's latest ploy had been to take knots of pine dipped in pitch, set them alight and catapult them into the castle. No doubt he hoped to set alight some of the timber and thatch structures which had been used to stand there. Of course, these had long since been pulled down on Benedict's instructions, and therefore the flaming torches could do no harm, unless they actually hit some unsuspecting man or woman passing below.

'What can we do?' said Reynold, trying not to let hysteria show in his voice. 'They are rapidly gaining the upper hand, are they not?'

'Why,' said Benedict. 'There are still many things that we can do. We can try throwing heavy boulders and cauldrons of burning pitch onto the leather shield that covers the ram. I thought we might have enough long timbers left to knock the pick out of the way, or hook the end up . . . but we haven't much left in the way of serviceable wood, and we're also short of ropes. We might be able to get some more from the town.'

'Short-term measures,' said Reynold. 'They'll be through into the outer gatehouse within twenty-four hours, I think.'

'I believe they will,' said Sir Henry. 'Benedict, what are we to do now?'

CHAPTER SIXTEEN

'That's all right,' said Benedict. 'Let them get in. They'll leave the ram outside, and rush in.

We'll set bars of iron in sockets across the only door out of the tower, the one that leads into the drawbridge pit. The only way they can go, once they break into the tower, is up the stairs. And there they'll meet the stone walls we've built, denying access to the ramparts. And at that point they're vulnerable, because they haven't got their leather shield over them.'

'But how can we fire at them there? The ramparts are on the same level all round.'

'We go one higher. I've had some stages of wood built, which can be erected on the battlements on either side of the gatehouse towers. From these vantage-points our archers can pick off anyone who appears on the roof of the gatehouse.'

Everyone relaxed.

'And then,' said Benedict, 'they'll remember that the gatehouse controls the portcullis, and they'll wind that up. Then they'll work out how to fill in the pit between them and the inner gatehouse—they may have timbers ready to throw in, even now. I mean, I would have prepared for it, if I were Hugo. Then, when they've filled in the pit, they'll push the ram under the portcullis and into the area between the two gatehouses, and they'll start on the inner wall. Reynold, we'll need more mattresses at that point. Then they'll break into the inner gatehouse, and once in there, they can lower the drawbridge . . .'

'God in heaven!' cried Reynold, looking

haggard. 'Can we not stop him, whatever we do?'

'Yes and no,' said Benedict, keeping calm. 'I don't think we can stop him breaking through the gatehouse if he has enough men to spare of sufficient calibre, and I think we can take it that he has. Whatever inroads the dysentery has made on his men, their morale is still high, and they are still a formidable army.'

Sir Henry said, 'Aylmer cannot possibly be here for another twelve days at the earliest. We have food enough to last. Our hearts are stout enough. Are you telling me that we cannot hold this place until Aylmer comes?'

Benedict rubbed the back of his neck. 'Oh, I think we can manage it without Aylmer's help. Yes, I really think we ought to be able to do so. Of course, there will be casualties. I can't guarantee that we won't lose some men . . . but, on the other hand, we'd lose many more if we get hand-to-hand fighting at the gatehouse.'

Ursula said, 'I will lead one party.'

Benedict blinked. Then he smiled. 'No, no. We will have volunteers enough without that. Sir Henry, will your men fight?'

'You must ask them, my friend,' said Sir Henry. 'Simon Joce, have all the able-bodied men in the castle who are not on watch, drawn up before the mounting block in an hour's time. And send the Peasmarsh men to me.'

* * *

Before the appointed hour, Hugo's men had brought up a second and much larger trebuchet and begun to throw boulders into the well between the two gatehouses. Before long this second trebuchet would have the range of the inner tower.

Benedict inspected the crumbling defences with Reynold before hurtling down the stairs onto the greensward, where the garrison awaited him. Not only the men from the town had come, but also most of the women, some of them nursing babies. Also a considerable number of older children. All looked towards the gatehouse and murmured when yet another boulder crashed into their defences.

Sir Henry stood on the mounting-block from which he had been accustomed to slide into the saddle of his war-horse in happier days. His figure was held upright in its corset, his yellow curls held firm in spite of the breeze, and his voice reached the farthest member of the crowd before him.

He explained their position simply. He reminded them of what they had suffered at Hugo's hands. He spoke with sorrow of Peter Bowman's death and of those who had been ill-treated in the jail. He asked them to consider what would have happened to them—short of food as they had been, and at the mercy of the mercenaries—if they had been left to rot in the town below. He spoke at some length of Benedict's foresight and skill as a leader. He said that Benedict had devised a plan whereby they—the people most wronged by Hugo—might strike a blow on their own account.

Then he turned to Benedict, who was showing signs of embarrassment at being praised before so many people, and beckoned him to come forward.

'Listen to him,' Sir Henry said to his people. 'As I do. Follow him as I do. And be sure we will prevail!'

He was cheered as he stepped down from the block, helped by Benedict and Ursula. Then Benedict leaped up into Sir Henry's place and told the crowd what he intended to do. Were they with him?

'Yes!' Lead on, we are with you!'

'Will you take up what arms you can find, and follow me?'

A cheer followed, and then another.

'Us, too!' cried one of the women, elbowing her way forward. 'We can fight, too!'

'I know you can,' said Benedict. 'Yes, band yourselves together, and send your leaders to join the conference we will hold at dusk tonight. Eat well, my friends. Sleep well. For we strike at dawn tomorrow!'

Their elation was soon stilled. There was a scream and a crash from behind them. They all turned to the gatehouse. Two sentries came running towards them, their mouths agape.

'More scaling ladders are being brought up . . . and they are nearly through into the gatehouse . . . May the Lord have mercy on us!'

* * *

Once more the garrison battled to break down or topple the ladders which had been set up against their walls. Once more Reynold directed his men to fire down at the unyielding leather roof of the ram. Once more Sir Henry found work for his sword to do, and at his side fought a man without armour, wielding a double-headed axe.

The assault was almost continuous for an hour. Twice during that time Hugo's men managed to leap over the battlements and turned on the defenders from behind. Sir Henry's lungs began to give out, and his legs to waver.

Three mercenaries closed in on him. He was surrounded. He was beaten to the ground.

Then Benedict hurled one man aside and stood over Sir Henry, swinging his axe with both hands. A man with a sword in one hand and a dagger in the other feinted at Benedict's head, and stepped aside as his companion lunged with a pike. Benedict lunged forward to deal one mercenary a crushing blow, but was himself caught off balance by the other. He side-stepped, staggering backwards. But, as he fell, he rolled to cover Sir Henry's body with his own.

And then a snake-like figure wormed its way up from the ground and the man whose sword had been raised to give the coup de grâce howled and hopped away, hamstrung by Barnabas's knife . . . and a tall man in full armour caught the second mercenary up and threw him over the wall.

'My thanks,' gasped Benedict, as Reynold pulled him to his feet. He tried to smile, but pain pulled his mouth awry. 'Sir Henry . . .?'

'Just . . . winded . . .' said Sir Henry, sitting up and reaching for the sword he had dropped.

'Blood!' said Barnabas. 'Master!' It was a cry of terror. He was pointing to Benedict's arm.

'Get out of here, you fool!' said Reynold. 'Don't you know better than to come up here without armour on?'

'Just what I said!' croaked Sir Henry, staggering to his feet and checking that his limbs still functioned. 'Leave this work to those who understand it. And that's an order, Benedict!'

Benedict leaned against the wall, his head bowed. He had dropped his axe.

Reynold peered over the battlements. 'That's the last of them for the moment, anyway. Better see to that wound at once, Benedict!' He hurried away.

Barnabas was making darting movements at Benedict, but not touching him. It seemed the lad wanted to help, but did not know how.

'All right . . . in a moment,' said Benedict.

'No, you're not,' said Sir Henry. 'Get down those stairs and have that wound attended to, before you meet our men at dusk. Don't want anyone saying you're out of the fighting with a serious injury. Take him away, men!'

A dozen men had run up to enquire if Benedict were hurt. He waved them away.

'A short rest. A graze, that's all.' He held his left upper arm with his right hand, to stop the blood welling out. He could walk alone, if he put his mind to it. Ah! He bit his lip to hold back a cry of pain.

Two men closed in, one on either side of him. They were big men, tall, fair-haired and strong. They linked arms, stooped and picked Benedict up as if he were a babe.

'His bad leg, doubtless,' said one. 'Tell no-one he's hurt, or we'll have the women wailing.'

'Tell them it's a graze and a twisted knee,' said the other. 'Someone's bound to see him being carried across the garth.'

'Where's the Lady?'

'Dressing wounds in the garden. Take Old Limpy there. He won't make any more stairs as he is now.'

'I am quite . . . all . . . right,' said Benedict, but was grateful that they heeded his words as little as the flies that buzzed about his ears. Or perhaps it wasn't flies, buzzing in his ears, but . . .'

'Hold hard, my lord!' said one of his escorts. 'You'll not faint in public. Or we'll have everyone throwing down their arms, and surrendering to Hugo.'

'Idiots!' said Benedict, which seemed to reassure them, for they grinned and continued to trot across the turf, bumping him along between them as if he were a sack of grain. But he was near enough passing out, all the same . . .

A cry of alarm.

He knew that voice. He was being laid flat. The sudden change from the vertical to the horizontal made him giddy. For a moment he closed his eyes.

Someone was putting something cold on his face. Something wet. He winced and tried to raise himself. Someone pushed him back again. Someone else was cutting away the sleeve of his tunic and orders were being ripped out by a hard-voiced creature above his head.

'No, leave him here. Get a tarpaulin, a tent . . . anything to keep the sun off his head. And bring down a bed of some description. We can't leave him on this bench. No, not like that, you fool! Cut it off with his knife: And send for Parkyn! No, Barnabas, you are being too gentle. Do it quickly—before he faints again. Did you ever see such a fool, to go out . . . Not even a helmet! I could box his ears!'

The voice was hard, but the hands were gentle, first bathing his face, and then bathing and binding up his arm.

''Tis his bad leg, surely,' said someone. 'He covered Sir Henry with his own body . . . right in the corner . . . with four men rushing at him with their swords and pikes . . . no, five men! But he never hesitated! Against the wall, twisting as he fell, Lady. He saved Sir Henry's life, for sure!'

'Out of my light, you numbskulls!' shrieked Ursula. 'Off with you! Have you nothing better to do . . .? That's right, the bed here . . . and the tarpaulin you can hook on there and there . . . and take the rest of the wounded into the Hall for the other women to deal with. Off, I say! No, not you, Barnabas. Nor you, Parkyn. That's right, lift him gently . . . yes, he probably will faint again, but . . .'

The voice receded. Then it came back.

'No, of course he's not going to die. He will be perfectly all right when he has had a rest and something to eat and drink.'

The pain had moved . . . was moving . . now in his arm and now in his leg. He made an experiment. He opened his eyes and lifted his head. The tarpaulin swung off into darkness about him.

'Oh, you fool!' Ursula pushed him back and he was only too thankful to close his eyes and rest again. Then he felt her hands about his knee, and stiffened.

'I could kill you for being so stupid!' said Ursula. Her voice sounded strange, as if she had something in her mouth.

He tried opening his eyes once more, but a sudden twist on his leg brought him such pain that he almost passed out again. He gritted his teeth. Ursula was calling to Parkyn to hurry with the cold water, and she was bathing his knee . . . the water was so cold that he drew in his breath . . . the pain was overwhelming . . . and then there was cold water on his brow, too . . . stinging cold. And after a few minutes he felt as if he could bear the pain without screaming, and opened his eyes again.

'You . . . idiot!' said Ursula. She was weeping. There were tears on her cheeks. They dripped off her chin onto his tunic. 'Worse than a small child!' She changed the cloth on his forehead for another, colder one. 'You are certainly more trouble than a child, going out there without any armour! Did you want to get yourself killed?'

He could only stare at her in wonder.

She seemed unaware of her tears. She poured some vinegar on a cloth and bathed the side of his face, where it was red-hot. 'All scratched and grazed, and in such a mess! You never did see the like! And entirely your own fault!'

He thought, 'Idonia never cried for me . . .'

She threw down her cloth and wiped her face with the back of her hand, sniffing. 'As if I haven't enough to do, without your getting into trouble and worrying the life out of me!'

He thought, 'She didn't cry for Aylmer . . .'

'I have a dozen men more seriously injured than you,' she said. 'I certainly can't sit here all day, bathing your brow. Barnabas and Parkyn will have to keep those cloths about your head and knee cold. You'll be perfectly all right, if you will only rest a while. And I will set sentries outside to see that you are not disturbed. Do you understand?'

He tried to say 'Yes'. She put her fingers over his mouth and then, with a swirl of her gown, she was gone. He closed his eyes and drifted into a doze. He was in a grey mist, half asleep, and half in too much pain to sleep. He knew the doze would lead to sleep if his knee were only slightly sprained, but he also knew that it would lead to a greater awareness of pain if he had done any real damage.

And eventually he did sleep and was only awakened when the flapping of the tarpaulin announced her return. Behind her came Barnabas bearing wine and some freshly broiled fish. Parkyn, who had been watching beside his master's bed, rose to report that Benedict had slept a little and that the swelling of his knee seemed somewhat reduced.

Benedict didn't open his eyes properly. In fact, one eye wasn't prepared to open to its full extent anyway. Ursula didn't scold him this time. She bathed his face and swollen eyelids without words. She inspected the bandage on his arm and gave a little nod of satisfaction. The bleeding had stopped.

Only then did she lift the cloths to look at his bare leg. It was purple from bruising and the cold of the water that had been on it. Benedict wondered how she could bear to look at it, so ugly and misshapen was it.

She touched his knee with her fingertips, so lightly that he barely felt them. She put her head on one side, considering both the area where the bone had been broken and badly set, and the newly-sprained knee.

She said, 'I suppose you thought to go down through the drain to attack Hugo. I don't think you'll make it. You'd best go with the boats, and have the men carry you up through the town. They'll do it, for you.'

'Going into battle in a chair?' He was surprised that he could speak, and even attempt a laugh; but it seemed that he could, even though his voice sounded strange in his ears.

She held a cup of wine to his mouth and helped him eat and drink. He felt better then, though still disinclined to move.

He said, 'If I could send Reynold down through the drain, I would. But he's never been in the town. He doesn't know what to expect. I shall have to go myself. I can walk with a crutch, I expect. Will you find one for me? I walked with a crutch before, for months. I can do it.'

'I have a better idea,' she said. 'You shall lead your men on horseback. Don't look so surprised. Have you never heard of horses being transported in boats before? It can be done, I assure you. We have boats in plenty now, thanks to you.' She looked out of the improvised tent, up into the darkening sky.

She said, 'It is almost dusk. I did not realise it was so late.' For the first time she looked worried. 'They will be waiting for you. If you don't go, they will think the worst. As it is, there are so many rumours running about the castle about your having killed a dozen men, defending grandfather, and about your being severely wounded . . . I cannot move about the place without people clutching at me, asking what is become of you. You ought to rest, I know. Perhaps I could bring the leaders of each group here to you . . .'

'No, I must go to them. Somehow.'

'I'll get them to carry you.'

'No, I must walk—or hobble along by myself. They must see that I am all right.'

'Well, I know you are not all right, but perhaps . . . if you can do it, it would be a good thing. The gatehouse . . .' She caught herself up, annoyed at having let the word escape her.

'They have not broken through, have they?' He found the strength from somewhere to sit up. He turned his head, listening. Surely the noises of the trebuchet and the ram had redoubled!

'They are through into the pit,' said Ursula, in matter-of-fact tones. 'They got the portcullis up, and they had timbers with them, to throw down into the pit. As you said they would. The ram is attacking the inner gatehouse now, but it cannot get through tonight. I am sure it cannot.'

Fear got him to his feet. To one foot. The air went black about him and then resumed its normal hue. He was not going to faint again. Parkyn propped him up on one side, Ursula steadied him on the other. And here came Barnabas, running up with a crutch.

Benedict fitted the crutch under his arm and tried it out. Hoppity-hop. Idonia had laughed herself silly, hands pressed to mouth, to see him hop around like this. Ursula didn't laugh. She held her hand near his elbow, frowning, ready to leap to his side if he toppled over.

'Yes,' he said. 'I can do it.'

* * *

The night seemed endless. He slept lightly, waking now and then to listen. He was afraid that Hugo might continue to operate the pick through the night hours. The man must have known that he was almost through . . .'

But the pounding had stopped, and there

were no night alarms.

Each time he woke he propped himself on one elbow to see how far the marked candle had burned down. He had to be up and dressed and down on the jetty long before dawn. Barnabas and Parkyn slept at the foot of his bed, curled up in their cloaks. Barnabas shivered and moaned in his sleep, perhaps reliving the moment when he had darted in with his knife to save Benedict's life . . . perhaps remembering the old days when he had been a ragged outcast, to be kicked by all and sundry . . .

Parkyn dragged himself up from the ground every now and then, to change the cloths on Benedict's leg. His movements were slow, his eyes gummed up with sleep, but he did his work efficiently.

I am indeed well served, thought Benedict. Of a certainty he would buy both men from Sir Henry, and set them free . . . if they came through this alive.

Once she came. He opened his eyes on hearing the brush of her dress against the foot of his bed. She had thrown a cloak over her gown and carried a dark lanthorn.

When she saw he was awake, she stood still, saying nothing, not even smiling. He was only half awake. None of his injuries were so bad at that moment that they screamed for attention. So he continued to lie there, looking up at her . . . and she to stand, looking down on him . . .

The next time he opened his eyes she was gone. She had moved the crutch away from his bed, perhaps to ensure that he did not try to rise unaided. It was a good crutch, stoutly made, and of the right height for him. No-one had laughed as he'd made his halting way to the mounting-block at dusk, though it seemed as if almost every inhabitant of the castle had come to see for himself that he could still lead them into battle.

There had been smiles here and there, but they had been smiles of welcome, and of relief; the smiles of friends. Benedict had barely had time to note their forbearance before his mind had turned to the problem of the moment.

He lay in bed and went over his plans once more in his mind; then he slept again.

* * *

He woke, and jerked to his elbow. Then he swore, for he had jarred his wounded arm. The candle had burned low, but it was not yet time to rise. Neither Parkyn nor Barnabas had woken this time. The tarpaulin stirred, and she came in, with her lanthorn. Had she not slept at all? She had not taken off her clothes, nor freed her plait from its silken sheath. Around her head the honey-coloured hair was roughened into a nimbus.

Once more she stood looking down at him. He had the oddest feeling that time had moved backward, and that it was still midnight, when she had stood looking down on him before. Only now she moved to put down her lanthorn and to bathe his face. He tried not to wince. His eye was almost closed, still.

He turned his head to look at the candle and she slipped her arm under his shoulders, to help him lie more easily. Now he could look at it without propping himself on one elbow. Her arm stayed around him. She sat on the side of the bed.

Surely she would move away in a minute. But she didn't. How it came about, he was not quite sure, but one moment there was only her arm beneath his shoulders, and the next his head was resting on her shoulder. Presumably she didn't object to this proximity, because she was holding the cold cloth to his face with her free hand . . and now she was drawing the covers higher over them both.

He thought, I must be still asleep and dreaming. Then he thought, I can't go to sleep now.

He stopped thinking. It was enough, just to exist.

Now and then he flicked a glance at the candle. Surely never did candle burn down so fast! Now and then she dipped her cloth into a bowl of cold water, to lay it against his eye.

As the minutes passed, he felt the pace of her breathing quicken. And so did his, too. He moved his head. He wanted to see her face.

It was pity, surely, that caused her to hold him like that! He struggled to sit upright. She dropped her cloth into the basin and stood, turning away from him.

'Is it time?' she asked.

'Not yet. Ursula . . .'

But their voices had roused Parkyn. Parkyn roused Barnabas, and sleepily pulled at his tunic, to make it lie straight. Ursula was looking at the candle, her hands twisting and turning.

Then she threw back her head. 'I forgot to ask about your knee.'

'It is well enough,' he said. 'I can get to the foot of the steps, anyway.'

His knee protested at every movement, but the protests were less urgent than they had been. Much of the swelling had disappeared. Parkyn was bringing up a razor and towels. He was yawning, but his eyes were properly open at last. Barnabas was floundering about, cursing under his breath.

'It is still quite dark,' said Ursula. 'I will go to see that grandfather is awake, and then I will meet you on the ramparts, to ensure that you are properly armed this time.'

CHAPTER SEVENTEEN

Everyone had to be in their place, an hour before dawn. At dawn Hugo's men would be roused in their camp, and come up the hill to start swinging the ram at the battered inner gate once more. At his current rate of progress, he would be inside the castle before noon, for the inner gate-towers had not been built as stoutly as their companions.

Sir Henry was to stay in the castle with Simon Joce, to defend the gate-tower as best he might.

Reynold was to lead the party which was to go down the sewer. No-one had been more surprised than Benedict when Reynold had volunteered for the task. Originally Benedict had intended to go that way himself, but his knee injury had put paid to the idea.

Reynold was to be guided by Merle. Once in the dell, Reynold and his party were to await a signal from Benedict, and then they were to release the men imprisoned in the two houses near Dead Man's Cave, thus swelling their ranks with some twenty or so more Salwarpe men. Six of Reynold's men were then to go to the jail and release the hostages there, while the rest made their way with all speed up the road and fell on Hugo and the men with the ram.

Benedict and his party would have the farthest to go and would therefore start first. He was going in the boats with Dickon and the Peasmarsh folk, together with all the fishermen who could be armed. They would sail or row round to the quay—depending on the wind—and there disembark. Dickon and a picked handful of fishermen would then take the boats back to the castle to fetch the next contingent—that of the womenfolk. These latter were also armed, though with a strange assortment of weapons. The women had been given the task of going through the houses one by one after Benedict had passed through the town, to seek out and deal with any mercenaries who might yet linger there. Much against her will, Ursula was to stay in the castle, and one boat was to be left at the foot of the cliff steps, for emergencies.

Benedict's task was to detour round the town, deal with any mercenaries who might have stayed behind in the camp there, and then hasten up the hill to join Reynold.

It had seemed a good plan when Benedict had outlined it to his men the night before. Now, in the uncertain hour before dawn, it seemed doomed to failure. He knew he must show nothing of his doubts. The men around him would despair if he did.

He took his crutch and set it under his arm, when the tarpaulin was drawn back and four grinning men came in with a chair which they had lashed to two stout poles. He was not going to have to walk anywhere. They put him on the chair, picked it up and carried him thus all the way to the steps, and thence out onto the ramparts by the postern. There Ursula awaited him, with his armour.

Files of armed men passed by and most saluted him as they went through the postern gate and down the stairs on the cliff-face. The flickering light of the torches held by Barnabas picked glints from their armour. He had forgotten how heavy the chain-mail of his hauberk was. It chafed his arm, despite the quilting of the jupon beneath. The metal greaves on his legs were almost unbearable, but he knew that if he tried to take them off, Ursula would only start scolding him all over again. And of course on horseback a man's legs were the most vulnerable point.

She was kneeling at his feet, buckling on his spurs. How strange it seemed, this ceremonial arming . . . when he had been knighted, Aylmer's wife Joan had buckled on his spurs, and now Ursula . . .

There, it was done. She handed him his sword. Her eyes were wide and dark. She moved like a sleepwalker, like a priestess . . .

He settled his sword against his thigh. As usual, it got in the way of his bad leg. After this—if there were to be any 'after'—he would have done with armour and battles and poking his nose into other people's business.

Parkyn was pulling the chain-mail hood over the linen bonnet on his head. Over that would go his helmet. Damn all helmets; never could see out of them properly.

Ursula said to Barnabas, 'Go out and see if they are ready for him.'

All around them was dark, but they stood in a circle of light . . . a charmed circle . . .

Benedict said, 'In a few hours, it will be all over.'

Will it?' It was a challenge. She was not referring to the siege.

'Yes,' he said. 'It must be.'

'What if I don't agree?'

He shook his head. How could he explain? Surely, she must understand.

She tore the silken sheath from her hair and bound it round his upper arm.

She said, 'There. I know you will say I ought not to do this, but surely it is only right. If ever there were a true knight, it is you. And should not a true knight be rewarded?'

'I have had my reward.' Was he thinking of the minutes he had spent resting in her arms, or the good opinion of the garrison?

Barnabas came back, to say that they were ready for Benedict.

He hesitated. It seemed that he had something else to say to Ursula, but was not certain how to express himself.

She stamped her foot at him. 'Go, now. Before I change my mind and forbid you to risk your precious life! Oh, go! Don't you see how it is with me? No, I will not cry! You must not be distracted, I realise that. Do what you have to do, and then . . . I will be waiting.'

He took the crutch which Parkyn was holding out to him and went out onto the cliff-face. There, at the top of the stairs, was the newly-built hoist that he had designed to bring sacks up from the jetty. Now a chair had been fixed to the hook at the end of the rope, so that he could sink down the cliff without effort. As he was lowered over the edge, so Ursula came out onto the cliff-top, holding a torch above her.

And then all was dark about him.

A man with a lanthorn met him on the jetty. Two more men lifted him into the Peasmarsh boat, and then they were pushing off and oars were being dipped into the water. Behind and ahead of them went the masthead lights of other boats, manned with fisherfolk. Round the base of the hill they went, and drew up to the quayside.

The place was deserted. Hugo's men had long since ceased to take any interest in the smashed boats that still lay there. A fine-looking horse was led ashore by means of some planking, and Benedict hoisted up into the saddle.

It seemed ridiculous to be so high in the air when everyone else was going to walk, but that was the way it had to be. He felt like a giant, riding amid a sea of pygmies. John Peasmarsh the elder led the way, letting his lanthorn shine out now and then to show the company the path. They did not go into the town, but skirted it on the side opposite the castle.

The journey was a nightmare. Benedict's leg ached. It was still dark. His horse was being led by someone who knew the way. He had nothing to do but sit on it and worry. He was good at worrying.

They didn't really need him at all. He was nothing but a dead weight, having to be picked up and carried here and there, having to be looked after at every turn. Ursula was quite right. He had been a fool to leap into the fighting on the ramparts yesterday without thinking about armour. But Sir Henry had been hard-pressed and Benedict had not thought before he leaped, any more than he had thought before leaping to throw Aylmer aside, so many years before.

Something was happening. They had come to a halt. His horse was being led in a circle and was now facing in a different direction. Something large and dense was on his left. Ah, the mill.

John Peasmarsh was giving whispered instructions.

They waited.

There was a frightened cry nearby. Someone snickered.

'Hugo set a guard on the mill. More fool

he!'

So. The first man killed that day was Hugo's. Benedict supposed that that was a good thing. He didn't wish anyone killed. He'd never seen the point of killing. Except that sometimes there was no alternative.

'All set,' said John Peasmarsh the elder, back at Benedict's stirrup. 'I've sent my son ahead to see if anything's stirring in the camp yet.'

Another voice. 'The night-watch are just turning in. The camp's quiet, and empty. You can hear men marching up the hill, and see their lanthorns. They've gone to set the ram going again. The camp should be easy to take, but there's something going on in the town, I think. Lights, and men shouting.'

'That's not our business,' said his father. 'Give the signal, lad.'

They didn't need Benedict, even to give orders. They knew what to do. Two of their men were already climbing up the stairs inside the mill, to set torches alight in its upper window. The mill stood on a hillock and could be seen by sentries atop the castle, and by Merle in the dell. The signal had been given.

'Forward!' screamed John Peasmarsh, raising his pike.

Benedict didn't have to give any orders himself. His horse started forward of its own volition. He certainly hadn't applied spurs to its flanks. Or perhaps it had been pulled forward by the groom. No, the groom had been left behind and now Benedict was being bumped up and down in a most painful manner . . . he thought he could probably hold on, but as to striking a blow for Sir Henry or anyone else . . .

He heard a startled cry, and a white face fell behind. There was a mace hanging at his saddlebow. He liked maces. If you hit someone with a mace, he didn't answer back.

Another white face, and a hand grabbing at his horse's reins. He swung the mace and the white face was tossed aside. His horse sprang forward once more.

There was a yelling, screaming horde at his horse's heels. He reined in, whirling the mace around his head, shattering the arm of a mercenary who was running ahead . . .

The alarm had been raised in the camp. An officer was rousing the men, sending them streaming towards the church, which was stone-built and therefore defensible. That couldn't be allowed. They couldn't leave an armed body of men behind them, when they went on up the road.

Benedict turned his horse's head and set spurs to its flanks . . . leaping, snorting, riding men down before him . . . and then he was between the main body of men and the church door, and something pricked at his thigh, above the greaves and under the mail.

Then the townsfolk, heedless of danger,

were falling on the mercenaries, and Benedict and his horse were being driven back against the church doors . . . those within were turning and trying to get out. Benedict contrived to close one leaf of the door and hold his position there, beset on all sides.

The thud and whimper of men at hand-to-hand fighting . . .

The gurgle of a man, coughing out his life-blood . . .

Benedict's arm was tiring, wielding the mace, but there was Barnabas, armed with iron cap and leather jerkin, wielding a long knife at one stirrup, and John Peasmarsh the younger crowing like a child as he turned his pike in the belly of a fallen soldier.

And then there was a space before the door. The townsfolk rushed into the church, and there was peace outside, if not within.

'That's about it!' said John Peasmarsh, the elder. He straightened his bloodstained tunic, and brushed off a piece of dirt in a gesture reminiscent of his master, Sir Henry. His pike had gone, but he had acquired a sword, and a shield. He didn't seem to know what to do with the shield. He slung it round his neck, where it bobbed up and down, getting in his way.

'Like me and the sword,' thought Benedict. 'I'm better off with the mace, and he's better off without that shield.'

'Are they all dead?'

'Nigh on.'

'We can't afford to . . .'

'Come, haste!' screamed John Peasmarsh to his men. 'Shut the doors, and leave a guard on them . . . yes, you and you! Leave them to the womenfolk! We have other work to do . . .'

'I think we had best . . .' began Benedict.

'Aye. Dowse the lanthorns, you two. No need to give Hugo warning of our coming. On!'

'Wait!' Benedict raised his hand and there was a seething silence around him. The noise which had attracted Benedict's attention was not far away.

'To the jail!' Benedict set spurs to his horse, and bent low. He thought, 'I ought to have known Reynold would mess it up . . .'

The square was thronged with soldiers, fighting with Reynold and his men. In the middle of the square someone had set light to a large bonfire, and in the midst of the bonfire, roped to a stake, writhed the grey-headed skeleton of a woman.

Benedict swung his mace, scattering burning wood. Screams followed, as the embers flew at the backs of the mercenaries. Benedict did not heed them. Swinging his mace again and again, he cleared the burning wood from around Mother Peasmarsh, while her son and grandson fell on her bonds with their knives.

And then Benedict bent down to hoist the frail old creature up onto the saddle before him.

'They had more men billeted nearby,' said Reynold, appearing at Benedict's side. 'They had the woman tied up overnight . . . they'd learned she'd tricked them . . she was to burn this morning, as a signal to restart the ram . . .'

The ram! Benedict had forgotten the ram.

He turned in his saddle, listening. Yes, there it was.

The boom of the ram was already picking away at the last defences of the castle, while he lingered below.

John Peasmarsh was waving his arms again and screeching. The shield swung as he summoned his men to action.

'Lock the rest of them in the jail . . . Merle, you take four men and see to it! Come on, men! What are you waiting for?'

And he set off up the hill, with the townsfolk streaming after him. As they left the square, the first of the women arrived, leaping along, knives in their hands. They barely looked at Merle and his fellows, who were dragging and pushing the last of the living soldiers in the jail. They ran on, past the jail, out of the square, and on . . .

On, up the hill. Feeling the pull of the slope. Knives at the ready, most already blood-stained. Eyes straining in the dawn, eyes flickering with thirst for blood and yet more blood.

Benedict rode along with them. He didn't think they even knew he was there. He rode among them like a ghost, with them and yet not of them.

The fisherfolk left the road and leaped up the hillside, swarming over rocks and up gullies, their eyes ever on the backs of the unsuspecting soldiery above.

And then a mercenary turned and saw them. He cried out in shocked disbelief. Another reached for his crossbow . . . and was knocked over in the rush of men and women, striding up and over him . . . overwhelming the enemy with the force of a tidal bore.

Benedict had nothing to do but pick off the few stragglers who managed to crawl out of the mêlée and run for it. Again and again he swung his mace, or pointed to Barnabas to deal with the fellow for him. Barnabas was laughing.

Then there was silence. The birds were singing above. Benedict looked up. The sky was blue and the sun well up.

He looked around him, and there was nothing to be seen but dead men and shattered masonry. The townsfolk had all disappeared within the castle. The portcullis was up and, although the drawbridge was not down, staging had been thrown across the pit, so that one could ride across it. There was a gaping hole in the masonry of the inner tower, large enough to accommodate a man on horseback.

Benedict urged his horse forward, past the still bleeding corpses and the much-battered framework of the ram, through the tower and into the castle itself.

There had been bitter fighting in the tower, but it was all over now.

Sir Henry was leaning against the mounting-block. He had taken off his helmet and was smoothing down his curls. Ursula was beside him, a helm on her head and a hauberk over her gown, waving her sword at him.

Eager hands reached up to take Mistress Peasmarsh from Benedict and to exclaim over her narrow escape from death.

They were all cheering.

At first Benedict had thought they were cheering for Mother Peasmarsh but then he realised they were cheering for him. He went red, and tore off his helm because he was hot inside it; and then wished he hadn't, for it seemed he'd collected a buffet or two on his way through the town, so that every movement hurt. He looked around for the Peasmarsh men, who had really been responsible for clearing the town and raising the siege, only to discover that they were cheering as loudly as anybody . . . John the elder was beating with his sword on his captured shield. Even Reynold was grinning, as he wiped blood from a hand that had been grazed through his chainmail mittens.

So Benedict had to endure the penalties of fame at last. He was given a triumphal tour of the castle grounds on his horse, before being allowed to dismount.

'For there is still much to be done,' he said, rubbing his bad leg. 'Where is Hugo?'

No one knew.

The cheering died away. There was a blanching of cheeks. Women and children were hustled under cover while armed men went seeking the man. It was known that he had been in charge of the ram when it pressed home its last attack at dawn. He had been seen. He always wore a surcoat of red and gold and was therefore easy to recognise. Many people spoke of the surcoat, but few could give any better description of the man himself than that he was dark and of medium-build, clean-shaven and of middling years.

The surcoat was found, stuffed behind a block of fallen masonry within the castle.

'That proves he's still here,' said Sir Henry. 'Find him! A reward to the one who brings him to me, alive!'

Benedict looked up. He'd been tying some linen round a cut on Barnabas's arm. A string of disshevelled mercenaries were being led past, to be housed in the dungeons. Some wore the full chain-mail of the professional soldier, some the heavy leather and metal jerkin. A few still possessed their iron caps.

'That man there,' said Benedict, pointing towards the end of the line. 'No, not him. The one that was looking at me. The one with the good leather boots. Bring him here.'

The man was extracted from the line and led forward. He did not speak, but stared at Benedict. And Benedict stared back. The man wore a poorly fitting jerkin and had a bloodied bandage round a dirty face.

'That's him,' said Benedict. 'Hugo de Frett.'

'What?' cried Sir Henry, peering at the sorry-looking creature. 'It can't be! Is it? I'd never have recognised him, myself. Though, come to think of it . . . By all the saints, but it is: Benedict, I've seen the man a half dozen times, but I'd never have guessed . . . he must have changed jerkins with one of his men and dirtied his face. When did you meet him?'

'I've never seen him before,' said Benedict. 'But when you've fought to the death against a man, you learn what he's like. I knew him as soon as he looked at me.'

The man tore off his bandage and threw it on the ground. He said nothing. He looked at Benedict as if to say, Yes, and I know you, too. Then he made Benedict a bow, and turned his back on Sir Henry as if to indicate that he had no further interest in the proceedings.

'He would have found some way to escape, if we had not identified him,' said Benedict. 'He must be securely guarded until he is handed over to the justices for trial. He will try bribery, of course. He will be a difficult prisoner. Best hand him over to Aylmer. And ask for a ransom or compensation of some kind. Someone's got to pay for all this.'

Benedict looked around him, imprinting the scene on his mind. Then he got to his feet, put one arm over Parkyn's shoulders, the other over Barnabas's, and limped away.

*   *   *

It was two days before Ursula could manage to come upon Benedict alone. At last she found him dozing in the garden, with an open book lying on the bench beside him. He was walking with a stick now, and got to his feet when she arrived, in order to bow. There was a blank expression on his face which should have warned her that he would not welcome a tête-à-tête.

She said, 'You have been avoiding me. Did you not hear I me say I would be in the garden this morning? Yet you came not.'

'I went to help Sir Henry, down in the town. The last of the dead were buried this morning. Tomorrow we are to christen a baby which was born during the siege; also Barnabas. Your grandfather has agreed to stand sponsor to Barnabas, along with me.'

'You were avoiding me. You have been avoiding me ever since Hugo was taken. You know that Aylmer will be here tomorrow, and my aunt.'

'Yes, indeed. Both Sir Henry and I will breathe a sigh of relief, when we hand Hugo over to Aylmer.'

'You are wilfully misunderstanding me! You know what I wish to say, Benedict.'

'Perhaps I do not wish to hear . . . whatever it is that you wish to say.' His manner was still distant, but he smiled, more to himself than to her.

She stared at him. There was something different about him today. An air of quiet confidence? He looked, he acted, as if he were a much older man than before. He was not hanging on her words as he had done once.

He said, 'May I sit down? My leg . . .' He tapped it, and sat, without awaiting permission. He picked up his book and turned it over in his hands. 'My old tutor lent this to me. Will you see that it is returned to him for me?'

'Why should you not return it yourself? You will be travelling back to Aylmer's court with us, surely.'

'No, I think not.'

She sat beside him and put her hand on his arm. 'Benedict, help me . . .'

He moved away, as if he had not seen her hand. He said, 'I can hardly help myself. So let us not set ourselves in the way of temptation, shall we?'

'Aylmer would understand if . . .'

'He would not!' Suddenly his voice was harsh.

But she was of fighting stock and would not accept defeat.

'If you went to him, and said . . .'

'I will not go to him, and I will say nothing.'

'You do not think of me!'

'You are only a child, but you will learn. We will do what is right.'

'But I love you!'

He started. 'No, do not say it. It is much better not to say anything, Ursula. Think of the future . . .'

'I am thinking of it! Do you think I wanted any of this to happen? Do you think I have not fought against it? I admire Aylmer, and I am grateful to him, but you are part of me in a way he can never be.'

'Enough!' He got off the bench and reached for his stick. 'I did not hear that. You did not say it.'

She caught his arm and hung on it. 'At least tell me, just once, that you love me. If it is impossible—which I do not admit—but if it is, at least you can tell me you love me. Look, we are standing beneath the honeysuckle. Your flower. My flower. Can you look on it unmoved?'

'The honeysuckle is over.'

'It is not. It will bloom again, and then . . . oh, then you will remember, will you not? Say that you will remember. Give me some comfort, Benedict. Give me something to live on.'

Benedict closed his eyes for a moment. Then he opened them and looked around. He said, in conversational tone, 'Barnabas, send for an axe, and some salt. A deal of salt, Barnabas.'

Barnabas, who had been curled up in a sunny place behind the bench, slid away. Ursula stepped back, biting her lip. She had not realised they might be overheard. Still . . . she threw up her chin . . . let all the world hear. Let Aylmer hear. She cared not.

A workman came running up with an axe. Benedict took it from him with a word of thanks, and the workman went off, grinning. Everyone was happy to do Benedict's bidding about the castle, nowadays.

Benedict lifted the axe, whirled it round his head and brought it down on the roots of the honeysuckle.

Ursula gave a cry, and put her hands over her ears, closing her eyes. Yet still she felt every blow, as if it were on her own body.

The axe rent the tough old roots apart. Benedict pulled the tangle of greenery down. He cast it aside. He chopped away at the roots, till chips of wood and earth flew wide about him. Still he continued with his work. The rosebush nearby went . . . and another, a sickly thing that had never bloomed well. Then the bench, his book skittering along the grass, to be trampled under foot.

He was breathing hard. He rested, leaning on his axe.

Barnabas came up with a crock of salt. Ursula turned away, hands over her face. She could not bear to watch, and yet she could not leave until he had completed his act of destruction. He seeded the earth with salt where the honeysuckle had once flourished. Nothing would grow in ground that had been treated with salt.

He rubbed his hands clean and sent Barnabas to pick up his book and stick.

She looked at what he had done. She thought he had destroyed more than just the garden. The pain was so intense she thought she would faint.

Then it was as if someone else was standing there in her shoes. Someone to whom the garden and Benedict meant nothing. Someone who had lost the power to feel. She walked past Benedict, looking neither to left nor right, and went up into the keep.

* * *

When Aylmer and his train of servants came riding into the castle, it was this new Ursula who swept down to greet him. She had left her girlhood behind her and become a woman. She saw that Benedict had prevented her from committing a terrible sin, but she did not think she would ever recover from the blow he had dealt her. She thought that Aylmer must surely read in her eyes that she was mortally wounded.

Aylmer came. But, instead of the big brown

creature she had been holding in her memory, she found him turned into a man with an anxious, lined face, and grey in his hair. As he took her hand and tried to make light of the fact the he had not yet thrown off the effects of his fall, she saw that he still loved her. And something moved within her, bringing tears to her eyes.

Aylmer needed her. She felt a rush of gratitude, and of something that was almost, but not quite, love.

She went into his arms and kissed his cheek, saying, 'Oh, Aylmer! I ought never to have left you!'

* * *

The castle seemed very quiet, when Aylmer and his bride had gone. The Lady Editha had ridden back with the newly-married pair, saying that she deserved a little gaiety after having been shut up in Salwarpe for so long. Hugo de Frett had also ridden away in Aylmer's train, under guard.

Sir Henry sought for Benedict, and found him leaning on his stick, in the devastated area which had once been a garden. Sir Henry signed to his valet to set down the stool he had been carrying and seated himself with care.

'This place reminds me of a graveyard,' said Sir Henry. 'Why don't you take a seat too, my boy?'

Parkyn, who had been hovering nearby, darted away and came back with a stool, and a cloak for his master. The wind was growing chill, though the sun was out.

'They plant yews in churchyards,' said Benedict. His thoughts were plainly elsewhere.

Sir Henry patted his back curls. 'My face feels as if it were going to crack, with all that smiling.'

Benedict gave a hoot of laughter. He looked around him. 'Sir Henry, I have spoiled your garden for you.'

'And saved my honour. I know. Do you want to speak of it?'

Benedict shook his head, resting his chin on his fist.

'My boy, I have a boon to ask of you, and here is a better place to ask it than anywhere else. And yet . . . I find that I am grown a little afraid of you . . . like Ursula.'

Benedict smiled and shook his head.

'Oh yes, now that you are fully come to man's estate, you are indeed a formidable person. Reynold noticed it. He said to me last night . . . but that is beside the point. My boy, you must rouse yourself. Your old way of life is finished. Will you go to the wars again? You know that Reynold wishes to go, next year?'

'I . . . had not thought. Probably not.'

'You can go no more to Aylmer's court. Like me, one part of your life is finished. Yes, I am in the same position as you. I had built my life round my granddaughter, and now she is gone, and I do not like the look of the years ahead. You should say that at my age I should be thinking of making my peace with God. Well, perhaps so. But before I do that I would like to see something of the world.

'You remember that book of tales from Ancient Rome? The one about the gods? They say there are many antique statues being dug up in Italy. And in Bruges they are making good books. In France they build cathedrals. Shall we go to see these things for ourselves?'

Benedict gave Sir Henry his full attention, but did not speak.

'Of course, there is Christmas to get over first,' said Sir Henry. 'And Hugo's trial. Perhaps you will invite me to your house on the Downs for Christmas? And we have some rebuilding to do here. But in the spring, we could be off on our travels. Couldn't we?'

Still there was no reply. But at least Benedict was listening.

'We have good men to oversee our estates, if we go travelling. We could see what there is to see, buy some books, inspect some statues, make love to a few ladies, perhaps . . .' He paused, but still Benedict did not react.

'And then, when we come home in eighteen months' or two years' time, I will arrange another match for you.'

Benedict studied his hands and Sir Henry studied Benedict. Did the lad not realise that Aylmer's days were numbered? That grey, worn look . . . the tremor in his voice . . . one hard winter, and Ursula would be a rich young widow of nineteen. Add one year for mourning. Yes, if Sir Henry could only keep Benedict occupied and out of the way of other women for a while . . .

'I would like to see Rome,' said Benedict. 'But as to marrying again, I think I have made her hate me.'

* * *

Sir Henry patted his widowed granddaughter's hand. 'You are looking well, my dear; though I do not think that black becomes you.' He removed the thick black mantle in which she had travelled home to Salwarpe, and stood back to look at her.

She submitted to his scrutiny with a smile. Her figure was a trifle more robust than it had been when she was eighteen, yet her close-fitting gown showed it off well. Her hair was just as clear in colour though it was now coiled up at the back of her head under a filmy veil.

She said, 'Travel seems to have suited you, too.' She slipped her arm within his and stood close, letting him know that the was glad to be back.

Sir Henry stroked his hair. At some point in their travels, Benedict had persuaded Sir Henry that he would appear more distinguished if he allowed his hair to revert to its natural silver. But his coiffure was as elaborate as ever, and his tunic a marvel of Italian damask.

He pinched her cheek. 'You will not remain a widow long, I swear.'

Her face hardened. 'Not you, too. Have I not had enough of that to bear from my aunt? How many times must I say that I loved my husband, and have no wish to remarry? If only we had had a child . . .'

'But you did not. Now, my dear, you have mourned Aylmer for a whole year. You have been on pilgrimages for his soul, you have fasted and made retreats, just as you should. Everyone praises your conduct. You have vacated your husband's castle and returned to Salwarpe. All very right, proper and dutiful. And so now I have another match to propose for you.'

She disengaged her arm from his. 'A widow need not remarry. That is the law. Besides, Aylmer divided his estates between me and his . . . his ward, so I do not have to take any of the needy knights who have been flocking around me these last few months.'

'The man I have in mind is already wealthy. The size of your dowry will not weigh with him.'

'And no doubt he is also the most handsome, the most noble . . .'

'No. He is not even straight. As you very

well know.'

Not a muscle moved in Ursula's face. She went to the window and looked out. 'I see the stabling has been rebuilt. And the gate-towers. You would think nothing had ever happened here. Perhaps nothing did.'

Sir Henry put his hand on her shoulder. 'Do you hate him, Ursula? He was afraid that you might.'

'No, I don't think so. It all happened so long ago. I was only a child, and foolish. Let us talk of something else.'

'Very well. Let us go and walk in the garden, shall we?'

For the first time colour came into her cheeks. 'There is no garden in Salwarpe.'

'If stabling and gate-towers can be rebuilt, why not a garden? We were walking about in Rome one day, and observed men at work, creating a new pleasaunce. He gave that little nod of the head, as he always does when he's solved a difficult problem—do you remember? And he said we should commission some Italian workmen to remake the garden here.'

She put her hand to her throat, and now she was as pale as she had been red before. 'But there was salt strewn in the earth . . .'

'The poor soil has been carted away, and good earth brought in to take its place. Come and see.'

'No!' She put her hands over her face. 'I am not well.'

He put his arm around her. 'I promise he will not come to you until you are ready to receive him.'

'He is here in Salwarpe? Oh, no!'

'Where else would he be?' said Sir Henry, meaning, Behave yourself, child!

'On his estates,' she said, in a breathless voice. 'He is rich and powerful now. He despises me. I thought he loved me once, but then he changed . . .'

'He did what he had to do. There could have been nothing but misery and shame for you, Ursula, if you had thrown Aylmer aside. He saw that more clearly than you.'

'But he hurt me! Oh, I cannot bear to think of it, even now!'

'Did he not hurt himself as well? He had only learned to smile naturally again by the time we reached Rome, and then we received news of Aylmer's last illness, and he was in a fever to return.'

'That was months ago!' Her tone was scornful.

'You think he did not want to jump on the first boat back to England? You think he did not wish to write to you? Only he had me round his neck, like a millstone, urging caution . . . an old man, unable to travel quickly . . .'

'He did write to me. It was a kind letter, I suppose. It didn't say anything about . . . anything.'

'Could you have borne it, if he had? He

knew you had transferred your love to Aylmer, and he knew you had to have time in which to mourn. But that time is over now. It is time to look forward. Time to visit the garden.'

This time she made no demur. He led her down the stairs and out into the sunshine. A beech hedge now surrounded the area which had been occupied by the old garden, and in the hedge was a gate. Sir Henry pulled on the latch and she passed within. A cloud of perfume rose from a bed nearby, which had been planted with lilies. The central area had been paved and a marble bench had been set where the old wooden one had been used to stand. Before her was a fountain, delicate and cool. On either side of her were beds of rich dark earth, filled with flowering plants, and above her head floated the trumpets of the honeysuckle.

She began to cry, but this time her tears were of joy.

The gate opened, and Benedict came into the garden.